The Stolen Guitar Case

A Pegasus Investigations Mystery

Brian D. Eyre

Swinging Cats and Blinking Hats Press
Dallas, Texas

Swinging Cats and Blinking Hats Press
www.swingingcatsandblinkinghats.com

Prologue

Success is just like love; the harder you search for it, the harder it is to find. The young man with the hungry eyes and the brooding good looks knows that very well.

For years, love has been easy to find. As a good looking musician, finding girls is easy. Sleeping with band bunnies may not be the same as true love, but it works for him.

For months, success has been eluding him. He quit his band to pursue a solo career, but it isn't going as planned. Everybody loves how well he plays guitar, but nobody seems to love his original songs. He doesn't want to play other people's songs forever.

For weeks, he's been playing his latest song to receptive applause. It's not exactly his song, but everybody thinks it is, and that's really what matters. Once he records a hit song, people will be more receptive to his next ones.

For days, he's felt a little guilty about stealing the song. He didn't really mean to steal it, and he did have to finish up some of the lyrics, but he still feels a little guilty. He vows that once he's a big star, he'll make it up to the guy who started the song.

For hours, he's thought about the hottie he dragged home from the bar last night. She was so hot; he even let her play his guitar. Of course, he was disappointed that she got cold feet, but some things are worth waiting for, and this babe definitely is.

For minutes, he wonders who is knocking on his door at such an early hour. He hopes she changed her mind and returned for a morning rendezvous, so he opens the door with a smile on his face.

For seconds, he feels pain as the bullet rips through his brain. He prays to a God he never really believed in that stealing a song isn't a cardinal sin.

As he dies, he thinks that stealing a song should not be a capital offense. He's right about that.

But, after enough Cardinal Sins, things like that don't matter!

Part 1 –Dallas Heat

"All my life I've been a sinner
And all my life I've been a winner…
There's not a damned thing you can do
You choose to die or choose to choose."

The American Tarot
'Where are you, Davinci?'

01   Freak Show

"My friends don't call me Freak anymore." I said to the beautiful, blue-eyed blonde sitting in one of our client chairs. It's not exactly true, but I've said it so much lately, I'm almost starting to believe it. Freak Show was my legal name for several years before I changed it back to the name my parents gave me.

"You'll always be Freak to me. I spent the three best years of my life watching you torture yourself for fun and profit, and now you want me to think of you as something other than Freak? Forget that!"

Bobbie Jo had a valid point. She's been my best friend for years. "Call me anything you want, just be sure you call me."

She laughed courteously, "It's been almost a year now, Freak. How are you holding up?"

Almost a year, actually it's only been ten months and twelve days. It seems like a lifetime, several lifetimes, in fact, since a totally screwed up person killed my fiancé and our unborn child. When it happened, all I wanted was revenge. Well, I guess I also wanted not to be framed for it. The police thought I killed them. Almost everybody did.

I answered Bobbie Jo, "As well as can be expected, I suppose."

She frowned, "Damn, I was hoping you'd be doing better than that."

"Me, too," I answered honestly.

She changed the subject, "How's business?"

"We're doing okay; my trust fund and my partner's reward money are pretty much still intact. I don't expect to have to get back into show business and he's not planning to go back to being a bike courier to make ends meet."

"That's good, at least. How is your partner, by the way? Are he and Emily still together?"

"Of course," I said

"Cool, I like her; she's not all priggish like so many straight women her age. By the way, you promised you would tell me how you met him."

"I did, didn't I? It was several months before Katherine and I hooked up. I was hanging out in Deep Ellum minding my own business, just being myself."

She laughed, "By which you mean you were strutting around like a manlier version of Marilyn Manson, scaring the Hell out of the tourists and turning all the college girls into your love slaves."

"Exactly, except one of the college girls turned out to be a high school girl who had run away from home. I didn't know that, and nothing happened between us. Anyway, Carl had followed her trail to a biker bar. Someone had seen me hanging out there with her, and he wanted to ask questions."

"Did he care that some of those bikers would kill their own fathers for asking questions?"

"If he did, he didn't show it. He's almost seven foot tall in case you never noticed."

"Sure, I know that. I also know that bullets are about fifteen dollars a case and aren't affected much by how tall the guy they rip through is."

"If he was worried by the surroundings, I saw no sign of it. I was the only person he was questioning, and I wasn't carrying a gun. I tried to break his nose with my fist. He swatted away my attempt like a parent deflecting a toddler's slaps. I've never seen anybody that quick."

"How did he react when his counterpunch didn't faze you?"

"He didn't even return the punch."

"Did he already know you couldn't feel pain?"

I don't feel pain because I really am a freak. I've never felt physical pain in my life. I never will, because I have a medical condition called Congenital Analgesia. Some people think that would be a cool gift to have, but really it's more of a curse. Okay, sure it has its good points, but it's not nearly as cool as might be believed. Not feeling pain isn't the same as being invincible, as I've learned all too well.

"No, he just didn't hit me. He knew I wasn't going to be able to hit him, so he just kept asking me questions."

"He's a good man. I guess I already knew that, but I don't know too many people who wouldn't hit somebody back in that situation."

"I only know one, Carl Jennings."

Talking about it got met thinking about how I helped Carl solve Katherine Elizabeth's murder The memory was bittersweet, at best. That, of course, got me thinking about how much I miss her. I don't know how long I spent reflecting before Bobbie Jo interrupted.

"I see your partner has taught you the silent trick."

"Sorry. I get quiet sometimes when I think about her. It's easier not to cry when I don't try to talk."

She reached across the desk and held my hand. "Sometimes it's better to cry, you know. Or do you think now that you're a private investigator, you have to be all macho all the time?"

"No, I don't have to be macho all the time, but it can't be good for business to be seen sitting at the desk crying with a beautiful girl in the client chair. Speaking of which, what brings you in from the suburbs, business or pleasure?"

"Both actually, there's a new arachnid exhibit at the Dallas World Aquarium I'm going to check out. Mostly though, I think I have a case for y'all. Is the Great Detective here?"

'The Great Detective' is one of several nicknames we have for Carl. He pretends to hate it just like I pretend not to like being called Freak Show, but I know better.

"Actually, he and Emily are in Florida, waiting to get on a cruise ship." I told Bobbie Jo.

"He's in Florida? He hates everywhere that isn't Texas. Why would they go to Florida to get on a cruise? Did he forget that Texas has a coast?"

"Not likely, Emily wanted to go to Florida, so they went to Florida. He loves her more than he hates anything."

"Except for spiders," she pointed out accurately. "I left my pets at home to keep from creeping him out, and he's not even here."

"True, but we are open for business. What's this case of yours? Maybe, it'll be my chance to finally make a contribution to Pegasus Investigations."

"The case really isn't mine; it's my brother's."

"How is Charlie Ray doing? I haven't seen him in ages."

"He's good. He says since Dad got home from the hospital, he's been at his most creative. He's sure one of the great new songs he's written is going to be his breakthrough hit. Or at least he was until somebody stole his guitar."

I don't know enough about music to know why having a guitar stolen would keep a great song from being a breakthrough hit, but I knew Charlie Nothing and his Nothing Special Band had recorded enough regional hits to afford Pegasus Investigations rates.

"If Charlie Ray wants to hire us, why are you here instead of him?"

"Because he doesn't realize he wants to hire you, yet. I have to talk him into it first. He says the guitar's not expensive enough to be worth hiring anybody to find. Also, he's still a little sore about having been a suspect last year. I just wanted to make sure you would take the case before I did."

"Nobody likes being a suspect, as I'm sure we both remember. However, he might be right. Stolen goods aren't often recovered, and we charge by the day, not on a finder's fee."

She laughed, "You obviously still have a little to learn about the marketing aspect of the business. Do y'all want the case or not?"

"We'd love to take the case. But you're my best friend, and your brother is also my friend. I haven't forgotten that he loaned us his tour bus last year, you know. I just don't want him wasting his money paying us to look for a guitar we might never find."

"I don't care about the money. He's been in a funk ever since it happened, and I can't stand seeing him that way. I'll talk him into coming down here. You keep your schedule free so you can help him, okay?"

I didn't bother telling her how easy it would probably be to keep our schedule free. After she left, I started thinking about how to find a stolen guitar. The best way to find one would depend on why it was stolen. If somebody stole it to sell it, then checking with pawnshops would be the first step. But, if it was someone who wanted to play it, you'd have to find that person playing it.

Dallas probably has about a thousand places to play guitar, and a million professional or semi-professional guitarists trying to play them. That doesn't even count all the amateurs playing, or trying to play, for their friends or by themselves in their rooms. If we got the case, it would be like looking for a needle in a haystack. Still, I hoped she'd be able to talk him into hiring us. If Carl called to check on the agency, it would be nice to be able to say we were earning money in his absence.

I really need to be more careful about what I hope for.

02   Lost Guitar

As expected, keeping our schedule free turned out to be very easy. Apparently, it turned out to be much easier than talking Charlie into hiring us. Bobbie Jo called or came by every day that week to reassure me that we would eventually get the case. I doubted her, but it wasn't like I was turning down other clients. It was one of those weeks when the waiting room in the office Carl loves so much was about as useful as the minimum speed signs on North Dallas Tollway.

Our office used to serve as his home and office, but that's not why he loves it. He loves it because it's a virtual fortress. All the walls and doors are steel reinforced and the windows are bulletproof. Even the window between the lobby and the exterior waiting room is bulletproof. It isn't noticeable from the waiting room and can be covered by a sliding panel on the inside.

Thursday afternoon, I was gazing out through the waiting room north window toward Neiman Marcus. Back when I had visible piercing all over my body, Katherine used to love taking me in there just to watch the sales clerks and society ladies react. As I reminisced, I saw Charlie Nothing walking toward the office. He had a tattered backpack draped over one shoulder.

He walked with his head down and his hands in the pockets of his blue jeans. His black hair fell in front of his shoulders instead of down his back since he wasn't wearing his trademark black cowboy hat and ponytail. I watched him as he approached and got to our stairs. He hesitated before climbing, and then stopped again at the office door. He started to ring the bell, but stopped himself. He put his hands back in his pockets, shook his head and turned back toward the stairs.

I may not have perfected the art of marketing a private investigation agency, but I know better than to let a potential client just walk away. I hit the remote to slide the panel over the window and hustled toward the door. I got to the exterior window just as Charlie got to the bottom step. I saw no sign of the hesitation he had shown at the door. He had made his choice and was leaving.

I quickly opened the door and shouted out. "Charlie Ray! How are you? Why don't you come back up and we can talk about it?"

"Oh! Hi. Sure, I guess I could." He hesitated again. "It won't cost me anything just to talk, right?"

"No, Charlie, it won't cost anything to talk. We offer free consultations. Even if we didn't, I wouldn't charge a friend just to talk about a problem. Come on up."

He laughed and started back up the stairs. "Of course, you never did have a head for business. That show you and BJ used to have should have been a license to print money and you barely kept it afloat."

Ignoring insults from potential clients is another thing Carl has taught me well, so I simply ushered him into the lobby and got him situated in a client chair. He slid the backpack off his shoulder and sat it in the other chair.

"How did you know I was out there? Do you have x-ray vision or something?"

"Of course, didn't Bobbie Jo tell you I have superpowers?"

"No she didn't mention that. But, she does say nice things about you. You're probably her favorite man."

"As Jennifer Engle would say, isn't that somewhat like being the world's tallest midget?"

He laughed, "Okay. I'll grant that BJ's list of favorite men is pretty damn short. But the way she raves about you and Carl Jennings almost makes it sound like she's thinking of going straight."

"I hope your dad's not still hoping for that. I don't think it happens very often."

"No, he's been cool about it ever since he got out of the hospital. I guess being in a coma for a few months helps a man get his priorities in order."

"Maybe any time in a coma can do that." I said, thinking of my own recent time in the hospital. "Why don't you tell me about the guitar that got stolen?"

"It's a Dillon Black Dragon acoustic electric. I've had it for a few years."

"Is it the one with the Texas flag on the body that I've seen you playing?"

"No, that's my stage guitar; it's a Taylor Dreadnought that a guy in Austin custom painted for me. If that one gets stolen, I'll round up a posse straightaway. Of course, since it's one of a kind, it wouldn't be as impossible to find as the one I lost."

Charlie Ray is one of only two people I've ever heard use the phrase 'round up a posse.' The other is my lawyer. The difference between the two is that Charlie really thinks that way. My lawyer is just trying to sound like a Texan when he says things like that.

If I was going to get to call Carl and tell him we had a case, I needed to find a way to convince Charlie Ray to round up a posse for the guitar that had been stolen. "Charlie, we're professionals. Nothing is impossible for us. We don't get cases finding things that are easy to find. If you want the guitar back, hire us to find it."

He laughed without mirth, "I don't give a tinker's damn about that guitar. I could buy one on eBay for less than y'all want for a retainer."

We hadn't discussed fees or retainer, but I figured Bobbie Jo had given him an idea what it would cost to hire us. Maybe, I didn't have a potential client in front of me. On the other hand, there had to be some reason he had come to Downtown Dallas and climbed the stairs to our office.

"So, if you don't care about the guitar, what do you care about? I know you love your baby sister, but not enough to let her talk you into coming down here just to appease her." I took a deep breath before I continued grasping at straws. "What got stolen with the guitar that you care so much about? Was it something of sentimental value? Our investigations are completely confidential. If there's something specific like a gift from a lover or something, we won't reveal what it is to anybody. When I say anybody, I mean anybody, including your family."

He laughed again; maybe I should consider stand-up comedy for my next career. I was wondering how soon I might have to embark on that next career when he said. "No, it's nothing like that, but you're right. There was something else. The guitar was in its case when it got swiped. Since I might well be dumber than Jessica Simpson, my notebook was in the case with it."

"Your computer was in your guitar case?" I asked incredulously.

For the third time in less than five minutes, Charlie Ray laughed at something I said. This time, I realized he wasn't the only one in the office who might be dumber than Jessica Simpson.

8

03   Reluctant Client

"Maybe the guys that work for the money factories in Cashville carry computers in their guitar cases. Me? I carry a blue Mead spiral notebook I bought at Wal-Mart."

"Of course. I guess I'm just a product of the digital age." I pointed with my eyes over to the computer desk. "I don't remember the last time I used a paper notebook to take notes."

"That's not an option for a songwriter like me. I have to be able to write stuff down as soon as I think of it. Willie Nelson may be sure he can remember anything worth remembering, but I'm not Willie Nelson."

The way he said it made it obvious that not being Willie was a source of much disappointment for him. "Maybe not, but you've had some success of your own. Why don't you tell me about the theft? Where were you when it happened? Who had access to it, and why do you think it was stupid to have the notebook in the case?"

"Well, I guess it really only seems stupid to me in hindsight. I jot down all my notes about possible lyrics or chord arrangements in that notebook. Since it's been gone, I've tried to reproduce as many as I can remember, but I'll never know if I lost some forever."

He said it the way an animal lover says he's not sure if he'll ever find a missing pet. As soon as I realized that, I realized that I probably was talking to our next client. I reached into the desk drawer and pulled out the Phillips PocketMemo 9350 I use for recording conversations.

"Charlie, do you mind if I record this just in case you do hire us? Like I said, taking notes with pen and paper isn't in my skill set."

"Sure, go ahead."

I checked to make sure it had a memory card inserted and started recording. I hadn't been kidding about not remembering the last time I used a pen and paper to take notes. Unlike the Great Detective, I'm a huge fan of technology. Since he learned the detective business before most of the technology I love was even a dream, he often dismisses them as my 'toys.'

However, he's come a long way since we've been partners. One reason is that cool technology helped us solve our big case last year. A more important reason is that we'd probably both be dead if not for a few of these 'toys.' Regarding the PocketMemo recorder, his only reaction was to tell me that it was probably illegal, and certainly unethical to record a conversation without both parties knowing it was being recorded.

He told me to always record the other person agreeing to have the conversation recorded to protect us from lawsuits. I normally take his advice. This time, I ignored it. I've known Charlie Ray long enough to know he wouldn't pretend later he hadn't agreed. Besides, if he did, his baby sister would kick his ass.

I sat the recorder on the desk and said, "So, somebody stole a Dillon Black Dragon acoustic electric guitar and a blue Mead spiral notebook from you." The Great Detective says that reiterating the situation can bring it into perspective and encourage a potential client to become a client. I continued. "The guitar itself is replaceable, but the notebook may contain treasure which no man can measure."

Charlie Ray interrupted, "Whoa, Hold on!" He started muttering to himself, "treasure, measure, treasure, more than you can measure; you are what I treasure. I treasure every measure of...."

His voice faded as he reached into his bag and grabbed a notebook and a pen.I watched him as he did so and his concentration was palpable. A bomb could have gone off in the street and he probably wouldn't have noticed. Of course, the way this office is fortified, a bomb could go off outside and I might not notice, either.

While he furiously wrote in his notebook, occasionally flipping pages back and forth, I thought about what to say to get him to hire us to find his other notebook. I knew he was serious about his song writing. With his looks and singing voice, he probably could already be a star if he'd just gone to Nashville and agreed to sing songs other people wrote for him.

Eventually, Charlie Ray looked up, "I'm sorry, what were you saying?"

"I was saying that before you had that notebook, you had another one like it. You are trying to decide whether to hire us to look for it. If you do, and we don't find anything, you will have wasted your money. If you don't, you will always wonder if the song or lyric that would have turned the Nothing Special Band into something special disappeared because somebody stole it.

"Damn, Freak! Maybe you do have a head for business. When did you learn the art of the sales pitch?"

I chose not to mention that my friends, and clients, don't normally call me Freak these days. I simply answered the question. "If summarizing the situation and pointing out the obvious is a sales pitch, I've always known the art. I know a little about irreplaceable losses. You want that notebook back. That's why you came down here in the first place. If you don't think we're good enough to find it, go hire somebody you think is better. Don't let yourself wonder forever if you could have gotten it back if you had tried."

"Like Hell! Bobbie Jo would kill me if I hired somebody else to look. I did mention that she thinks y'all hung the moon, didn't I?"

"Something to that effect might have come up in the conversation." I nodded at the pocket memo, "I don't think I was recording when it did, though."

"It doesn't matter. I do want that notebook, and the guitar and case for that matter, back. I also want to get a few minutes alone with whatever no-account polecat stole the damn thing."

When he said 'no-account polecat', he again sounded like my attorney, Larry Joe McCoy. Charlie sounded mad, though. I've never heard Larry Joe sound mad. Hell, Larry Joe didn't even sound mad when he called me a liar and said he wouldn't represent me at my murder trial last year.

I said, "Sounds like you've made a decision. Let's talk about fees and a retainer, Mister Nothing."

Suddenly, I was Mister Salesman getting ready to close a deal. Wouldn't Carl be proud? Charlie's demeanor went from angry to nervous when I said the word fees. He relaxed considerably when we discussed the actual fees involved.

Within minutes, Pegasus Investigations had a new client, a check for the retainer, and I was about to start my first case acting alone. For the first time, I actually felt like I was a real private investigator. That meant it was actually time to start acting like a private investigator and ask some pertinent questions.

Before he left, Carl told me he knew I could handle things. He also left me a cheat sheet of what he called right new client questions. It was one of about seventy-five cheat sheets he left me. I very much doubted that I'd need the one on how to tell how long a body has been dead by measuring the size of the maggots, but you never know.

04   Song Writing

The cheat sheet is designed to help the client remember details that might have slipped his or her mind. I started with the most obvious, "When did you first notice the guitar was gone?"

"The guitar was stolen three weeks ago Saturday, the last day of March sometime between 2:30 and 4:15 in the afternoon."

Charlie's memory seemed clear. I put the cheat sheet in a desk drawer. "Why don't you just tell me what happened?"

"I was at a DSA songwriter's workshop over on Live Oak all day. When I got ready to leave, I went to pick up my guitar and it was gone. It was 4:15 when I went to leave, and I know it was there at 2:30 because that's when I put it in the storeroom."

"Why did you put it in the storeroom?"

"Well, it's not really a storeroom; it's just a small room where people store things when we use that venue. In the winter, people put their coats in there. We had a pretty big group for a workshop, so there wasn't a lot of room in the main room. When we all have material to perform, those of us who don't need our instruments store them in the other room to make for a more comfortable and realistic performing venue."

"Realistic? How is a venue realistic or not realistic?"

"It's kind of hard to explain, but these workshops; at least the ones the DSA puts on are very nurturing. Some even say too nurturing. We all try to support each other, even though some of the members can't write a song or play an instrument to save their lives. A guy can come in there with a poem he wrote to his high school sweetheart that doesn't even make sense, and somebody will tell him it has potential."

I laughed, "So it's a profit deal, huh? Make everybody think they can be a songwriter, and everybody will keep paying dues."

"No, it's not like that. Music is a weird business, man. Sure I know you have some experience with weird businesses, but you have no idea. Some of the biggest hits are worse than the worst poem I've heard presented at one of those things. You have heard of 'Who Let the Dogs Out', right?"

"Yes, okay, so everybody gets encouragement, just in case they might write the next terrible song that everybody wants to dance to and/or download. I think I get that. What does that have to do with putting the instruments in the storeroom?"

"Well, that's how it works until we get to performance time. Then, the workshop ends and everybody with enough guts performs a song for the group. Then, the group becomes the audience. If the song is great, the group applauds. If it isn't great… well I'll just say that silence in that room is more devastating than boos or catcalls from a bunch of drunks in Deep Ellum."

"So you put your guitar aside, because you weren't performing?"

"No, the theme of this workshop was co-writing duets. I had spent the morning working on a duet with a woman who plays the piano like an angel plays a harp. There was no reason not to perform the song with her instrument instead of mine. Even if the song sucked, at least her playing was sure to bring some applause."

"Did it?" I asked, genuinely curious. Sure, I've been a performer, but our acts never really led to critiques that might hurt our feelings. I couldn't really imagine the gut-wrenching pressure involved in performing a song hoping people would love it. Maybe that's why Bobbie Jo started her spider act; to keep from having her looks compared to those of other beautiful women and critiqued.

Charlie shrugged, "Was the song any good? I don't really know. What we wrote isn't really my style. We got some applause, but like I said, she could play Chopstix and get applause. If she ends up doing anything with the song, I'll be credited as co-writer. More likely though, it will just disappear like all the other songs that get written at these workshops."

"So, if nothing ever comes from them, what's the point of the workshops?"

"Good question. The idea is to get a better idea of how to write a song, do a little networking, and maybe stumble across a spark of an idea that might someday lead to a breakthrough hit song. Does my teaching you the music business in any way help you find my notebook and guitar?"

I noted that he listed the notebook first, "Only in that your description of it matches almost perfectly the way we go about solving cases. The idea is to get a better idea of what happened, do a bunch of networking, and eventually stumble on the clue that will lead to breaking the case."

13

Charlie didn't look happy with that, "I hope it works more often in your business than it does in mine. Otherwise, I'm not likely to ever see that notebook or guitar again."

"We only need it to work one time, to find your notebook and guitar. The performances ended at 4:15, and you went to get your guitar and leave. What did you do when it wasn't there?"

"Actually, the performance session ended at about 3:45. I talked to a couple of people before I left. When I saw the guitar missing, I went back into the main room, thinking maybe I'd left it by the piano. I hadn't, of course, but you know how it is. Like when you come out of a mall and can't find your car. Even if it's been stolen, your first thought is that you must have parked somewhere else."

"I don't drive, Charlie, but I think I understand. The idea that it had been stolen was too improbable to believe, so something else must have happened."

"Exactly, so I looked around. I even looked in the bathroom and kitchen. By this time, the only other person there was the workshop facilitator. I told her I was going to call the police, but she talked me out of it. She thought somebody must have picked it up by mistake and promised to have the association president put a note on the website to try to find it."

"If someone had picked it up by mistake, there should have been another left behind. Was there?" I asked.

"No, but I wasn't thinking clearly at that point. Anyway, they put the note on the website, and even sent out an email blast to all the members asking about it. When there was no response by Wednesday, I called the police and filed a report."

"And the cops thanked you for coming by and assured you they'd find your guitar without lifting a finger, except to enjoy a celebratory donut." I tried not to sound overly sarcastic, but I probably failed.

"Actually, the cop shot pretty straight with me, told me there wasn't much chance of finding it. He said he'd check the database of pawned goods, which he said turns something up once in a while. He even went over to the Center with me and looked around."

This time I didn't even try not to be sarcastic, "Our tax dollars finally paying off. Did he find any useful clues?"

Charlie started to smile, but suppressed it. "If he did, he kept it to himself, which is why I signed the check that's on your desk. When you finish mocking the police, what's your plan to find my notebook?"

"Actually my first step is to talk to the police. Did he give you a case number?"

Charlie gave me the case number and his cell number and asked me to keep him apprised of how things went. I followed him to the stairs and watched him as he walked north past Neiman Marcus. When I turned back to the office, I glanced at the brass plaque that the Great Detective had recently installed.

Pegasus Investigations, LLP
Est. 1959

Carl Jennings
Franz Scholes

Even if most of my friends do still call me Freak, the plaque serves to remind me that it's not really my name. It also suggests that I'm a detective now. I looked forward to proving that by investigating Charlie Ray's missing guitar case. Of course, when I used to be Freak, I also looked forward to suspending myself by meat hooks thirty feet above a stage. I sometimes look forward to things that I should dread.

05   Community Cooperation

"So, the absolutely incredible Freak Show needs help from the law. I love it!" "Where's my old friend, Larry Bird, today? Why isn't he here to hold your hand?"

"His real friends don't call him Larry Bird." I didn't bother adding that mine don't call me Freak. He already knew he wasn't my friend. "Mr. Jennings is attending to other matters. I guess my apprenticeship is over."

I was sitting in an office at the Jack Evans Police Headquarters building on Lamar Street across the desk from a cop named Woodbury. His clock read 12:45, but it was at least 15 minutes fast. Woodbury made his reputation by being tough enough to go into Deep Ellum and pretend to enforce the law. Apparently, that was enough to get him promoted. In reality, he mostly enjoyed a few complimentary beers and shook down some suburban kids and SMU students who tried to prove how tough they were by fighting each other.

He doesn't get along with any man he can't intimidate with either his badge or his vaunted stare. That eliminates just about every man with a backbone. For that matter, he never managed to intimidate Spineless Spicoli, the pot-smoking contortionist who spent two months with my show before he moved to Amsterdam, either.

"So what brings you here?" Woodbury asked me, not bothering with the stare he likes so much.

"I'm wondering how close you are to finding Charlie Nothing's stolen guitar?"

He flinched as if I'd slapped him. "Damn, why'd that redneck hire you guys? If he wanted to hire a private firm, I could have recommended a real agency."

"I'm sure you could have, for a nominal percentage of said real agency's fee."

"Freak, you better hope I don't take that as an accusation!"

"Sure, Officer, just don't expect me to take that as a denial."

"You can call me Detective or Detective Woodbury. I wouldn't have this nice office if I were still just an officer."

16

"So when I report you to your superiors for soliciting finders' fees you want me to be sure to call you Detective Woodbury? I'll make sure to do so!" I stood up and started toward the door.

Detective Woodbury reacted as I expected. "Freak hold on, you're taking everything out of context. Come back, have a seat, and let's talk about this."

I returned to the chair without saying a word. The Great Detective's been teaching me the value of not saying a word for the last nine months.

Detective Woodbury ended the silence quickly, as I knew he would. "I meant no insult to you or your partner. All I meant was that I could have put Charlie in touch with a larger agency with more resources. You guys are good, considering how small an agency you run, but a guy like Charlie with his money can afford to hire real professionals."

"Maybe once he saw the results the real professionals at the Dallas Police Department were getting, he was looking to go in a different direction, Detective."

"Ouch! Okay, I'll admit we weren't getting very far. Hell, I'll even admit we weren't trying very hard. First off, how hard did he expect us to look for a $2000 guitar and secondly, how many real professionals do you think we have down here?"

I noted that Charlie had learned the art of the police report/ insurance fraud game and made a mental to note to ask him about that. I chose not to tell Detective Woodbury that including present company, I counted zero real professionals on the force. Instead, I tried to forge an alliance. The Great Detective's been teaching me the value of doing that, too.

"Of course, Detective," I said being careful not to sound sarcastic. "If the police force had time to waste searching for every missing item in Dallas County, our little agency would never have any clients. And by the way, I'm sure Charlie would have asked you for a recommendation, except that his sister and I go way back, so she recommended us."

"His sister, huh? I didn't know he had a sister. Is she hot? Is she single? Maybe, I should spend a little more time on this case."

I knew Bobbie Jo well enough to know she wouldn't mind. "Yeah, his sister is single and she's smoking hot. That is, if you're okay with a blue-eyed blonde with an hourglass figure. Plus, you two have a lot in common. As soon as we find Charlie's guitar, I'll introduce you to her."

"Of course, the allure of the hourglass figure always depends on how much sand is in the hourglass, but I'll take you at your word. The one thing I've always respected about you is your taste in women. If she's so hot and you go so far back, why haven't you hooked up with her?

Telling him the truth about Bobbie Jo wouldn't help get his cooperation, so instead I told him the truth about me. "I'm still in mourning. Nobody can compare to Katherine, so I'm not even looking."

"You're too young to mourn this long, but I understand. I'm sorry I asked." Woodbury almost sounded like a human being as he said it, but he soon reverted to his normal self. "Of course, if you ain't getting any poontang, what's the point of going to bed at night or getting up in the morning?"

"At the moment, my point is to find Charlie's guitar. Are you going to help me or has DPD closed the case?"

"Shit, we never close an unsolved case; we just ignore some of them longer than others. I bet there's still an open file somewhere on the Kennedy shooting. What kind of help do you want? I'll help you until I find out this sister of his weighs 200 pounds or is tore up from the floor up."

"In the spirit of cooperation, I promise not to tell her you suggested that about her. All I'd really like right now is to review the case report so I can avoid repeating steps you've already taken."

"Oh Hell, I can do more than that. Sit tight a minute." With that he turned to his computer and started typing. Pretty soon, his printer kicked in and he turned back to me. "As I'm sure Charlie told you, the theft, if it was a theft, occurred at the Center for Community Cooperation over on Live Oak. Have you been there, yet?"

"Not yet, I wanted to see the report first."

"And you just assumed I'd love to cooperate?"

"Of course, besides I didn't see anything on the internet this morning indicating that the Freedom of Information Act was repealed. I'm pretty sure it will be a big story nationally if it happens, even the Morning Snooze will have to cover it."

Woodbury laughed, "I suppose they will, assuming anybody left over there even knows what it is." He pulled the stack of pages

off the printer and handed them to me. "I'll take you over there; you can read it on the way. I can't wait to see how much you love the place."

I had no idea what he meant by that, but I followed him to his car as if I couldn't wait, either. His Ford Mustang was parked illegally on Lamar Street between two police cruisers which were also illegally parked. I got in and skimmed the report as he drove. Even as I concentrated on reading the report, I could tell that Woodbury was ignoring almost every traffic law as we made the trip.

Thanks to his aggressive driving, the ten minute trip to the Center for Community Cooperation took just a little over nine minutes. It wasn't enough time to really study the report, but at least Woodbury let me read it in silence. As he ushered me into the lobby of the main building of the Community Center, I saw immediately why he couldn't wait to see my reaction.

The nameplate on her desk said her name was Lisha McDonald.

06 Striking Resemblance

Lisha wore her hair curly, short and black, exactly the way Katherine wore hers when we were in high school. But even if her hair had been different than any style Katherine ever wore, she would still have been the spitting image of Katherine. She had the same semi-arched eyebrows, the same high cheekbones, the same dimple and the same hallucinogenic hazel eyes. As we approached, she smiled with the same almost perfect smile that my late fiancée had dazzled me with when she first won my heart.

It was like seeing a ghost and it felt like I'd been hit. Rather, it felt like being hit would feel like if I could feel physical pain. I fought through the emotional pain and sat in a chair beside Woodbury across from the desk at which Lisha sat in front of a computer. She typed with great concentration and an indirectly proportional lack of speed. She stopped typing as soon as we were both seated.

"Hi, Richard, I mean Detective Woodbury; how nice to see you." She said in a voice that sounded exactly like Katherine's.

Hearing a ghost was more than I could handle. "Air! Excuse me, I need some fresh air." I tried to not run, or at least to run with a modicum of dignity, but I'm sure I failed on both counts. The last thing I heard as I went through the door was Lisha giggling exactly the way Katherine used to giggle.

I was sitting cross legged in a grassy peninsula between two empty parking spaces trying to breathe normally when Woodbury came out. "Are you okay?"

"You knew, didn't you? You knew who she looked like and you knew I wouldn't be able to handle it. You Mother…"

"Easy there, tough guy. Yes, I knew who she resembled. I'm sorry. What the Hell was I supposed to do? You're looking for Charlie's guitar. It disappeared from here. There's no way you were going to look for it without running into Lisha at some point."

"You could at least have warned me or something."

"Could I? What could I have said that you would have paid attention to? It's no secret you don't like me. You haven't liked me since we tried to shut down your act years ago."

"Tried to frame us on drug charges, you mean."

"Not me, man. That was my dumb-ass partner. Internal Affairs fired him and cleared me completely. I even got an accommodation for helping them nail the dumb son of a bitch."

"Whatever." Obviously not the most original thing to say, but it was all I could think to say. I decided to say it again, "Whatever."

"Look, I know you hate me. I'll even admit you have a good reason to dislike me. I'll also admit you're not my hero, but I don't dislike you, and I do like your partner. He may be the most upstanding person I've ever met.

"So when you told me y'all were on this case, I knew this was going to happen. I knew I couldn't prevent it, and I knew I couldn't make it any easier for you. I couldn't let you come here alone, and nothing I could have said would have convinced you that you shouldn't. So I brought you myself. I ask again, what the Hell was I supposed to do?"

I was trying so hard to pull myself together that I didn't even try to answer. Here I was on my first case alone as a real detective and I couldn't even get through the first interview with the first person who might be able to help without losing control. Sure, there were contributing circumstances, but I wasn't happy with myself.

Woodbury squatted on the grass by me, "Freak, look at me!"

I did.

"It's always going to be hard, but it'll get a little easier as more time passes. Coincidences like Lisha will make it harder, but you'll be okay. You've got people who care about you, you've got a career. And right now, you've got a damn guitar to find."

"And if I have to talk to Lisha to find it?"

"Then, you'll have to find a way to talk to her without having another conniption."

"And if I can't?"

"Then your partner will have to talk to her, or I'll do it. Other than the fact that she looks exactly like your late fiancée, she is a wonderful girl. I explained a little about your issue, and she gave me the key to the building where the guitar was stolen and agreed to let us look around without joining us."

He reached down and grabbed my arm tentatively and pulled me up, "Come on, let's go be detectives and study the scene of the crime."

And that is exactly what we did. For over two hours we studied the building where the DSA holds its workshops and meetings. We agreed that there wasn't much chance that a fairly ordinary guitar would be the target of a premeditated theft. Therefore, we were evaluating every possible way that an opportunist might have taken that opportunity to steal that guitar at that time.

We used his stopwatch to determine how long it would have taken to get from the performance room, steal a guitar and stash it in a car in the parking lot. We timed how long it would take to come inside from a car and steal it and get back. We evaluated sight lines. Some of the things we measured I didn't fully understand, but I helped measure them all. We walked the perimeter to see what a passerby might have seen.

A window in the storeroom faced Oak Street. But if somebody saw something they wanted through that window, it would have been easier to break the glass and take it than to go all the way around to the entrance, hoping to sneak in unnoticed. Besides, nobody ever walks on Oak Street. It leads from one street nobody walks on to another street nobody walks on. It might as well be in L.A. for all the foot traffic it gets.

All the while, Woodbury took notes. I didn't learn much about who took Charlie's guitar, but I learned a little about police work. Finally, I asked him, "Did we just do all this to clear my mind?" I pointed to his notepad, "Isn't everything in there already in the report?"

"Hah. We weren't even sure the guitar was stolen the first time we came out here. You wouldn't believe how many stolen goods cases are actually just attempts to get a police report for a phony insurance claim. I'm not saying we thought Charlie was doing that, but sometimes simply filling out an initial report is the only requirement of the job."

"So what have we learned today that isn't in the report?"

"I don't know what we've learned, but here's what I think. Charlie wouldn't have hired you if his guitar hadn't really disappeared. I don't know what you're charging him, but it's got to be more than he can collect from an insurance company. If somebody picked it up by mistake, they'd have returned it by now."

"All of which we knew before we came down here."

"Well, I think we ruled out somebody walking in off the street to steal it. It almost certainly had to be somebody who was at the workshop, so now you get to earn your fee. I'll update the report and make you a copy, and I'll search the pawnshop database more thoroughly and let you know what I find."

I suspected I knew the answer, but I asked anyway, "How many people have you questioned who were at the workshop?"

"None, we didn't go that far." He tried to sound apologetic, but didn't quite succeed, "Also, the list in the report isn't complete. Only those that pre-registered are on it. Let's go. We aren't going to find anything else here."

I followed him to his car. When we got there, I made a decision. "Wait here, I'll be out in a minute."

As I walked to the main building, he called out to me, "Are you sure about this?"

Of course I wasn't sure, but I was doing it anyway. I steeled my nerves and walked to Lisha's desk. My eyes were on her nameplate, maybe trying to remind myself that she's not Katherine. When I got to her desk, I held out my hand and introduced myself.

She shook my hand, "Nice to meet you, I'm Lisha."

"I'm sorry about wigging out earlier."

She handed me a business card. "Don't worry about it. Richard told me about your loss and how much I look like her. I can't imagine how difficult things are for you, but I'm sorry. If you ever need someone to talk to, call me. I wrote my cell number on the back. I've been told I'm a world-class listener and maybe on the phone it won't be so bad for you."

I put her card in my pocket and we parted ways on much better terms than we started. On the way to Woodbury's car, I realized that I did need to talk to somebody and not on the phone. Fortunately, the girl I needed to talk to didn't look anything like Katherine.

Woodbury didn't ask how it went; he just put the car in gear as soon as I was seated. "I'm done for the day. Can I drop you somewhere?"

"Walt Garrison's Rodeo Bar,' I said.

Woodbury smiled and started driving back downtown. "Of course, like I said, I do admire your taste in women. Give my best to April."

07   Stolen Kiss

Woodbury dropped me off at the Rodeo Bar just before 4 o'clock. April was behind the bar looking as stunning as always. She didn't see me enter. It was early enough that the bar wasn't packed, and I briefly considered taking a stool at the bar. Then I remembered how busy bars get on Fridays as early afternoon turns into evening and went to my usual table in the corner under a television.

I had barely seated myself when a waiter came over, "Hi, I'm Chris. Welcome to Dallas. What can I get you to drink?"

I didn't bother telling Chris that I wasn't new to Dallas; coming alone to a hotel bar obviously leads to certain assumptions. So, I just said, "Nice to meet you, Chris. I'll take a Coke and if you could, let April know I'm here."

He smiled at me the way a pimp smiles at a trick and walked toward the bar. With his bleached blond hair and Primetime Sanders swagger, he reminded me of the kids I used to see in Deep Ellum posing. as tough guys. He was almost certainly a college student, probably SMU, but possibly one of the schools at the Universities Center on Main Street.

He talked to April, and she glanced my way and smiled. Even from twenty yards away, her smile is dazzling, to say the least. She poured a Coke and brought it to me. As always, every man in the bar watched her walk. I noticed with amusement that Chris was the least subtle member of her admiration society.

"Goodness, Baby, you look terrible!" She sat beside me and gave me a side hug. "Tell Dr. April all about it."

"Bartender, actress, detective, and now Doctor; aren't you a little jack of all trades?"

"Of course I am. After all, I am a woman. Now tell me what happened before the customers have time to notice that Chris doesn't know shit about tending a bar."

"I take it you're not a fan. He seems to think highly of you."

"He thinks highly of anybody in a skirt; almost as highly as he thinks of himself. Now, kindly quit trying to avoid the subject and tell me why you look so depressed."

I realized that I had been delaying the inevitable. I told her about the case and the encounter with Lisha. I wasn't proud of my 'conniption' as Woodbury had called it, but I told her about it. She

24

listened, as she always did, hanging on every word. I think they teach that at the bartending academy.

When I finished, she asked, "Which was worse, being reminded of Katherine or letting a cop see your human side?"

I was saved from having to answer by Chris' interruption. "April, Frank wants another beer, but he insists that you bring it to him."

"Men, worse yet, regulars," April sighed. "Sure, Baby," she said to Chris "I'll take care of it." Turning to me, she said, "Regulars, you've got to show them some love, if you want them to show you the money. Sit tight, baby. I'll be right back."

April calls everybody 'Baby', even people she doesn't like. I think she learned that at the bartending academy, too. Chris winked at me as she got up, then turned and followed her. Even from behind them, I could tell that his eyes never drifted from her butt. Chris had already poured the beer, so April picked it up and took it to her regular, Frank Arrington. Regular was a good word for him. I don't think I've ever seen a more regular looking guy.

The fear of turning out like him is one reason I changed my name and started the 'Freak Show Revue' in the first place. April stayed at his table long enough to ensure that he'd show her the money when he left his tip. She also laughed at a couple of his jokes for him. I drank a little of my Coke and thought about why it bothered me so much meeting a girl who looked and sounded like Katherine.

April finished with Frank, made the rounds of her other customers and walked back to my table. As she sat down, she hugged me again and said, "How's the patient?"

"A little better, I think."

"Okay, then answer the question. What bothered you so much?"

"Even before I knew her name, I knew Katherine was unique and special, so the fact that she loved me made me think I was unique and special. When I saw Lisha sitting there looking exactly like her, it shook me to the core. What if she loves somebody exactly like me? That would make me just another clone like Frank over there."

"Oh baby, you know better than that. I never met Katherine, but do you really think her looks and voice made her special? You're not that shallow. Her heart, and the love you two had for each other, made her special. Besides, everybody has a look-alike somewhere. It's not surprising that Katherine would have one in her own hometown. Maybe Lisha's her sister."

I objected, "Katherine didn't have a sister, just the one brother who looks nothing like her."

"Are you sure about that? Her daddy wasn't exactly the poster boy for fidelity in a marriage. There's no telling how many half-sisters Katherine might have. He'd be my baby daddy if I'd let him have the chance, remember?"

I shuddered, "I hadn't thought of that."

"Of course not, you're too shook up to think straight. That's why you came to see Doctor April."

"Maybe if I see her again, I should ask Lisha if her mom had an affinity for assholes."

April gave me a courtesy laugh like she'd give any of her regulars. "Or better yet, you might try asking her a question that will help you find that guitar. I believe solving cases is a better way to become a successful private eye than insulting girls you don't know."

"Sure it is. Any thoughts on what question that would be?"

"That's not my department, Baby. Did you forget the Pegasus Investigations organizational chart? My job is to look pretty, boost morale and occasionally seduce a suspect. You and Mr. Jennings are supposed to come up with the right questions and get the right people to answer them."

I returned the courtesy laugh. "Sure it is, and you do all three jobs well. Unfortunately, I have no idea what questions to ask or who to ask; and Mr. Jennings is either waiting for a boat or on one, blissfully unaware that we even have a case."

"You didn't call and tell him? We finally talked him into getting a cell phone and taking it with him, and you didn't call him when you got a case. Why not?"

"I don't even know how much it costs to take a call wherever he is, and he wouldn't want us to spend more on roaming fees than we get for solving the case."

The bar was filling up and a group of five was waiting at the entrance for a table. April saw them and waved them over. She picked up my coke and smiled her Cheshire cat smile. "You go back to your office and call your partner. The Coke's on me, but you better call me tonight and tell me you called him and have a plan to find Charlie's guitar."

I couldn't think of one good reason not to follow her suggestion. I stood up, smiled at the group taking the table and hugged April. I was almost to the revolving entrance door, when I heard April call my name.

"Wait up!" she said.

I turned around, and April was right in front of me. She put her hands on my shoulders, stood on her tiptoes and kissed me. "You've always been unique and special. You always will be. Don't ever forget that!"

She walked away before I could think of anything to say. It was the first time I'd been kissed since the last time I saw Katherine. It came very close to being the last time.

08   Phone Calls

Fifteen minutes later, I was back at the office with three things I needed to do. I needed to call the Great Detective, find a stolen guitar and check email since I'd been out all day. Since I didn't have a clue how to do the second and felt very uncomfortable about the first, I started with the email.

First I deleted and tried to block and report some of the spam. I also deleted a few catalogs advertising products I hadn't needed since I shut down the revue. I can't bring myself to block them since I used to be a customer, but I don't think Pegasus Investigations will ever order many suspension tethers or cat-o-nine whips.

I was deleting unsolicited email so fast that I almost missed the important one. My filtering software had filed Charlie Ray's email as junk. I opened it and read:

"I'm glad you're looking for the notebook and guitar. I know you may never find them, but knowing that you're trying has cleared my mind. Even Bobbie Jo has noticed that I'm out of my funk and she's so heartbroken over Kim dumping her that she doesn't always notice anything."

"Anyway, I found other copies of a lot of what was in the notebook, including the files on my computer that JoJo entered for me before she decided if she was going to be a groupie, she wanted to be a groupie for a famous band and went to Nashville. I don't know why I haven't written a song about that yet; maybe I did and it's in the damn stolen notebook."

"Anyway, I've attached them to this email. I don't know if it'll help you search, but if nothing else, it might help me establish copyright if that polecat does try to steal one of my songs."

There were seventeen attachments to the email, which explained why it ended up in my junk folder. It also gave me something to do other than call Carl. Since he was on a cruise ship by now with his lovely chameleon lady, I figured he wanted nothing more than to spend a few weeks with no interruptions from anybody associated with Pegasus Investigations.

After printing out 42 pages of complete and incomplete lyrics and chord progressions that I barely knew how to read and had no way to learn anything from I realized I was going to need some expert help on this case. From my years in the entertainment business, I knew my share of musical experts. I wondered if I knew any who would help for free.

That got me thinking about how the Great Detective could always get people to help him, usually without even asking. I sighed to myself in the empty office; put down the stack of papers and picked up the phone. I logged into my MySpace page while I dialed.

As I dialed, I half expected the call to go straight to voice mail since I doubted if he'd remember to keep it charged. To my surprise the phone rang; to my greater surprise he answered on the third ring having obviously checked the caller i.d.

"Freak, what's going on? Is everything okay?"

"Sure man, calm down. I just wondered if we knew any musical experts who might help us on a case for a client who really can't afford to pay too many expenses for expert assistance."

The line was silent while he thought about the question. By this time I was used to silence while he thought. I expected him to ask about the case or the client, but instead he was focused on answering the one question. He's always been good at that.

He answered sooner than I expected. "That should really be your area from your time in show-business. Bobbie Jo's brother might help if he's not still mad at me. Maybe you can get Bobbie Jo to ask him. Have you talked to Sam The Man? He might be able to put you in touch with somebody who owes him a favor or wants to be on the good side of a 7 foot, 300 pound Nigerian."

"Damn, I should have thought of Osalumense." I liked calling him by his real name because hardly anybody else can pronounce it. "He's a bouncer, he has to know somebody. Aren't you going to ask about the case?"

"Sure, but first, I need to tell you something so Emily will quit elbowing me in the ribs."

"Okay, go ahead."

I wondered how long the silence would be this time. Apparently, he already knew what he wanted to say and how he wanted to say it. "We got married. This cruise is our honeymoon."

Nothing could have blind-sided me more, but I knew what I was supposed to say, "Congratulations." I said keeping my voice steady, "to you both."

"Freak, are you okay. You sound like you're about to lose it."

So maybe I didn't quite keep my voice steady. "I'm fine. It's just been kind of a rough day."

"Well, Emily's not hitting me any more so tell me about it. Tell me about the case, too."

I told him everything, except I left out the kiss from April. When I finished, he was silent for closer to his customary time. He had his thoughts organized when he did speak, "Okay, obviously this was a bad time to spring the wedding news. We're both sorry about that. You did the right thing going to talk to April; she could cheer up Marvin the Robot even if she looked like a Vogon Commander."

His analogies often varied depending on which movie he most recently watched. Obviously, he'd screened Hitchhiker's Guide recently. I ignored it and let him continue.

"I think you're right that we're going to need a music expert. The guitar is going to be hard to find, but if we can find somebody performing something from the notebook, we'll have a lead. I like Charlie Ray's music, but I don't think I could distinguish it from anybody else's. By the way, did Charlie Ray sign the contract."

That question surprised me, "No, I didn't think we'd need that from him."

"Good. That means there is nothing in writing saying we have to bill all expenses to him or that he has to pay them. If we have to hire a musical expert, we can pay it ourselves and call it a tax deduction."

"Not sure that's a great way to run a business, but if you're okay with it, I am. What should I do next?"

He answered immediately, "Call April; then find Charlie's guitar. Don't spend all your time on the computer; you may have to solve this case in real life. When I get back from my honeymoon, we'll all celebrate your first solved case."

After he hung up, I closed out my MySpace page without even checking my New Friend Requests and looked over the papers I'd printed out from Charlie's email. I realized that the expert didn't have to be a music expert. I had two calls to make. I called April first. I figured my morale could use a boost almost as much as Adams' manic depressive robot.

She answered on the first ring, "Did you do it?"

"Did I do what? Make that phone call or hatch a plan to find the guitar?"

"Both, I guess, but I meant did you make the call?"

"Yes, I did. He offered some good advice as always. I've got a couple of things to do that might help find the guitar."

"And?"

"And what?"

"Did he tell you anything about the cruise? Have they done anything fun or life changing?"

"Oh, you mean like getting married? I think he did mention something about it."

She shrieked, "I knew it! I knew they had a reason for going on a cruise. Tell me all about it."

"For a girl who can wrap any man around your finger in a matter of seconds, you sure don't know much about men. He said they got married; then we talked about the case. You'll have to get all the details from Emily."

"Men," she sighed. "Maybe Bobbie Jo has the right idea after all."

I presumed she was kidding, but I didn't ask. I had another phone call to make. The thing about running a freak show is that you get to meet freaks, such as The Amazing Raymond. Unfortunately for Ray, our audiences preferred tortured people or nearly naked girls swallowing spiders over the most incredible mind I've ever encountered.

I'd heard Raymond retired from show business and was living as a recluse, so I wasn't surprised when he answered after one ring, "Hello."

"Raymond, how have you been?"

He interrupted, "Freak! I don't know where you're playing or what you're paying. I'm not interested. I'm retired from public life. I make a good living doing Medical Transcription on my home computer. They mail checks to my house; nobody ever laughs at me and I haven't been booed in over a year."

"I guess you didn't hear. I closed down the revue. I'm retired, too. I'm a private eye now. I'm on a case for Bobbie Jo's brother."

I heard a sharp intake of air on the other end of the line when I said Bobbie Jo. I'd forgotten that Raymond's reaction to Bobbie Jo was exactly the opposite of the Great Detective's reaction to her pets. I optimistically explained what I wanted him to do.

He considered briefly before responding, "Memorizing all of Charlie's lyrics should take me about a minute. But hanging out in bars listening to bad singers until I hear a match will take longer. How do you plan to make that worth my while?"

"How much do you want?"

Raymond laughed. "Freak, there's not enough money in the free world to get me to put myself through that. I haven't even been to one of those places since I left show business. I'm much happier here with my computer. But, if Bobbie Jo goes with me as my date, I'll go to every bar in Texas until you solve the case."

I had already used Bobbie Jo's looks once today on this case, but I couldn't do that to Raymond. "Raymond, you haven't forgotten that you're not really her type, have you?"

"Oh, you mean because I'm a guy. No, I haven't forgotten that. I never forget anything, dummy. But, my god, have you ever considered what a wing girl she can be?"

I've heard of wing men and wing girls, but I'm not sure I really understand what one does. Nevertheless, I agreed to ask Bobbie Jo if she'd be willing to do it to help her brother. By the time, I finished with Raymond, it was late enough that I decided to just spend another night on the couch in the office lobby.

My first order of business in the morning was to call Bobbie Jo and ask her to be a wing girl. Knowing that she is much more of a morning person than most performers, I set the alarm for 8 a.m. just in case I slept for a change. I looked over the police report one more time and made sure the office was secured. Then, I laid me down to either sleep or count sheep all night.

09   Fiery Night

I dreamt I was enveloped in fire. It was a nightmare I often had when I did sleep. In real life, even fire can't cause me physical pain, but in my dreams the pain always feels real. Recurring dreams usually have meaning, but I have too many broken dreams to worry about one nightmare I can easily explain.

Tonight's dream was loud, but lacked the usual pain. As always, it felt real. I listened to the sirens and tried to use the blanket to protect myself from flames that weren't there like I always did. I was reflecting on the irony of only feeling physical pain when I was asleep when I realized that I was actually awake.

I looked out the north window and saw real flames. I wasn't having a nightmare; the intersection of Wood Street and Ervay was aflame. I grabbed the fire extinguisher and ran though the waiting room. Fortunately, my ROTC training kicked in, and I felt the outer door before I rushed out.

It felt a little warm. Given that it's a thick steel security door; even that warmth almost certainly meant the flames had reached it. That meant it would be smarter to wait for the fire department to put out the fire. I retreated back into the office. I had no idea what started the fire outside, but I knew I was glad the office was a virtual fortress.

It took the fire department less than half an hour to put out the blaze. I realized that I had no chance of actually sleeping now, so I went outside to access the damage. As I started down the staircase, I saw four fire trucks and at least ten police cars. As I reached the ground, I heard somebody call out, "Freak!"

I turned toward the sound of the voice and was surprised to see a large, black man named Blake Harrison standing beside one of the fire trucks talking with a short, pudgy white man in a wrinkled suit. Blake is a rising star in the Dallas County's Sheriff's department, whose official title isn't exactly clear. He's also the Great Detective's best friend.

Since fires aren't generally county business, I guessed he wasn't here officially. "Blake. What brings you to this part of town at four in the morning? Get kicked out of all of Deep Ellum's after hours joints?"

33

Blake laughed, "I could ask you the same question, except I'd be afraid of the answer I'd get. Maybe you didn't notice, but there's been a bit of a fire."

"Has there? Maybe you didn't notice, but I've been training to be a private eye. As part of the training, I've learned that the Dallas County Missing Person's department doesn't usually work arson cases."

Blake put his arm around my shoulder and walked me away from the guy in the suit without introducing us. When we got to the Neiman Marcus window, we stopped, and he asked, "Do you know something you ought to be sharing?"

"Me, I was just working late and decided to crash in the office. It doesn't take a forensics' expert to deduce that a fire might be arson when there are more cops than firemen at the scene. Besides, empty streets don't usually spontaneously combust."

Blake pointed to a floral patterned dress in the display window, "Do you think Jade would like that?"

"If you bought it for her, she'd love it. Unless, of course, she found out how much you paid for it. She'd much rather you buy her a similar dress from Nordstrom at a more reasonable price."

"Yeah, you're probably right. It would look good on her, though."

"Of course it would. So you're down here window shopping. That makes sense; no better time to avoid the crowds."

"No, I'm here because the county database still lists your office as Carl's residence. An acquaintance of mine in dispatch wanted me to know what was happening. The first calls to 911 sounded like this might be serious."

"Might be serious; aren't all fires serious?"

"No, I mean serious! Like terrorist attack or gang war. You crashed here because you were working late on a case. Tell me about your case."

"I'm looking for a missing guitar." I told him, leaving out any details about whose guitar it was or how we got the case.

"No, seriously, tell me what you're working on. Even if it's not a terrorist attack, fires being set in Downtown Dallas are serious. I need to know what you're working on if I'm going to be able to help y'all."

"Help us?" I had a hard time not laughing. "You're going to help find a guitar? We're a half mile from Deep Ellum and this is as close to the Dallas music scene as you've ever been. I don't think you can tell the difference between an acoustic guitar and an electric one. How in the Hell do you think you're going to help me find a guitar?"

Blake put his arm around my shoulder and turned so we were both facing the office of Pegasus Investigations and the rubble which surrounds it. "Fuck the guitar case, or whatever the Hell case you're really working on. How do you plan to explain why your office is the only part of your building left undamaged by the explosions?"

For some reason, my mind went to something my dad used to say whenever a sensationalistic weather forecast called for winter storms, and instead Dallas succumbed to about three snowflakes. "I guess the storm missed us," I said.

"The storm didn't miss you, Freak. Your building was the eye of the damn storm and people are going to wonder why only your office is still standing."

Technically, the vacant office below ours was also still standing, but Blake had a valid point. I'd known the office was a virtual fortress years before it became my office, but I had no idea why. The Great Detective never said anything about it, and always changed the subject when it came up.

It was starting to sink in just how close I'd come to being blown to pieces, and I just stared at the rubble trying to gather my thoughts. The one thought I kept having was how much better my chance would have been to actually sleep if I just hadn't been too lazy to walk home last night.

Blake interrupted my reflection, "Okay, Freak, I know your mentor is the silent assassin, but you need to talk to me. What's going on?"

"Blake, I have no idea. All I know is nobody blows up an entire city block over an $800 guitar. Besides, I really haven't even started looking for it. I talked to the investigating officer today, and tonight I was trying to map out a plan.

"I watch enough movies to know that crooks don't blow up detectives until they find a clue. In this case, I don't have a clue." I knew I'd left myself open for an easy insult, but Blake passed.

"Your case really is a missing guitar? That's about as small-time as a case can get. Almost sounds like something Encyclopedia Brown would take." Blake's tone was sad, not mocking. I was still so happy to have any case, I didn't care.

"No job too small," I said.

He smiled and looked at the rubble again, "I guess not. Okay, I'm not even involved officially, but I'll keep my ears open and try to let you know how much heat, make that pressure, you guys should expect about the building. You should call Carl first thing in the morning. I don't know what it takes to get back from a vacation cruise, but he may want to get back soon."

I doubted it, but I promised Blake I would make the call. He shook my hand and walked north on Ervay. I wondered how far from the scene he'd parked his car to make sure it wasn't noticed. I couldn't think of any reason to go back to the office, so I walked home.

As I put the key in my front door, I noticed something hanging from the door knob. I grabbed it and looked at it. It was a metal dog tag necklace with the inscription '1 Corinthians 6:18'. I draped it over my neck, tucked it under my shirt and went inside.

I never was much into religion, but Katherine was very devoted. Her influence and some things that have happened since she died have me at least leaning toward faith. I made a note to look up the scripture in Katherine's Bible sometime. It was after six in the morning, so I blew off the idea of trying again to sleep.

Instead, I made breakfast and waited for a decent hour to start making phone calls. I had promised Blake I'd call the Great Detective first thing, but I wasn't going to do that. I had no intention of calling him on his honeymoon without something positive to report on our case. The office is just a building; solving cases is our business. It was clearly time for me to start solving one.

10   Wing Girl

I called Bobbie Jo at eight and explained that I wanted her to be Raymond's wing girl and why. She was, to say the least, incredulous. "You seriously want me to go clubbing with the Amazing Raymond? Are you insane? Even women who like men can't stand to be around him for more than a few minutes at a time."

"Hey, I'll admit he looks a little nerdy, but he's not that bad. I've seen bigger geeks than him with hotties hanging on their arms."

"Oh God, Freak. I'm not talking about his looks. What would I care about his looks? The man never stops talking about himself, never."

"Maybe he's changed. Now that he's out of show business, maybe he's learned to talk about something other than himself. Hell, he's doing transcription work out of his home. Surely, even he knows that nobody is interested in that."

"I doubt it. He's always been the center of his own universe and he always will be. Don't you have any other way of finding Charlie's guitar?"

"If I did, would I be calling you at eight in the morning?"

"No, I guess not. I'll do it, but I'm not letting him pick me up. I'll meet him at the clubs and hang out with him, but that's it."

I told her that should be fine and that I'd call her and let her know as soon as we had the details worked out. Now I had a case, and at least a plan to start solving it. It was time to call the Great Detective and tell him the good news.

While I was at it, I would need to mention that our office building exploded. Then, I could mention that he was a horse's ass for not mentioning that he was going on the cruise to get married.

I hate telephones. I hate making calls like this. Worse, I couldn't think of a single reason to keep putting it off.

Again he answered on the third ring, causing me to wonder about his honeymoon. "Hey Freak, did you already find the guitar?"

"No, but I've got a plan that might work." I told him about the plan.

He listened to the plan and responded in his own due time, "Sounds like it might work. It also doesn't sound like anything you need my help to implement. That means you called for some other reason. Since you didn't start with the other reason, I'm presuming it's not good. I'm sitting down. Tell me what's going on."

"I saw Blake this morning; he seemed to think I should call you."

"You've seen Blake this morning. It's what 10 o'clock there, and you've already seen Blake?"

"Actually, it's not quite nine. It was about four when I saw Blake. We stood in front of Neiman Marcus looking at what was left of the office buildings which surround our office. Apparently, our office is every bit the fortress you thought it was, but everything around it is rubble from the explosions and fire."

As I expected, he did not reply quickly. In fact, he didn't reply for a long time. I started to say something several times, but stopped myself. For one thing, I didn't know what to say. Plus, I wanted him to know I was learning how to use silence to my advantage.

"Okay, the office is still listed in my name. Somebody at the 911 dispatch center knows that Blake and I are friends and called him when the fire started. That part I get, but why did Blake go down there? He knows I'm on a cruise and he knows I don't live there. Besides, he knows enough about the building's modifications to know I wouldn't have been hurt even if I'd been there. For that matter, what were you doing there at that hour?"

"I was using the office computer to do some research until pretty late. Since I knew I wanted to call Bobbie Jo first thing this morning, I just decided to crash at the office."

"You decided to crash at the office because it was late? Your place is a twenty minute walk from the office, fifteen if you hurry. Are you sure you just didn't want to spend the night somewhere other than the house where all your memories are after seeing Lisha?"

I hadn't even thought of that, but it made sense. "Maybe, I don't know. I'm okay now though. Something about being in a building as it exploded around me took some of the edge off the coincidence of seeing Lisha." April may have helped some too, but that didn't need to be mentioned.

"That's good, I guess. Did Blake tell you why he was there?"

"He mentioned how good a floral dress in the window at Neiman's would look on Jade, but I told him it was too late for window shopping."

"Jade does look good in spring colors, but she would kill him if he spent that much on a dress. Blake's worried about the building, isn't he? He thinks we, make that I, did something that could cause trouble."

"Now that you bring it up, he did mention something about that. I didn't exactly know what to tell him. You always change the subject when it comes up. Are we in trouble?"

"No, we aren't in trouble. I just like being mysterious. All the modifications were made before I leased the building. If there are code violations, we aren't responsible. Feel free to check that with Larry Joe if you want, but as far I can tell, we're just law-abiding tenants who happened to rent the right corner of that old building. That is, unless the explosions had something to do with us. Did they?"

"Blake asked about that too, but I don't see how. Even if somebody wanted to blow up an entire city block over a guitar, it's not like we're on the verge of finding it. Random acts of violence aren't exactly rare in Dallas."

"True, but this one's pretty violent, and the police don't like to concede anything is random if they can help it. You'll probably have to spend some time talking to cops for a few weeks until I get back. Try not to irritate them too much; you never know when we might need their help."

"A few weeks," I asked. "You mean you aren't rushing back to take over for your junior partner? Blake was sure you would."

"If either of you think I'm rushing back from my honeymoon to find a guitar, you're crazy. Goodbye, partner."

I was so relieved about the building, and so happy to still be working my first case alone that I hung up without bitching about him getting married without telling anybody. I also didn't ask for any details about his wedding. April was almost certain not to like that.

As soon as I hung up, I called Raymond and told him Bobbie Jo had agreed to be his wing girl, but only if they meet at the clubs."

"No way, I've been stood up too many times to go sit at a bar and hope she shows up."

Somehow, that didn't surprise me. It also didn't sound promising. I offered a compromise. "What if y'all meet at my house, first? I'm only a few minutes from most of the clubs. If she shows here, then you can reasonably expect she'll meet you at the club. Plus, wouldn't it look good if you walked in alone, then a hot blonde showed up later and picked you out?"

"Okay, that might work. I'll try it once, but if she no-shows one time or treats me like shit, that's it. I'm not going to waste time listening for your stolen songs, if I'm not getting something in return. I'm a businessman, you know."

"That sounds fair to me. I'll call Bobbie Jo and see if she's okay with it."

"One more thing," he hesitated, and I was worried about where he was going. "No spiders, I don't mind them, but most chicks don't like them. A wing girl with a tarantula isn't much of a wing girl."

I wasn't sure he was right about that, though I'm sure the Great Detective would agree. I've never fully understood what does or doesn't impress girls. When I was torturing myself on stage, some girls seemed to like it. Besides, Bobbie Jo never has any trouble meeting girls, and the spiders are hers. Regardless, I agreed to ask Bobbie Jo to leave her beloved pet spiders at home.

11   Pet Sitter

Having made the necessary phone calls, I returned to my comfort zone: the PC in my bedroom. Raymond had agreed to go to clubs to listen for lyrics that might be Charlie's, and Bobbie Jo had agreed to accompany him as his wing girl. Now, all I had to do was find some clubs where people from the workshop would be playing.

I had skimmed the list, and it wasn't exactly a who's who of local singer/songwriters. In fact, it seemed to me that Charlie was the most successful one in attendance. It occurred to me that maybe that in itself was a clue. Maybe the guitar hadn't been the target after all. If so, maybe we weren't on as much of a wild goose chase as I feared.

One great thing about the internet is that everybody who wants to be famous is using it in the hopes of becoming famous. The fact that it's never really worked for anybody other than Tila Tequila doesn't keep everybody from trying. I already knew that everybody with a song, a poem, a video, a talent or even one stupid human trick like my own has a MySpace page to share it with the world whether the world wants it shared or not.

Of course, I'm no exception, so I simply logged on and started searching for the names on the list. As expected, within an hour I had found a MySpace page for twenty-one of the twenty-two people on the list. From these I found upcoming appearances for all but two. I made a list of every appearance and worked out a schedule for Bobbie Jo and Raymond that would allow them to see all nineteen performers over the next two and a half weeks.

I wasn't sure how many days or hours even that Bobbie Jo was going to be willing to put up with Raymond. Therefore, I decided which entertainers seemed most likely and tried to get their performances early on the schedule. That process was more guesswork than scientific evaluation, but at least I tried. By 3:30, I had a schedule and more phone calls to make.

I called Raymond first, "It's me. Are you ready to start clubbing and finding a stolen guitar?"

"You mean tonight?"

"No better time to start. Can you be at my house at 6:30?"

"Okay, I guess I'm as ready as I'm going to be. Bobbie Jo's not bringing the spiders, right?"

I hadn't actually talked to her about it, but I assured him that she wouldn't. Then, I called Bobbie Jo and asked her to meet us at 6:30 at the house. She agreed readily.

"One more thing," I said hesitantly. "Raymond doesn't think your little lovelies should come along. No offense, but I think he may be right. If he's distracted by them, he may miss something."

"Why Freak, you're becoming a real diplomat. I'm impressed. Actually, I assumed that. I've been trying to find somebody to baby-sit with no luck. Charlie's got a gig, my parents are out of town and Sam The Man is working tonight. Can I bring them and leave them with you?"

"Sure, but in that case, come a little early and we'll put them upstairs until Raymond leaves. I don't know how squeamish he may be. If he's like the Great Detective, just knowing he'd been in the same house with them could throw him off all night."

"Yea, I'll come early. I still can't believe that Mr. Jennings, who's such a giant of a man, in so many ways, is scared senseless by a couple of three ounce bundles of joy. I'll see you at six. I'm going to the grocery store in a little bit. Do you need anything?"

Bobbie Jo knows I don't drive, and she worries about me quite a bit. "No, I'm fine. I stocked up at the Urban Market a few days ago. Thanks for asking, though."

"No problem. By the way, that wasn't your office that got blown up was it? I saw just a little bit on the news and it looked bad."

I didn't need her distracted, so I answered her sort of honestly, "No, our office wasn't damaged, but the fire was in our neighborhood. It may be a few days before we can get back in, though. They've pretty much cordoned off the area."

For the first time, it occurred to me to check the news reports on the fire. I went to the website of the Morning News which is and has always been the slowest downloading and least well organized website on the net. Eventually, I found the story and read it. A police spokesperson assured the citizens of the city that terrorism was not suspected, but declined to put forth any other explanation for the explosions.

The report also mentioned that there were no casualties or injuries since nobody was in the area at the time of the explosions. I didn't know whether to be insulted at being nobody or grateful that

42

Blake had apparently succeeded in diverting attention away from Pegasus Investigations and our fortress of an office.

Bobbie Jo arrived about fifteen minutes past five with her little lovelies in their purple carrying case/playpen. She also had a bag full of groceries from Tom Thumb. She handed me the purple case and I took it upstairs. I left it closed for now. It wouldn't do to have one come downstairs looking for Bobbie Jo while Raymond was here.

When I got back downstairs, Bobbie Jo had just finished putting some things in my refrigerator. "Bottled water and T.V. dinners do not count as 'stocked up'. You have to start taking better care of yourself. I know you're a freak of nature. I also know that you miss Katherine, but you have to occasionally mix some fruits and vegetables into your diet."

She threw me an apple. "You like apples. You ate them all the time when we were on tour. Have one."

I caught the apple and started eating it. She was right. She took one for herself, and the lecture ended. For the next forty minutes, we talked about other things; her current lack of a love life and how long that might last; my current lack of desire for one and how long that might last being two of the major subjects.

The third topic of conversation was the mission. Bobbie Jo expressed her concern that Raymond might be using this opportunity just to hang out with a pretty girl. Raymond was never a chick magnet, and advancing age and increasing bitterness couldn't be helping him in that regard.

"Look, I know he's a bit weird and somewhat self-absorbed, but he does have an amazing mind. I think he's doing this just as much to show off as he is to meet women. He certainly knows you well enough not to be harboring any crazy ideas."

Bobbie Jo nodded her head. "I know. He never seemed like a bad guy when he was with the revue, just extremely self-absorbed. I may just be nervous for no reason. What exactly is a wing girl supposed to do, anyway?"

"God, I don't know. I know a wing man is supposed to help his buddy hook up, but I don't even know how that works. How would I know how a wing girl does it? Just do what you can to keep Raymond on the case. If he asks you to do anything you're not comfortable with, just bail. If this doesn't work, we'll find another plan."

"Sure, you will. If you had another plan, we wouldn't even be trying this. You already told me that."

"Maybe I did. Charlie hired me to find the guitar and notebook. I asked you to help and I'm glad you are. But, that guitar is less important to me and to Charlie than you are. Don't do anything that makes you uncomfortable."

The doorbell rang at six fifteen and I answered it. Any concerns about Raymond's commitment to the actual case ended when he entered carrying a stack of notebook binders. He headed straight for the kitchen table and spread things out. He acted like it was his investigation and his plan we were implementing. Since he has the most incredible mind I've ever met, I didn't let it bother me. Or, at least if it bothered me, I didn't let it show.

He handed me some notebooks. "Here you go; I've recreated Charlie's notes in various orders. Each notebook is alphabetized by first word. The white notebook is his hooks; the blue one is choruses, the black one is verses and the red one has lyrics which could possibly be more than one."

Bobbie Jo rolled her eyes and asked, "How the Hell do you know a verse from a hook from a chorus?"

Raymond grinned, "Google sweetheart, I am the Amazing Raymond, and I've had over twenty hours to work on this."

Bobbie Jo looked at me and we both pretended not to be impressed. Raymond went back to his presentation. "The green notebook has all of the chord progressions and key changes that were in the notebook. The black one is all of the above sorted by titles. Titles can't be copyrighted and chord progression and key change similarities are seldom actionable, but we're only looking for leads, right?"

I nodded.

"Every page and every line in every notebook is numbered. Pick one up and turn to a page." He looked at me expectantly,. "Go ahead, read a line, Freak."

I obliged him, "The only three things I'll ever need are grace from God, love from you, and a nice cold bottle of beer."

"Okay, that's on page nine, line 12 of the white notebook, page 15, line 7 of the blue notebook and page 25, line 1 of the black notebook under the title 'Three Things'. It doesn't have a corresponding chord progression or key change."

I couldn't even pretend not to be impressed at this point, but still I asked, "How does this help?"

"When, and if, I hear something that might be stolen, I'll call you, tell you where to look and let you listen to the singer. If it's hook or chorus, it will come up again in the song. Just be sure you answer quickly. A typical song is only three to four minutes, maybe a bit longer live."

"Okay, I'll be here with the notebooks ready to answer on the first ring." I handed him the list of artists and the schedule. "Our first suspect is opening at the Double Wide in Deep Ellum at eight. You go ahead and Bobbie Jo will meet you there as we all agreed."

Raymond spent about 45 seconds reading the schedule and looked at Bobbie Jo as he handed it back to me.

"Okay, I've got it. I'll be at the Double Wide by eight. See you there, Bobbie Jo." I walked him to the door. As I opened it, Bobbie Jo surprised both of us. "If you don't mind, Raymond, I'll ride with you. I'm not exactly sure where the Double Wide is and we can talk a little about what we're planning to do on the way."

Apparently, I wasn't the only one who could be diplomatic. Raymond agreed readily, and I watched them walk to his BMW. He opened the door and held it for her like a true gentleman. I hoped that was a good sign, but I didn't have much confidence.

12   Romantic Liaisons

I spent next the few hours baby-sitting Bobbie Jo's spiders while she and Raymond went clubbing. I knew Bobbie Jo would be mad if I didn't let her little lovelies crawl around the place, so I brought them down and let them crawl around on the table with Raymond's notebooks.

At 11:25, the phone rang. I herded the spiders away from the notebooks as I answered, "Pegasus Investigations."

Bobbie Jo laughed, "How professional, I thought I'd called your cell phone, though."

"Sure, just wanted you to know we're on the job. Make sure you tell Charlie Ray we're on duty 24/7."

"Sure thing, I'll tell him that when I talk to him."

I could hear music in the background, so I presumed they were still in Deep Ellum. "How's it going? Is Raymond acting right, or do I need to head over there and kick his ass for you?"

"Yes and no. Raymond's been a perfect gentleman. He says the next performance on your list is at Adair's tomorrow afternoon. That's true, isn't it?"

I had to shoo one of her pets off my list to confirm it, but it was true. "Yes, your job is through for the night. Let me talk to Raymond."

"He's not here; he left right after the performer we came to see finished his show."

"Of course he did, he hates being out. Why did he leave you there? Is he bailing on the search or are you bailing on him?"

Bobbie Jo laughed softly before answering, "You do remember that I came here as his wing girl, right? Did you think I'd fail? Your genius boy wonder left me here to see if he and his new girl could get in the Ghost Bar. Do I rock or do I rock?"

It took me a minute to process what she'd said. "I guess you rock, but how do you plan to get home? And will Raymond continue the search tomorrow?"

"I'll find my way home, or at least I'll find my way somewhere." There was a slight pause before I heard her talking to someone, "Mandy, say hello to my friend, Freak. Promise him you'll take care of me or he'll worry all night."

46

There was a short silence as she handed off the phone before I heard a sultry feminine voice, "Is your name really Freak?"

"Some people think so, is your name really Mandy?"

She laughed, "Some people think so. How well do you know Bobbie Jo?"

"Well enough to care about her. You girls have fun, but if you hurt her, I'll find a way to make you hurt."

Mandy laughed. "She told me you'd threaten me, but I thought she was joking. That is so cool. I wish I had a friend like you."

"Any friend of Bobbie Jo is a friend of mine, so I guess you do."

"Unless I hurt her; I'll make sure I don't. That is, unless she wants me to. Hold on."

There was another silence as Mandy handed the phone back to Bobbie Jo. "Raymond and I will be at your house tomorrow at noon to continue the search. If you talk to his girl, try not to threaten her. Straight girls are such wimps about stuff like that."

"I'll try to remember that. I didn't realize you were such an expert on straight girls."

"Hey, I hooked up Raymond, didn't I? Only an expert could pull that off."

She had a valid point, so I let her have the last word. I went back to watching her three ounce bundles of joy crawl around. If there are easier pets to baby-sit than her tarantulas, I don't know what they are. Mostly, it involves watching them crawl around the house without stepping on them or screaming and running away.

The Great Detective wouldn't be able to do it, but for me it was pretty easy. The only thing troubling me was the fear that Raymond might not continue the quest now that Bobbie Jo had performed so well as his wing girl. Maybe, I should have warned her not to succeed too early.

Shortly after midnight, I rounded up Skipper and Skippette and returned them to their purple home and went to bed. It was a comfortable bed to not sleep in and I was comfortably not sleeping in it again when I heard the doorbell ringing at two-thirty in the morning. I got dressed quickly and went downstairs to answer it.

When I opened the front door, there stood Bobbie Jo and a petite redhead I presumed was Mandy on the doorstep arm in arm.

47

The redhead was certainly drunk, and Bobbie Jo was pretty close. I ushered them in and they sat together on the couch. I knew better than to vocalize assumptions, so I asked Bobbie Jo, "Aren't you going to introduce me to your friend?"

Mandy answered, "She already did, remember. We talked earlier. I'm Amanda and you're the world famous, incredible Freak Show." She slurred her words a little, but now that she was sitting down, she could almost pass for sober.

Bobbie Jo gave her a playful slap on the face, "You messed it up. He's the absolutely incredible Freak Show. I think you're drunk."

"I'm not near as think as you drunk I am. And you promised to introduce me to your eight legged pets."

New love, I can handle. New love shared by two beautiful girls, I can handle. New love, two beautiful, drunk girls and two spiders were more than I was ready to deal with at three o'clock in the morning. "Skipper and Skippette are upstairs. Why don't you two lovebirds go upstairs and spend the night with them. Neither of you is any shape to drive."

Mandy protested enough to prove her toughness, but it was easy for Bobbie Jo to talk her into staying. My couch isn't as comfortable as my bed, but I could not sleep on it just as easily as I could not sleep on the bed, so I didn't mind. I do care about Bobbie Jo, and it was nice to see her happy again. I wondered how long it would last, but that's always a question when the subject is love. The seventeen pictures of Katherine which still hang in my living area reminded me of that fact as I tried to sleep.

My fear about Raymond bailing proved unfounded. At twenty minutes before noon, Sunday morning he was in my living room with another notebook. "I realized that in a loud bar with a bad sound system, I'd never be able I to recognize the chord progressions or key changes, so I downloaded some guitar playing manuals. Now all I have to do is watch the player's fingers."

I was again impressed by his effort, but skeptical about his plan, "I didn't realize the 'amazing' in The Amazing Raymond was your eyesight. How do you plan to be close enough to the stage to see the performer's fingers?"

"Just like last night, I plan on Bobbie Jo and Mandy being able to get us wherever I want to get. Speaking of which, did Bobbie

Jo tell you when she was going to meet us here? I have a couple of questions for her before we go back to work."

On cue, Bobbie Jo and Mandy appeared at the top of the stairs. "Where's your girlfriend, Raymond?" Mandy asked.

Raymond blushed; then turned to me. "Can you give Bobbie Jo and me a few minutes alone?"

Just like that I went from lying on my living room couch while Bobbie Jo and Mandy shared my bedroom to sitting in my bedroom with Mandy while Raymond and Bobbie Jo talked in my living room. I wondered if this classified as the type of irony that always amused the Great Detective.

"You love her, don't you?" Mandy asked.

I looked at the picture of Katherine on my dresser and nodded, "Yes, I always will. I don't think I'll ever love another."

Mandy looked at the picture. "Oh my God, I'm such a ditz. I meant Bobbie Jo." She picked up the picture, "Who is this?"

For some reason, I didn't want to go into detail. "Katherine, she's gone."

"You and Bobbie Jo aren't, I mean, she's really a les... I mean she's...she's not..."

"Mandy, you made more sense last night when you were drunk. What are you trying to ask?"

"I got the feeling that you and Bobbie Jo were an item and I was just a game she was playing to try to shock you."

"Bobbie Jo loves to shock people, but she knows I'm not that easy to shock. Besides, I don't think she plays games like that. We're definitely not an item. You're her type; I'm not. But I meant what I said on the phone."

"If she doesn't play games, what was she doing at the Double Wide with that loser?"

"Did you ask her?"

"Yes, she said, 'I could tell you, but then I'd have to kill you' like she's some kind of secret agent or something. That's one reason I thought she was playing games."

I laughed, "That figures, she probably thought that would shock you. The truth is I'm a private investigator. She and Raymond are helping me on a case." I didn't see any reason to mention the triviality of the case or the fact that Bobbie Jo's brother was my client. I did hand her a Pegasus Investigations business card.

"Get out of here! Seriously? She really is doing something secret?"

"Well, it's not a secret government project or anything, but discretion is important in this business."

"Wow! And she still took time to hit on me." Her face glowed as she hugged me and kissed my cheek. "I won't hurt her, I promise. I just hope she doesn't hurt me."

After ten months without being kissed, I'd now been kissed twice in three days. I knew why Mandy had kissed me, but I started wondering about April's motivation. Was it just to cheer me up or something more? I'm pretty sure April is straight, although I can't remember seeing her with a man since I've known her.

Bobbi Jo came in the room and ended what was probably an awkward silence. "Amazing and I are headed to Adair's as planned. Want to come with, Mandy?"

"I'd love to, but Freak explained to me that you're working, and I don't want to be in the way. You'll call me?"

She sounded a little desperate; like she was still afraid Bobbie Jo wouldn't call. Bobbie Jo picked up on it. "Raymond, can you come up here a minute?"

Raymond appeared at the doorway, "What?"

"You've got the schedule memorized. I need to arrange my social life. What's the next night we don't have to work?"

"There's nothing Thursday."

Bobbie Jo turned to Mandy, "I'll call you Monday and you can tell me what you want to do Thursday night. You name it. I'm all yours Thursday."

13 Pawn Shops

Raymond and Bobbie Jo followed the schedule all day Sunday with no luck. I knew looking for a needle in a haystack could be a slow process. Still, by the time Bobbie Jo picked up her car and headed home Sunday night, I was frustrated. I didn't expect to find the guitar the first place we looked, but I had hoped to get a lead or two that I could pursue.

Monday morning, I rode the Dart Rail over to the Jack Evans Building to pay a visit to Detective Woodbury. I probably would have walked it, but the rain dissuaded me. The rain also gave me confidence that Woodbury would be in his office. Beat cops who get promoted don't tend to spend much time on the streets once they get an office. Beat cops who haven't been promoted usually manage to be in an office somewhere when it rains.

He greeted me as I came in, 'Freak, how's it going? Find the Hope Guitar, yet?"

"Hah. Not yet, but the search continues. Did you check the pawn shop database like you said you were going to do?"

"Actually, I did. I found two Dillon Black Dragons which had been pawned. I went and looked at both. Neither matched the description of Charlie Ray's."

"Thanks for checking. We appreciate it. Can you tell me where they are, so I can go look myself?"

"Sure." He turned to his computer and typed for a little bit. "One was at Value Plus on Montfort. The other was at Tony's on Irving Blvd."

"Thanks, I'll check them out."

"You do what you want, but like I said, I already checked them out." He got up and walked around behind me and closed his office door. When he was back at his desk, he said, "If I hired a Private Investigator to look for something, I'd expect him to look places the cops haven't already looked."

"Of course, who wouldn't? Do you have any suggestions?"

"Actually, I do. You know state law requires that pawnshops report every purchase they make to the police, so we can check it against the stolen goods database."

"I know that. That's how you found the two guitars you're sure aren't Charlie Ray's."

"Exactly, let's just say that some pawn shops are more conscientious about the process than others. DPD doesn't have the manpower to visit every pawn shop with a spotty reputation on the subject looking for one guitar, but somebody billing a client for his time might want to make the effort."

I smiled, "Sure, I wonder if there's a list of pawn shops that meet that description that I could have."

It was Woodbury's turn to smile. He turned back to his computer and started printing something. "Of course not, even if I had such a list; sharing it with a civilian would probably be actionable. Besides, we probably aren't even allowed to have a list like that. If we can't convict, we aren't supposed to accuse."

He stood up again and walked back to his door. This time when he had it open, he pointed at his printer, "Could you throw that away for me when it finishes printing?"

He was out the door before I could answer, which saved me the burden of pretending I was going to throw the list away. I picked it up and left the building. The rain had stopped, so I walked back home. I thought about walking by the remains of the office on the way, but thought better of it. I knew from the news that the area was still cordoned off while the authorities investigated the explosion, and I had no desire to be a part of that investigation.

There are over 400 pawn shops in the Dallas area. Of those, only 47 were on the list that Detective Woodbury officially didn't give me. As I read through the list, I wished I wasn't the rare private detective who didn't drive. After a couple of hours with the list and the Dallas Area Rapid Transit website, I realized it wasn't going to be a problem.

Forty-six of the forty-seven pawn shops which weren't fastidious about reporting their purchases to the police department were within a short walk of a bus stop. As I mapped out my visitation plan, it occurred to me that this probably wasn't a coincidence. More likely, it was a direct result of the human condition.

Not surprisingly, several of the pawn shops on the list were on Harry Hines, so I walked over to the East Transfer station and got on the 44 northbound. The fact that the 44 goes by the Sizzler

Steakhouse in Farmers Branch had no impact on my decision to check the pawn shops on Harry Hines first. It did, however, cause me to ride the bus out to Farmers Branch for lunch; then check the pawn shops on the way back downtown.

Monday afternoon, I checked eleven pawnshops with no success. I spent the evening at home hoping Raymond would call to say he'd heard something from Charlie Ray's notes. Tuesday was a repeat of Monday without the great lunch. The exciting life of being a detective was boring me to tears and the frustration of not finding anything wasn't helping matters.

By mid-morning Wednesday, I had checked all of the pawn shops on the list, as well as the two that Woodbury said he checked and looked at hundreds of guitars, none of which were Charlie Ray's. I decided to do what the Great Detective would do in this situation; I went to talk to Blake.

As I entered the George L. Allen building, it occurred to me that I should have called first to see if he was there. Luck was with me though; he was there and had time to talk. "Come on in, Encyclopedia Brown. Have you found that guitar, yet?"

"Not yet, the search, thus far, has turned up nothing on every front." I filled him in on what actions I had taken and asked him if he had any advice.

He considered for a few minutes before answering, "Actually, it seems like you've done everything you can do. It probably doesn't make you feel any better, but I am impressed. Either you have a knack for this, or you've been trained well."

"Thanks. But I really hoped you would tell me I had overlooked some obvious course of action."

"Sorry, if you missed something, I'm missing it, too. I'll let you know if I think of something. Hey, I do have some good news for you, though."

"I can use some good news right now. What?"

"You should be able to get back in your office by the end of the week. They're about finished with the investigation."

"What did they decide?"

"Well, they're chalking the explosions up as random acts of violence. They'll keep the case open, but no arrest is likely."

"What about our office's modifications?"

"Apparently, when those modifications were made; somebody greased some palms at city hall. Everything there is on the building permit. The fact that some of it hadn't been invented yet, when the building permit was issued raised a few eyebrows. But, nobody has any interest in looking into it very closely."

"Let he who is without sin, cast the first stone, huh?"

"Something like that. I've got to get ready for a meeting. Tell Carl I said 'hello', when you talk to him."

I promised I would and went back home to get ready for another exciting night waiting for a phone call that probably wouldn't come. I felt like an unattractive teenage girl. I doubted though that very many teenage girls waited for the phone to ring while watching two tarantulas feed on roaches from a Ziploc bag.

14 Highway Patrol

The phone rang at twenty minutes to eleven. In keeping with my imitation of a teenage girl, I eagerly answered on the first ring, "Hello."

Raymond said, "It's me. Listen to this and turn to page fourteen in the white notebook. Keep listening and read lines twenty-one through twenty-four."

Raymond quit talking and I could hear a male singer belting out what sounded like an old time country and western trucking tune. As I listened, I read the lines in the notebook. "There're sights all around in each Texas town, but I've no time to see them as I roll. As I speed right by, what catches my eye are armadillos and Highway Patrol.'

I'm no musical expert and cell phone technology hasn't advanced to the point where listening to a musician over one is an acoustic delight, but the guitar playing sounded really good. Then, the singer went into his next verse, 'There are scenes to be found, in each Texas town, but I don't see them as I roll. As the miles rush by, all that catches my eye are dead armadillos and the Highway Patrol.'

I listened to the rest of the song, which closed with a repeat of the same verse. Raymond came back on as soon is it ended. "We've got him, don't we? There's no way that's a coincidence, is there?"

"I don't see how. It's not the most original lyric I've ever heard, but it certainly seems unique enough that two people wouldn't write the same thing." I glanced over the schedule and continued, "So, you're at Poor David's Pub and that's Rick Taylor's band, right?"

"Actually, he's solo. He can play a guitar, I'll give him that. It's a Fender though, so it's not Charlie Ray's. What should I do now?"

"I don't know. I've been so consumed with hoping we find something, I haven't thought about what to do next. Is Bobbie Jo with you?"

"She was until I called you. She has a friend who works the bar here. She went to ask her what she knows about Rick Taylor."

"If you're still up to helping, why don't y'all both come here, and we'll discuss my next step."

"Our next step, Freak; I'm in this now. I want to see how it ends."

"Great, see y'all when you get here."

Raymond and Bobbie Jo got to my place a little after midnight. Bobbie Jo immediately went and picked up her pets while I offered Raymond a beer. He accepted, and I got myself a Coke while I had the fridge open. Raymond sat down at the table and had the green notebook.

As I handed him a beer, he pointed to the notebook. "He used this chord progression at least once in almost every song. You'll have to get somebody else to tell you if that means anything, but it's the only thing I noticed until he started singing the Highway Patrol song."

Bobbie Jo came into the kitchen, helped herself to a Dr. Pepper and sat at the table with us. I didn't see either of her pets. I didn't know if she'd put them to bed, or they just weren't visible. With the Great Detective not here to have a conniption fit, it didn't matter. I asked her, "What did your friend say about Rick Taylor?"

"Nothing shocking; he's a typical musician, make that a typical man. He chases anything in a skirt, and she thinks he's hot. Even I have to admit, he's pretty good looking."

"Did she mention a current flame?"

Bobbie Jo laughed, "According to her, he doesn't have flames, he has conquests. She said his relationships last from sundown to sunup, no longer."

"Oh, that kind of typical man; you do realize that really isn't that typical, right?"

"I know you don't think so, but you've never tried to have a relationship with a man. You want to believe most men are like you."

I noticed that Raymond was hanging on every word. I also noticed that the conversation had quit being about Rick Taylor. I steered it back, "Anyway, Rick is that kind of guy. Did she know of any recent conquests that might be able to tell us if he recently acquired a new guitar and a blue notebook?"

"As far as she knew, his last conquest was her just over a week ago. I didn't ask her about the guitar and notebook. I figured that was best left to a professional like you. She said he promised her she wasn't another one-night stand, then made it clear the next morning that she was."

She flashed me one of her lower watt smiles before continuing. "Since Hell has no fury like a woman scorned, she told everybody she knows that he couldn't get it up and had some visible sores down there. Since she knows almost everybody, she's sure he's been having a little trouble in his search for conquests recently. Did I mention that Nikki can be a bit of a bitch?"

Raymond cringed, "At this point, I don't think you need to mention it. I can't really blame her, but wow!" He turned to me, "What now? Do you have a plan? Can I help?"

"Actually, I think I have a plan. Let me sleep on it to make sure I know what I'm doing. I'll call you if I need your help." I looked at Bobbie Jo, "Should you be calling Mandy?"

"I called her earlier. We're going to Sue Ellen's on Cedar Springs tomorrow night." She looked at Raymond, "Did you call Deborah like I told you?"

Raymond beamed, "Yes, and I followed your instructions completely. We're going to the Cinemark IMAX on Saturday night. You should really think about being a wing girl/dating coach professionally."

By the time they finished discussing her possible future as a dating coach and his possible future with Deborah, it was after two o'clock. After they left, I locked the door and went to bed. I did have a plan. It wasn't a particularly original plan, but it was a plan. I set the alarm for nine thirty so I could be at Walt's Rodeo Bar when it opened at eleven without having to rush. For the first time since I saw Lisha, I actually slept enough to need the alarm clock in the morning.

15   Seductive Plan

At five minutes past eleven on Thursday morning, I walked into Walt's Rodeo Bar and sat at the usual table. April was behind the bar and smiled when she saw me. I smiled back and she poured two cokes and said something to Chris. Chris laughed and April brought the Cokes to the table and sat down beside me.

"You look better than last time I saw you, Baby. Either my kiss is as potent as Snow White's prince or you found Charlie Ray's guitar."

"Maybe both, but we need to be sure. You want to help?"

"Are you asking me to kiss you again, or help you find the guitar" She smiled the smile that could cause a thousand car wrecks and continued, "Or both?"

Looking at April sitting there glowing in anticipation reminded me of how she had helped us solve the murder of my fiancée and unborn child. A lawyer I know named Daniel Leeds once said that April's beauty was matched only by her joie de vivre. For the first time, I understood what he meant. I wondered briefly how she'd have reacted to a loss such as mine.

April interrupted my rumination. "Hey, Baby! Don't fade on me now. Tell me what you found out about the guitar and how I can help you find it."

I told her about Rick Taylor playing a song that sounded like Charlie Ray's. I gave her the gist of what Bobbie Jo told me about him and his relationship with Nikki. April shook her head when I mentioned that Nikki thought he was having trouble hooking up because of the rumors she was spreading.

"Poor Nikki, I don't know the girl, but she clearly doesn't understand how the game works. If Rick is half the player she thinks he is, her talking bad about him won't even affect him. He might have only scored women Nikki doesn't know last week, but he's scoring somebody. At best, she can hope he's had to settle for less gorgeous women than he's used to having."

"What makes you sure he's ever scored beautiful women?"

"For one thing, he's a good looking guy. If Bobbie Jo is willing to admit that, then we have to accept it as fact. Plus, he's a musician, so even if he's not good looking, he's going to get girls.

Since you're here, I presume the plan involves me seducing him. Tell me your plan."

"Well, you pretty much just described it. I guess I should have worked out the details before I came here to talk you into it."

She got up from the table and picked up both our glasses. "Probably, but you talked me into it. The regulars will be pouring in soon, Baby. Go work out a plan, and let me know what to do."

Once I started thinking about it, the plan was pretty easy to develop. Rick's MySpace page said he was sitting in on guitar Saturday for a band playing at Wizard's in Richardson. All April needed to do was go to the club, convince Rick to take her to his place and find the guitar. First, though I wanted to talk to Nikki about Rick.

I called Bobbie Jo and she gave me Nikki's number. "Do you want me to tell her you're going to call?"

"No, I'll do this without you. Depending on how things go, we may not want her to know that we know each other."

"Okay, then. Let me know if you need anything."

I promised her I would and called Nikki at ten-thirty Friday morning. Since she's a bartender, I wasn't surprised that she didn't sound like she'd been awake for long when she answered, "Hello."

"May I speak to Nicole Lloyd?"

"This is she, but it's Nikki, not Nicole."

"Fine, Ms. Lloyd, I'll make a note of that." I gave her my name and started the act I had rehearsed. "I'm with Pegasus Investigations and we're conducting a routine background check on a musician named Rick Taylor. I understand you are a friend of his. I'd like to make an appointment with you to discuss Mr. Taylor and your friendship."

I knew she and Rick weren't exactly friends, but she didn't know I knew. She hesitated before she replied, "I guess I can talk to you. I don't know Rick all that well, though. How long will it take?"

Bobbie Jo had told me that money was pretty tight for Nikki, so I answered, "It won't take long, but if you'd like I can buy you lunch while I interview you, so I won't be wasting any of your time."

As I'd expected, she liked that idea. She suggested a Bennigan's on Northwest Highway in Garland. I said that would be fine, and we made plans to meet there at two o'clock. It might be an unnecessary expense, but I wanted to know everything I could about Rick Taylor before April convinced him to invite her to his place.

Nikki arrived at the restaurant at about ten past two. I explained to her that the background check was pursuant to employment as a musician on a cruise he was seeking. I asked about fifteen questions and told about twenty lies while we ate lunch. As she was finishing her dessert, I told one more lie and asked the question I most wanted answered.

"The cruise line which is considering hiring Mr. Taylor was sued recently over an alleged sexual assault committed by one of its employees. It very much wants to avoid a repeat and wants us to thoroughly investigate the possibility regarding Mr. Taylor, who we understand has a reputation with the ladies."

After a pause, Nikki answered my lie with a laugh and the truth. "Honestly, I only agreed to meet with you in the hopes that I could say something bad about Rick that might cause him trouble. His reputation with the ladies is one he has earned by being a self-centered jerk. He played me for a fool, and I'd like to get revenge."

She paused for sip of her Coke, before she looked up at me again. "When you called and said you were doing a background check on him, I thought it might be my chance. I guess it is, but I can't do it. Rick can be a jerk, but he would never assault a girl. I don't know if any girl would ever tell him no. He is too gorgeous to hear it often. But if one did, he'd just move on to somebody else. Even on a cruise ship, there's always somebody else."

I asked a few more questions just to maintain the charade. After I paid the check, I walked Nikki to her car and thanked her for her honesty and cooperation. As she got in the car, I told her, "Our investigation isn't complete, but if Mr. Taylor played you for a fool, my initial impression is that he's the fool. I doubt if he'll be playing his guitar on a cruise ship anytime soon."

It may not have been honest, but at least it was true. It also made Nikki smile. Her smile didn't have the honest warmth that Katherine's always had or the pure mischievousness of April's, but it was a nice smile nonetheless. I hadn't learned enough to be sure that April would be safe, but I decided to go forward with the plan. After all, April has always been able to take care of herself.

I convinced myself that I was being overly protective. As it turned out, I wasn't. I was just being protective of the wrong person.

16   Guitar Player

As I rode on DART bus number 164 toward my house, my phone rang. Answering a call on the bus is always a dicey proposition. Since there wasn't much noise on the bus and it was Blake calling, I gave it a shot. "Hello, Blake. What's up?"

"Good news, my friend. Your office is officially available to you."

"So when I wrap up this case, I can bring everybody to the office and you'll take out the bad guys? That is good news."

Blake laughed politely, "Your partner leaves you for three weeks and you completely change how Pegasus operates? Just like that, you go from being Philip Marlow to being Nero Wolfe. I'll let the press know that your future celebrations won't take place in hospitals."

I laughed for real. When I could finally answer, I said, "I'm hoping if we stick to guitar thefts and avoid double homicides, we can minimize the hospital stays."

We both realized the conversation was drifting from light to dark and an awkward silence ensued. Finally, Blake said, "How are you holding up? You always seem so in control, it's easy to forget you've been through Hell. I'm sure you feel the need to maintain a façade for some people, but don't think of me as one of them."

At that point I realized that 'guitar thefts' and 'double homicides' had been heard by my fellow riders, another argument against answering the phone on the bus. I decided the sooner the conversation ended, the better it would be. "Thanks, Blake. I'll remember that. Give my love to Jade."

At the next stop, three people moved to seats closer to exits and farther from where I sat. However, nobody called 911 or ran screaming from the bus in terror. It was, after all, the bus going to downtown Dallas.

Since our office was now available, I decided to go there Saturday afternoon to finalize the details of our plan to catch a guitar thief. That left me a Friday night with no spiders to baby-sit, no phone calls to anticipate and no leads to pursue. I had the evening to do with it as I wanted, without feeling guilty about not making any progress.

At home, I relaxed for almost fifteen minutes before I went completely stir crazy. I walked back to the DART rail and rode to Mockingbird Station to see what was playing at the Angelika Theater. I could have looked up the movie listings online, but that would have defeated the purpose.

I ended up screening an Italian film with English subtitles and a plot so convoluted and illogical that I probably would have left after thirty minutes if it had been a Hollywood production. Since it wasn't, I stayed with it and the conclusion made just enough sense to explain the good reviews the Dallas Observer gave it.

As planned, I was at the office by 12:30 Saturday afternoon. April called at a quarter after one, "Do you have a plan yet, Baby?"

"I'm getting there. Rick Taylor is playing a gig at Wizard's tonight at eight. Are you ready to work your magic?"

"I will be. I work until six. I'll meet you at your office after that, okay?"

That left me six hours to work out details of the plan to find out if Rick Taylor had stolen Charlie Ray's guitar. That's all we were trying to do. All of the emotional baggage aside, it was a simple question to answer. Did he steal a guitar and claim a lyric from the notebook as his own? As I sat in the office pretending to be a real detective, I thought about how many ways the question could be answered without asking April to seduce the suspect.

Blake had compared me to Nero Wolfe and Phillip Marlowe. He was joking, of course. Still, I wondered if either of those detectives would ask a bartender to solve their case for them. Of course they wouldn't. Marlowe would harass Rick until he either confessed or tried to kill him, then he'd beat the shit out of him and make him return the guitar. Wolfe, on the other hand, would simply tell Archie to get Saul and break into Rick's place and see if the guitar was there.

As I thought about how Wolfe would solve the case, I thought about Archie's photographic memory. That reminded me that my memory wasn't as reliable. I updated the case notes in the computer and backed them all up to the virtual server I recently convinced Carl we needed. I may not be a great detective, but I do know how to use modern technology.

I pulled up Rick's MySpace page and printed a couple of pictures for April. It would be embarrassing if she seduced the wrong guitar player. While I was surfing, I printed out a couple of blogs he had posted. April's looks would probably be all it took, but it wouldn't hurt for her to know some of his likes and dislikes. I also printed out the description of Charlie's guitar and case from my notes for her.

April arrived at the office at six-fifteen. She parked in the street and I watched from the waiting area as she climbed the stairs. She wore her typical work jeans and white top. She had a tan purse with multiple side pockets over her left shoulder and a pink bag with the word 'Dance' in cursive in her right hand.

Pointing at the dance bag, I asked "Are you planning to stop off at a Jazzercise class on your way to Wizard's?"

"Just carrying the tools of the trade," She answered. "You don't expect me to seduce him in this outfit, do you?"

"It seems to work on all the regulars at Walt's."

"Wizard's isn't Walt's, baby. I'm going to need to take his attention away from all the wait sluts in schoolgirl outfits, plus any other customers with dreams of scoring a guitar player."

"Far be it from me to tell you how to do your job." I showed her the pages I had printed out.

"I'm glad I came prepared. If these pictures aren't airbrushed, I'm going to have a lot of competition. Can I change in your office? Your ladies' room is a little cramped."

"Of course," I said.

April did just that. When she came out, she wore a pink minidress with a wide white belt. She carried a pair of pink high heels with ankle straps,

I whistled. "There may be other girls interested in Rick, but you won't have any competition."

She blushed. Among her many talents, April can blush on cue. When she had her shoes strapped on, she said, "Walk me to my car, Baby."

I did. I told her to be careful and she promised she would. She also said she would text me as things develop. "I've changed your name to 'mom' on my phone, so if Rick notices me texting, he won't be suspicious. He'll just think I'm letting her know I won't be home."

"Why didn't I think of that?"

"You didn't think of it because you're not as paranoid as I am. Some guys like to read over your shoulder when you text. Don't forget that if a message doesn't exactly make sense. Let me have your phone."

I handed her my phone and she typed something before handing it back to me. "The scene is set and all the actors know their parts, right mom? Oh, by the way, check this out."

She opened one of the side pockets on her purse and showed me the taser and mace canister inside it.

"Wow," I said. "Maybe I should be warning Rick to be careful."

"Maybe so, Baby. As long as he doesn't do anything stupid, he'll be fine. If he does, I have more than one surprise in store for him." As she said this, she reached into the purse and pulled out a small pistol.

"Damn, April. I guess you are prepared. I hope it doesn't come to that."

"I'm sure it won't. But these days a girl can't be too careful."

I agreed and she went off to seduce a guitar player. On the walk home, I read the text April sent to herself from my phone, 'made big pot of gumbo. too much 4 me and dad, wanna come over 4 some?'

I wouldn't have thought April's mom would be big on gumbo, since she'd never mentioned any Cajun roots. Of course, I'd never heard her mention any other roots, either. I figured this was part of setting the scene to prepare the actors and actresses for their roles.

At home, I popped Mallrats into the DVD player and settled in for another exciting evening waiting for phone calls and text messages. Mallrats isn't Kevin Smith's best film, but it doesn't have subtitles and doesn't require the viewer to think. That made it a perfect choice for me to watch while I waited for April to work her magic.

17   Femme Fatale

The first text message came at half past eight, 'Cant v and i bout to go shoot pool. tom?'. V would be her friend Vanessa. April and Vanessa shooting pool at Wizard's would certainly get attention; especially if Vanessa, a statuesque brunette, dressed anything like April.

I texted her back, 'have fun be careful CU tom'. It sounded like something a mother would tell her adult daughter on a Saturday night. Plus, I meant it; at least I meant the part about being careful

By ten-thirty, I was watching Clerks 2, the only Kevin Smith film with Tracy Phillips in the cast. I wondered how the new coach of the Dallas Cowboys liked watching his daughter dancing in a green miniskirt and fishnets.

The rest of the city probably cared more about how Wade planned to get the 'Boys to win their first playoff game in over a decade. Of course, the rest of the city wasn't sitting alone watching Clerks 2 on a Saturday night waiting for a phone call. Or if they were, it wasn't for the type of call I was waiting to receive. The phone rang at eleven ten. I hit the pause button before answering in a falsetto voice, "Hello."

April said, "I hope you're not tired, Baby. It looks like it could be a long night."

"Since when do you call your mom, 'Baby'?"

"I'm in the ladies room lounge. As I'm sure you can hear in the background, the band, and therefore our suspect, is playing. This call won't blow our cover. The band is playing right up to closing time, so it'll be after two before he leaves. You going to stay up or should I just report in the morning?"

"I'll be up; great detectives like us never sleep when on a case. Any luck yet, making sure you leave with him when he goes?"

"Enough, I think. He knows we're here and is interested. He spent the break between sets hitting on Vanessa. It shouldn't be hard to redirect his attention when it's near closing time."

"He's hitting on Vanessa instead of you? I didn't realize he was blind."

"Maybe he just lacks confidence. Anyway, it shouldn't matter. As long as his focus stays on one of us, we'll make it work."

"If his focus doesn't stay on one of you, we'll have to presume he's gay and come up with a new plan."

April laughed, "We won't need a new plan. We'll just have to switch roles. I'll get to sit at home watching a Kevin Smith movie marathon and you can be the femme fatale."

She hung up before I had a chance to ask her how she knew I was watching Kevin Smith movies. At a quarter before one, I was watching Chasing Amy, wondering how Bobbie Jo and Mandy were getting along when I got a text message from Vanessa, 'alone again, guitar guys prefer blondes. call u bout 2'

So, they'd managed to turn Rick Taylor's attention from Vanessa to April. It's nice to work with true professionals, even if they are actually amateurs. Not for the first time, I wondered why I'd never known April to date anybody or even flirt except when she was using her feminine wiles to help solve a case.

I replied to Vanessa's text, 'least no one calls u Barbie...lol...nights still young'

She replied, "so are we. too bad ur workin and not into me...even when ur not." Unlike April, Vanessa flirts often. In fact, she pretty much flirts always and with everybody. In person or on the phone, Vanessa is likely to be flirting with somebody. Apparently, the same is true when she texts.

I sent back, "u 2 are working, I'm JAFO waiting for ur call'

As I expected, she didn't respond. I went back to my personal Kevin Smith film festival. True to her word, Vanessa called shortly after two in the morning. "It worked, April and Rick are on the way to his place. She's following him in her car, and made him give her the address to give me. Do you need it?"

I thought about the arsenal April showed me before replying "Probably not, April can take care of herself. But since you have it, why don't you give it to me?"

I wrote down the address and apartment number as she gave it to me. The apartment was The Dakota in the Villages complex off of Northwest Highway. The complex isn't the singles scene I've heard it used to be, but it still has its reputation. I was not surprised to learn that Rick lived there. "Thanks, Vanessa. We appreciate your help."

"It's okay, I'd do anything for April, and she'd do anything for you guys. I don't think either of you appreciate her as much as you should, but she never complains about it, so I guess I won't."

I didn't see anything to gain by mentioning that she had, in fact, just complained about it. Instead I asked, "Does April ever complain about anything? If she does, I've never heard her."

"Nothing she'd want me to tell you about. Good luck with the case. If you talk to April before I do, tell her to call me."

She hung up before I could answer. Apparently, I'd asked a question that irritated Vanessa. I didn't know why, and I didn't have a strong desire to figure it out. Throughout history, men have tried to figure out what will or won't irritate women without much success.

That was one thing I always loved about Katherine. She never got upset without a reason that made sense to me. It was only one of many things I loved about her, but it was one. I didn't realize I'd spent two hours reminiscing about all the things I'd loved about Katherine until I got a text message at ten after four in the morning from April. 'he is it call me'.

She answered on the second ring, "Baby, you've done it again. Charlie's guitar and case are on the floor in Rick's spare bedroom. A blue notebook is on a student desk in his living room beside his laptop. I thought about trying to steal it back, but decided against it. He was disappointed that I didn't put out for him on our first date, but not so mad I can't get another invitation if you need me to go back."

"That's great. Where are you, now?"

"I'm almost home, but I can come to your place if you want. Do you need me to do anything else?"

"No, you've done plenty. Hell, you basically solved the case. I'll take it from here. I know you well enough to know that he has no idea that you were interested in the guitar or notebook. I'm sure they'll still be there when Charlie Ray and I talk to him about it."

By five thirty in the morning, I was in my bed hoping to get a few hours sleep before I could call Charlie Ray and tell him we found his guitar. I didn't know if I'd actually sleep, but I looked forward to giving Charlie Ray the good news. Two hours later, I was still in bed hoping to get some sleep. At seven-thirty, my phone rang. Almost immediately, I wasn't looking forward to calling Charlie Ray.

18   Deadly Irony

"Dude, what the fuck is going on? I thought I was helping you find a guitar. You didn't say anything about committing a damn murder!"

"Raymond, calm down. What are you talking about? Nobody's been murdered."

"Like hell they haven't! A well known local musician was found dead of a gunshot wound early Sunday morning on the porch of his apartment in the 6500 block of Shady Brook. Richard Kelvin Teasdale, who performed under the stage name Rick Taylor, was a guitarist and songwriter best known for his work with the Nothing Special Band."

"What are you saying? Why would you say something like that?"

"I'm not saying it, Freak, I'm repeating it. I read it on Dallasnews.com. What have you dragged me into, man?"

"I don't know." I told him honestly. I tried to think and found that I couldn't. "Raymond, I had a long night last night and this isn't how I expected today to start. Let me get myself together and I'll give you a call."

He agreed reluctantly and I tried again to think. Rick Taylor had been shot at home. He lived in the Dakota apartment complex, which was almost certainly named after the Dakota in New York City. I wondered if Rick had chosen to live there because John Lennon had lived in the other Dakota.

If he wasn't dead, I could ask him. Since he was, I could only reflect on the irony of him dying there in a manner eerily similar to the way Lennon died. Granted, it wasn't a great thought or one that was likely to help me, but at least my brain was working again.

I sent April a text message, "call me ASAP". Then, I got on my computer to find the article Raymond had seen. I had just found it when April called. "What's up, Baby?"

"Did anything happen last night you need to tell me about? Did you have to use anything in your self-defense arsenal?"

"No, not at all; he was a perfect gentleman. In fact, I got the distinct impression that what mattered most to him was that his band buddies saw him leaving Wizard's with me. Once we got to his place, he did try, but he wasn't overly persistent. A girl with less confidence might have been hurt by how easily he took no for an answer. Why do you ask?"

"According to the Dallas Morning News, Rick was found shot to death this morning."

"No way! This... can't be happ... not... no, He's in... it's, no it's not .... It ca...

Her sounds weren't getting any more coherent, so I interrupted. "April, calm down! What are you rambling about?"

She hesitated before answering and I could hear her trying to get her breathing under control. "Sorry, I'm okay now, just shocked. I didn't kill him, if that's what you were thinking."

"Well, I had to ask, but I believe you. Now, we just have to hope the police do, too."

"Why wouldn't they?"

"You said it yourself, all his buddies saw you leaving with him. From their perspective, that's going to make you his girlfriend and the last person to see him alive. Either one would make you a prime suspect; the combination may be enough to keep them from even looking very hard for other options. Remember, I do have some experience with what happens when cops don't look for other options."

"Okay, I see your point. What do we do?"

"First we get you a damn good lawyer. Then I find out who did kill that no-account polecat."

"No-account polecat? Since when do you talk like that?"

"It's something Charlie Ray said when he hired us. Thinking about Larry Joe made me think of it."

"Freak, are you insane? I couldn't afford Larry Joe McCoy if hiring him was the only thing between me and the hangman's noose."

"That's not your problem. I got you into this; I'm going to get you out. I'm not letting anything happen to you over Charlie Ray's stupid guitar."

"Speaking of Charlie Ray, you don't suppose...?" She trailed off, not willing to say out loud what she was thinking.

"I don't see how. I haven't even had a chance to tell him we found his stuff. You didn't tell him, did you?"

"No, I don't even know how to reach him. I have Bobbie Jo's number, but not his. And before you ask, I didn't tell her either.

What do we do?" She had calmed some, but her voice was still tense.

"Mostly, we need to stay calm. Let me talk to Larry Joe and see what he thinks we ought to do. Just do whatever you were planning to do until you hear from me. If the police try to talk to you before I get back to you, tell them that your attorney has advised you not to answer any questions. Don't admit to anything or answer anything about last night."

"Sounds like what I'd do if I were guilty. You do remember that I didn't do it, right?"

"Sure, but I also remember how much time two innocent people spent in jail when Katherine was murdered. Just trust me on this, okay?"

"Okay, I will." She had calmed down considerably. Her voice was back to normal, "Let me say something. The first time I ever helped The Great Detective on a case, I knew there were risks involved. He made it clear and warned me over and over. I agreed to help you with this, because I like doing it, and I still knew there were risks."

"Do what you can to get this worked out, but don't beat yourself up over involving me. I volunteered to help you just like I volunteered to help your partner last year when you and I met. I'm a big girl; I make my own decisions. If they arrest me for something I didn't do, I'll go to jail until somebody gets me out. There are worse things that can happen."

"I don't think they'll arrest you any time soon. But if they do, call Larry Joe's office and mention your past association with Pegasus Investigations. Somebody there will get you bailed out." I gave her the number and reminded her again not to panic and not to answer any questions or even admit that she knew the victim or had been at Wizard's on Saturday night.

Then I did something I hadn't done since high school. I called my Godfather, the famous and infamous Texas defense attorney Larry Joe McCoy at his home on a weekend about a legal matter. It wouldn't be completely accurate to say the man raised me, but nobody alive has known me longer than he has. He's also the closest thing to family I have.

19   Legal Counsel

"…Childish, hayseed, greenhorn whippersnappers! What in tarnation were you thinking? Ain't either one of y'all got the brains God Almighty gave to rocks?"

April and I were sitting in Larry Joe McCoy's office on Monday morning. He'd been ranting for the ten minutes it had been since we finished telling him what we knew about what happened to Rick Taylor. I've heard him rant like this since I was in middle school, but it was new for April. If it bothered her, she didn't show it. She listened intently, but her face showed no emotion.

Larry Joe took a breath, and I decided to end his rant the way I've been ending his rants for several years. "No Sir, Mr. McCoy, Sir! God gave those brains to the rocks and there were so damn many rocks there weren't any brains left for us."

McCoy has to have heard me say that a hundred times, but he laughed heartily like he always does.

As far I know, April has never heard it. She didn't even pretend to laugh. Instead she looked at me like I was crazy. It's a look I'm not unaccustomed to receiving. I didn't say anything as I waited for Larry Joe's latest retort.

"I reckon that's all for the good. The rocks'll put 'em to better use anyhow."

He sighed and looked at April. His trademark, affected Texas accent was noticeably absent when he addressed her, "I'm sorry Junior here has put you in this mess. I know how much help you've been to Pegasus Investigations and the cause of justice in general in the past. That should put him; make that us, in your debt. Instead, he has foolishly called upon you again, and put you in peril."

"It wasn't foolish, Mr. McCoy. A crime was committed, I used the gifts God Almighty did give me to help solve it. Whatever else happened was a coincidence that he couldn't have anticipated. I know you're the best lawyer in the state, but if you can't help us without yelling at him, I think I'll take my chances with a public defender. Not that it matters, I can barely afford this free consultation. I could never pay your fees."

Larry Joe smiled, "Yelling at the boy is one of the responsibilities I accepted when I agreed to be his godparent. Another is fixing the problems he causes with his naive belief that he can right every wrong and solve everybody's problems. This certain…"

April looked at me as she interrupted, "He's your godfather? Why the hell did you never tell me your godfather is the legendary Larry Joe McCoy?"

"Don't you think the shame of being his godson is enough to bear without broadcasting it to everybody?"

"Sure, Baby, I wouldn't tell *everybody* either." She turned back to Larry Joe, "So, how do you plan to get me out the mess 'Junior' got me in?"

While I tried to figure out why April was mad at me for not telling her I was Larry Joe's godson, he returned to form as the famous attorney with the down home Texas accent. "Well Missy, that'll depend on a couple of things."

"Junior promised me yesterday that you didn't kill the picker, but he ain't always been able to think straight when it comes to pretty little things like you. I'm a little, make that a lot, less easily charmed. Why don't you try to convince me that you're as innocent as a newborn foal?"

"So the concept of innocent until proven guilty is just a fairy tale for primary school students?"

"I see it more as a rope out of quicksand. I ain't hankering to rely on it if you ain't in quicksand. If you didn't kill the boy, then we won't need it. Did you?"

"No, he never gave me a reason. He was a perfect gentleman. I was even a little disappointed when I found Charlie's guitar there. He seemed like a nice guy, so I hoped he wasn't a thief."

"How well do you know Charlie?" Larry Joe often slipped out of his Texas accent when taking a deposition; apparently he was doing that now.

"I've met him a few times through Bobbie Jo, but I can't say I really know him. Why?"

"If y'all have a relationship, a jury might believe you'd be willing to kill somebody for stealing his guitar. More importantly, a prosecutor might think he could get a jury to believe it. Have you ever gone out with him or been anywhere with him where somebody might think y'all were an item."

"I already told you I've only met him a couple of times."

"True, but you only met the victim once and everybody at that bar thinks you and he were an item. That's why we're having this conversation, Honey."

"Ouch, okay. I get it. No, I've never done anything, anywhere to suggest that I have an interest in Charlie Ray. I've never attempted to seduce him, personally or professionally. Also, he's never once hit on me. I think since I'm a friend of Bobbie Jo's, he thinks he's not my type."

Larry Joe smiled, "That's more likely than the chance that he doesn't find you attractive. Tell me about the gun you had with you that night."

"I carry it for protection. It's licensed and I have my CCW permit. Why shouldn't I have had it with me?"

"Easy there, gal; just tell me about the gun. I'm on your side, remember."

"Sorry, what do you want to know?"

"What caliber is it? What brand? How long have you had it? When did you last fire it? Anything else you can think of that I should know."

"It's a 9mm; Springfield xD subcompact. I've had it for a couple of years. I'm sure I have the receipt some place if you need the exact date. I fired it Saturday morning at the firing range to make sure I remembered how. I didn't shoot Rick Taylor with it. Does that answer your questions?"

"Do you own any others?"

"No, I only need one."

"I reckon that's true. You said you didn't shoot Mr. Taylor with it. Have you shot anybody else?"

April had been tense through the entire interview, but she tightened up even more before answering this one, "The only person I might shoot is serving a life sentence. He'll die in prison, so there's no need for me to do anything."

Many people think a life sentence means staying in jail for life. I used to think the same thing. I've learned recently that it doesn't, but this didn't seem like the right time to explain the U.S. Justice System to April. Apparently, Larry Joe agreed.

"Fair enough; I don't think you killed Rick Taylor. Go about your business as normal, while I see what I can find out over on Hall Street. If they're focusing on the girl he met at Wizard's, I'll probably advise you to come forward. We'll decide at that time, if we want to mention Charlie Ray's guitar or keep that as our hole card."

It didn't sound like much of a hole card, but I don't play the game as well as Larry Joe. I had no choice but to trust him on this. I walked April to work, then went to the George Allen building to see if Blake was available. I knew I was putting off calling my partner, but I wanted to have something good to say when I called him. I forgot that if you put things off too long, sometimes you never get a chance to do them.

20   Unfinished Business

"So you've found Charlie's guitar, but you can't give it to him because the thief is dead, and Dallas' finest aren't going to just hand you the guitar on your word of honor." Blake can state the obvious as if it's a revelation.

"That's the crux of the matter. Another fine mess, as they say in the movies."

"That's not your biggest problem, though. Your biggest problem is that you found out on Saturday night that Taylor had Charlie's guitar, and they found him dead on Sunday morning. It won't be easy convincing anybody that's a coincidence."

I thought about it, "I'm having a hard time convincing myself, but I know I didn't do it, and I'm pretty sure April didn't."

Blake nodded, "I've known April a few years now. She's capable of it, but she'd need a damn good reason. Besides, I don't think she'd lie to you about it."

"Why not? She doesn't know me well enough to assume I wouldn't rat her out."

"Would you?"

That was a good question and I gave it some thought before I answered. "No, I don't guess I would."

"That's April's unique talent. Her looks are impressive. But what sets her apart, and the reason she's helped solve so many cases, is her ability to know people better than they know themselves."

"Except her superpowers failed her regarding Rick Taylor. She says he seemed really nice. She was surprised and disappointed when she found the guitar in his apartment."

Blake looked at me intently, "That bother you as much as it bothers me?"

"I hadn't thought about it. What do you mean?"

He looked at me for a little while longer. "I'm just wondering. Your case, such as it is, involves two musicians and a stolen guitar case. The only thing of significant value in the case wasn't the guitar, but a notebook full of songs."

I agreed, "Right."

"How do you know who owned the notebook and who stole it?"

"Charlie described it to me." I began to understand where Blake was heading and I was shocked. "You're accusing my client of setting me up?"

"It's a thought. Do you have any evidence other than Charlie's word to suggest that I can't be right?"

"No, but that doesn't make you right."

"No it doesn't. But, it's worth investigating. Usually, when a crime is committed, no matter how small, the perpetrator has a plan for getting away with it. How would Rick expect to get away with singing a song Charlie wrote without Charlie knowing about it?"

I thought about it. "I don't know. Isn't copyright hard to prove? Maybe, he hoped Charlie wouldn't press it. People write similar songs all the time. He probably hoped Charlie would think it a coincidence if he ever heard it."

Blake reached into his desk drawer and pulled out a compact disc and held it out to me. Check out the liner notes. I took it from him and read it. It was Charlie Ray's first release, 'Charlie Ray Nothing and the Nothing Special Band'. I quickly saw what he wanted me to notice.

"Okay, Rick Taylor played with Charlie on his first C.D. We knew that. What's it prove?"

"It would explain how Charlie knew what his guitar, case and notebook looked like. It might also mean the motive had nothing to do with the song or the guitar." He handed me two other discs. I took them and read them. Rick Taylor did not appear on either of Charlie's last two releases.

"So, they had a fight a few years ago, and now Charlie decides to kill him and use Pegasus Investigations to get away with it? I still don't see it. How does this help him get away with it? All he's done is given himself a motive."

"That bothered me, too, but I think I know. He would know that Pegasus uses April's talents when the need arises. He'd also know that Rick Taylor has a reputation as a player. Put two and two together, and he would safely reason that eventually April would be seducing Rick."

"It's a theory. It makes more sense than anything I've come up with. I'll keep it in mind."

"Do that. Run it by your partner when you talk to him, also. When are you planning to to tell him about the murder, by the way?"

"How do you know I haven't told him?"

"You were shocked when I suggested your client might have set you up. Carl's more cynical than I am and always leans toward the conspiracy theory. He surely would have already suggested the possibility to you if you had."

"You're probably right. I'll call him when I get back to the office. Do you have any other theories? I'm particularly interested in any theories that might involve us actually getting to bill our client and getting paid."

"I don't, do you?"

"Actually, I do. I'm thinking Rick might have had an ex-lover who was stalking him. She goes to the show at Wizard's hoping to regain his attention and affection."

"Sounds good; so why does she shoot him?"

"When she sees him leave with April, she realizes she can't compete with April and decides to kill him. She follows them to his apartment, and waits for April to leave. Then; she knocks on the door and shoots him when he opens the door."

"I can see why you like that theory better. It seems consistent with the way his body was found. It might just be right. All you have to do now is find her. I have missing persons the County's paying me to find." He stood and we shook hands. I exchanged pleasantries with his assistant, Ana Marie, on my way out.

I exited the building and turned right on Commerce. It was lunch time and I hadn't been to the Renaissance Cafeteria in a while. As I walked, I thought about what Blake had said. I knew if Charlie had set me up, Bobbie Jo wasn't in on it.

However, she adores her brother. If he tried to fool her, it would probably be pretty easy. She'd believe anything he told her without question. But I just couldn't believe it. He loves her, too. He would never use her like that.

As I reached my decision, I heard a ping like a hammer hitting metal below me. I looked down to see what it was, but all I saw was red. All around me, I heard people yelling.

Someone screamed, "He's been shot!" Abruptly, I realized I was on my back, and they were talking about me. Finally, I didn't realize anything.

Part 2 –Honest Deceptions

"I'm the lady they call Texas,
You carry part of me within.
Wherever you may travel,
You can come home again.

Charlie Ray Nothing and
the Nothing Special Band
'Home Again, Part 2.'

21   Honeymoon Cruise

I've been called many things in my life, but I wasn't ready for the latest one. When Emily called me her husband, it really struck me for the first time that we were married. Okay, maybe I'm not real smart. After the preacher said, 'I now pronounce you man and wife', I probably should have realized I was her husband.

Even so, it still shocked me seven nights later when Emily told a table of friends, "My husband and I need to go now." By friends, I mean people we'd spent a couple of hours with in the dining area. That's how she is. If not for her, I'd still call them strangers.

As we left the table, I asked, "Where exactly is it that we need to go?"

"We have to go back to the stateroom, of course. It's our anniversary, dear husband."

I had no idea what my new bride was talking about, but I was happy to walk with her back to the stateroom. After we entered, she ended the silence. "It was exactly a week ago at this time that we consummated our marriage. Let's consummate it again."

I could have pointed out that we consummated it years before the wedding and several times since, but I chose to say nothing. We consummated our marriage again that night and a few times into the morning. That's the excuse I'm using for still being too sleepy to grasp that the phone was ringing the next afternoon.

"It's for you, dear husband," Emily said as she handed me the phone, "It's April."

Even in the middle of the ocean lying in a small bed with my lovely new bride, April's beauty crossed my mind as I took the phone. I don't think I'm a bad man, but I am a man and April is April. I muttered a greeting as I tried to calculate what time it was in Dallas, which was impossible since I wasn't even positive what time it was on this ship.

As soon as April spoke, it no longer mattered.

"Freak's been shot! I think he's going to die!"

I was wide awake now, and not thinking of anything inappropriate. I asked, "What happened?"

For the first time since I'd known her, April sounded scared, "I don't know, but he's at Parkland and nobody wants to tell me

80

what's going on. I don't know what to do, and I'm scared. I haven't been scared in a long time, and I'm really scared now."

"Have you talked to Blake?"

"Yes, he's the one who told me, but he doesn't know much either He can't, or won't, even tell me what room Freak's in. I'm sure he's trying to help, but we need you here. When are you going to be home? We need you. Really, I need you! I can't deal with this! Not after everything else that's happened. You need to be here."

I didn't bother asking what else had happened. Freak being shot was the only thing that mattered to me. We'd been sure the explosion at the office was a coincidence, but now that seemed less certain. My brain finally transitioned from honeymoon cruise mode to detective mode.

"You're right. I need to be there right now, but I don't know how quickly I can get there. I'll make it as fast as possible. In the meantime, I need you to do something for us."

Emily was listening to my end of the conversation. As soon as I said I needed to be there, she left the stateroom. I knew she'd be finding out how fast we could get off the boat and get to Dallas. I also knew she'd convince somebody to make sure it happened quickly.

While Emily went to see about getting us back to Dallas, I explained to April what I wanted her to do. "Larry Joe McCoy is Freak's legal guardian; he'll know where Freak's being treated. Call his office and tell them that you're acting as my agent. If he hesitates, tell him I said, 'Ithaca'."

"What the hell does Ithaca mean?"

"Nothing, but it will prove to Larry Joe that you're working with me on this. Once you have the room number, you need to find Sam The Man and tell him everything. Last I heard, he's still working the door at Reno's. Even if he's not, someone there will know where he is. It's important that he knows the situation and the room number."

April sounded much calmer when she replied, "Okay, I'll take care of it. I saw Sam in Deep Ellum last weekend; I'll be able to find him. What the hell is going on?"

"I don't know, but apparently somebody who doesn't know Freak is really Superman is trying to kill him. Tell Sam to do what he can for Freak."

"I get that!" April's exasperation was palpable. "But, what does this have to do with the late Rick Taylor?"

It wasn't the first time I hadn't understood a question from April, but it was the most confused I'd ever been from this far away. "Who is Rick Taylor, and what does his not being on time have to do with anything?"

"Damn it! You don't know anything about your own agency's case. Please get off that boat and get back here soon. I'm going to go get bodyguards in place for your partner."

She hung up before I could answer, which was fine, since nothing I could answer would help anything. I hadn't told her that I wanted Sam The Man to act as a bodyguard for Freak, but she figured it out quickly enough. If I were as quick on the uptake, I probably would have realized that someone named Rick Taylor was dead, not behind schedule. I was still trying to figure out who the late Rick Taylor used to be and what he might have to do with Pegasus Investigations, when Emily came into the stateroom.

"We can be off the boat in an hour or so. With any luck, we'll be back in Dallas by morning. Tell me what's going on while we pack."

I told her what little I knew about the situation. I knew better than to verbally thrash myself for not being in Dallas when Freak was shot while talking to my newlywed bride. I did allow myself to mention the explosion at the office and wonder if I should have taken it more seriously.

"Of course, you should have known something sinister was afoot, darling. Only omniscient people should become detectives. I'm sure Sherlock Holmes wouldn't have let Watson get shot, just because he wanted to enjoy a honeymoon with his wife."

Holmes wasn't the marrying kind, and Freak certainly isn't the Watson type, but her sarcasm brought me out of my funk. "I don't know about all that, but I do know one thing. I am going to find out what happened and somebody is going to answer for it."

Emily smiled her Nora Charles smile, "Yes we will, darling, we most definitely will."

22 May Day

Getting off the cruise ship wasn't as hard as I expected. The captain steered us into a port and helped us get a cab to the airport. Getting back to the U.S., on the other hand, proved to be an ordeal I wouldn't wish on my worst enemy, even if I had one. We took a puddle jumper from the island we were on to a slightly larger island where we got an even more rickety plane to an airport in a Puerto Rican city I still can't name.

From there we flew to San Juan in relative luxury on a Cessna that was certainly older than April and might have been older than me. The only thing worse than the planes themselves was the hour or more we waited for each one to take off.

At almost eleven o'clock local time, we boarded an actual Continental Airlines flight back to the United States. One more transfer and eight hours later we landed at Dallas Fort Worth International Airport. As we deplaned, Emily gave me the keys to her Bronco. "Go see what's going on. I'll see how much of our luggage I can rescue."

I kissed her goodbye before I sprinted from Terminal E to Terminal C where we had parked the Bronco. At that time, an elopement to Florida, followed by a two week honeymoon cruise had seemed like such a wonderful, romantic idea. Now it felt like the worst mistake of my life; not the marriage; that was the right thing to do. But it should have been possible to get married without leaving my partner on his own to get himself shot.

Somewhere over the Gulf of Mexico my cell phone battery died, so I plugged it into Emily's car charger. I guess that's another advantage of buying matching his and her phones on a family plan. As I drove out toward 183, I called April.

She still sounded scared when she answered, "Hey, Baby. Please tell me you're in Dallas!"

"I am. We landed a few minutes ago. I'm leaving the airport as we speak. Have you found a room number for Freak, yet?"

"Yes, but they won't let anybody in to see him. Even Larry Joe couldn't get in. Sam and one of his friends are standing guard. Oh, and a couple of cops are standing guard, too."

"That should be interesting; especially if Sam's sidekick shares his opinion of the police department. Did you notice if the cops were city or county?"

"No, is it important?" She asked like an eager student who'd been told her homework wasn't complete. "I'm not far from Parkland; I can go check if you need to know."

"No, it's not important. I was just wondering how much Blake had to do with getting the official guards. I'm only fifteen minutes away, so I should be there within an hour in this traffic."

"Okay, but Larry Joe wanted me to have you call him before you go to the hospital."

"Did he say why?"

"No, but he made it sound important."

"Did he sound more like a redneck or a lawyer when he told you?"

April laughed, but it was a strained laugh. "He sounded like a lawyer, and I do know what that means. That's why I said he made it sound important. I know you still don't like Larry Joe, but we all need to work together for Freak's sake."

I assured her that I was willing to cooperate, and she gave me Freak's room number at Parkland. As expected, traffic heading downtown from the airport was stop and go. Amid the sounds of car horns and motors idling, I jotted down the room number on a notepad. Then I called the famous attorney, Larry Joe McCoy.

When his secretary Adriana answered the phone, I asked to speak to Lawrence.

"I'm sorry Sir, Larry... I mean Mr. McCoy is in a meeting." She continued tensely, "May I take your name and have him call you?"

I gave her my name

"Oh, it's you. I should have recognized your voice. Hold on, Mr. McCoy is waiting for your call."

"Hello, Pardner. Are you back in town, I hope?"

"I am. What's going on? Why did you need me to call before I go to the hospital?

"What I really want is for you to come to my office first, but I know you'd rather not, and I know April already told you the room number. I can't think of anything I can say to convince you to come here."

"Maybe you should just tell me why."

"I reckon I should, but I can't... not over the phone. Pardner, please come here first. I'm willing to beg if I must. Just once, can you just trust me on something? Please!"

I thought about it as traffic began to unwind a little. Larry Joe and I aren't friends, but we aren't enemies, either. If he thought it would be better for Freak if I stopped at his office before I went to the hospital, it probably was. Also, April was right, he definitely sounded more like a lawyer than a redneck. Clearly, he was very worried.

"Okay, I'll stop by your office. I just passed Loop 12. It shouldn't take too much longer to get there."

"Park in our garage, I'll have Adriana validate your ticket for you."

If the lack of a Texas accent hadn't told me how worried Larry Joe was, the fact that he was willing to pay for my parking certainly did. He's not exactly a miser, but he doesn't often pay for anybody else's expenses.

"Thanks. That should save me a few minutes. I'll see you around nine-thirty."

"I doubt it, Pardner. Traffic ain't let up none around here since y'all went off to get hitched."

I'm never a big fan of Larry Joe's fake Texas accent. His accent and rush hour traffic was a combination I couldn't take at nine in the morning. I especially couldn't take it after what I'd been through just to get back to Dallas. I ended the conversation and called April to let her know I'd be going to Larry Joe's office before going to the hospital.

Her relief when I told her was so apparent that I couldn't help wonder what was so important about me seeing Larry Joe. I thought about pressing her on the subject, but decided against it. Driving in Dallas rush hour traffic is bad enough without compounding it with a long drawn out telephone conversation.

Traffic began to lighten a little as I passed the American Airlines Center, which helped my pace, but made me glad I wasn't on the phone. My fellow drivers all seemed to think they could make up for lost time by speeding up, slowing down and changing lanes randomly. Eventually, I managed to get onto Woodall Rogers, happy to be alive. Larry Joe's warning about the traffic proved to be correct as I again ended up crawling stop and go through the arts district on Pearl Street.

Finally, I turned off Elm Street into the Thanksgiving Tower parking garage at nine-fifty. The machine spit out a parking ticket and the gate lifted. I found an open spot on level three and eased Emily's Blazer between a Lexus and a Mercedes. As I waited for the elevator, I noticed the date on the ticket, May 1st.

The irony of finding my partner, my agency and me in distress on May Day amused me a little, but not as much as irony usually amuses me. If I'd known I'd be planning Freak's funeral by the end of the day, it probably wouldn't have amused me at all.

23   Immaculate Deflection

Adriana smiled as I entered Larry Joe's office. Her black eyes glistened with just a hint of humor as she spoke, "He's expecting you in the conference room. Go on in."

I followed her instructions and was surprised to see Blake and a stout woman with shoulder length gray hair sitting at the table with Larry Joe. The woman appeared to be in her early fifties and had probably been quite athletic in her twenties. I doubted that she'd ever been particularly attractive, even before age had added the weight it so often does.

Blake introduced her as Detective Randall, and she shook my hand firmly, "Nice to meet you. I've heard good things about you from Blake."

"Well, everybody needs somebody to say good things about them. Thanks, Blake."

Detective Randall smiled broadly, "Oh, I've heard good things about you from other people, too. Blake's just the most recent."

I managed not to blush, and looked at Larry Joe, "Why am I here instead of checking on my business partner at Parkland?"

"Cuttin' to the chase like a true straight-shooter; I reckon that's the million dollar question." Larry Joe looked back and forth at Blake and Detective Randall expectantly, but neither seemed inclined to speak.

Larry Joe eventually continued, "I guess one reason is that the boy ain't at Parkland. But that ain't really a straight answer. We reckon somebody done tried twice to kill him, so they'll likely try again if'n they know they ain't got it done."

"Twice? When did they try again?"

Blake answered, "The explosion at your office hasn't been cleared up, but it doesn't seem likely to have been random violence in light of these recent developments."

"You really think somebody blew up an entire city block trying to kill Freak? That doesn't make sense. I can see how somebody might try to shoot him, but that's pretty extreme, isn't it."

Randall answered, "No more extreme than shooting him in broad daylight with top notch sniper rifle. The bullet that hit your partner is a .338 Lapua. We believe the shot was fired from over

1500 yards away, and it hit him dead center in the chest. We aren't dealing with a typical Texas shootout. Somebody wants him dead, and is an expert at making that happen."

"I know how he survived the first attempt. How did he survive the second?"

"Pure luck; the bullet hit his dog tag and deflected away from any vital organs. Apparently, the shock kept him from passing out from the pain and he managed to stop the hemorrhaging enough to keep from bleeding to death before the paramedics arrived. It's nothing short of a miracle that he's still alive. We'd all like to keep him that way if we can."

Apparently, neither Blake nor Larry Joe had felt the need to explain to Detective Randall why Freak hadn't succumbed to the pain. I also didn't see a need. "So, what's the prognosis?"

Randall answered, "Incredibly, it appears he might live. The doctors aren't promising a full recovery, but they aren't ruling it out, either."

Larry Joe spoke, "Course, that's assumin' we don't let the varmint take another run at him. Even the luckiest cat runs through all nine lives at some point, and that boy ain't guarded his too much, even before he became somebody's target."

Randall continued, "Which is one reason we wanted you to come here. Knowing your persistence, we weren't sure our officers could keep you from going in the room without shooting you, and we didn't want it to come to that, at least most of us didn't." She gave me a hard stare as she asked, "How good are you at keeping your mouth shut when you need to?"

Both Larry Joe and Blake laughed out loud. Blake answered for me, "Last year when he had a secret to keep, District Attorney Kenth had him in jail for a week thinking he'd break. If you don't trust us as references, call Kenth."

Randall looked at me again, but it was a very different look. "That was you? I withdraw the question. Kenth ranted and raved for that entire week swearing that he was going to break you or die trying. Unfortunately, he stopped short of dying." She turned to Blake. "Okay, I agree we can tell him everything. You want to do it or should I?"

"It's your case, you tell it."

"About five minutes before your partner was shot, a patrolman reported an SUV with the driver acting suspiciously. As he was waiting for instructions and/or backup, he saw the back window roll down and thought he saw a flash and heard a shot being fired. He pursued, but the SUV got away. It was found the next day parked at an abandoned warehouse in south Irving."

Randall looked at her notes before continuing, "The owner of the SUV reported it stolen at 4:30 when he got off work. He was in a meeting from 10:30 to noon with twenty people. We're not ruling him out as a suspect, but that's a lot of alibis to impugn. For now, we're accepting that his SUV was stolen for the express purpose of being used to kill your partner."

"Makes sense to me," I said. "Do we have any actual suspects in the shooting or the explosion?"

"Not really, but we think it's related to the Rick Taylor shooting.'

I asked, "Who?"

Larry Joe turned sharply toward me, "Oh, crap! Are you telling me the son of a bitch didn't tell you he was working on a case?"

"I know we have a case, I just don't' know who Rick Taylor is. Maybe somebody should just tell me about it instead of insulting a man who's currently in a hospital."

"I reckon that's right, sorry." Larry Joe's Texas accent disappeared almost in mid-sentence, "Freak decided Rick Taylor might have the stolen item and enlisted the aid of your friend, April Rose. On Saturday, April 28th, Ms. Rose seduced Mr. Taylor, and went to his apartment to look for the guitar. She left his apartment at fifteen minutes before four on Sunday morning and reported to Freak that the guitar was indeed in Mr. Taylor's possession."

As usual, Larry Joe had no notes to consult, He continued without breaking his stride, "At five-thirty a.m., Rick Taylor's body was found on his front porch. He was shot one time in the forehead from close range with a small caliber weapon. The crime is still unsolved, but I believe Ms. Rose is a prime suspect. Is that correct, Detective?"

"Yes, she's still a suspect, but I wouldn't say prime suspect. Nobody that I know really likes her for it, and Kenth is pushing hard for us to find somebody else." She looked at me with her hard stare again. "The more likely suspect is your client, Charles Nottingham. So far, though, we haven't been able to establish a motive. All the evidence we have suggests that he didn't know Mr. Taylor stole his guitar until after the shooting. If you find anything to suggest otherwise, we'd appreciate being the first to know."

"Of course, I always do what I can to get our clients arrested. Do you mind if I collect our fee first before I give him to you?" She started to smile; then thought better of it. I continued. "Seriously, why is Kenth pushing for somebody else? That's not like him. He's usually gung-ho to convict anybody the police decides to arrest."

Randall paused before answering, "I'll deny I repeated this if it comes up, but Kenth said he wasn't sure he could get a jury to convict that girl of murder if eleven of them saw her do it and the twelfth was her worst enemy. Also, her gun is a nine millimeter and the bullet they pulled out of Mr. Taylor's head is a thirty-two."

"If any of the jurors are straight males, I suspect Kenth is right about that. Back to my partner, if he's not in Parkland, where is he?"

"We had him taken by CareFlite to LBJ General in Houston. The room your large friend is guarding is empty."

"I'm not sure he's my friend, but I know he's Freak's. If the killer is smart and cases the room, he'll notice that nobody goes in and figure out the room is empty even without me barging into it."

Randall smiled, "You think this is the first target we've ever tried to keep alive? We do know what we're doing. That's why we're also casing it, and have undercover people going in and out on a routine nurse's schedule. It's also why you're going to put an obituary in the Morning News, while we make arrangements for his funeral."

"I am? How did I get elected?"

Blake answered, "You didn't get elected. It just makes sense. Who'd do it if he really died? Do you think Sam The Man or one of his other Deep Ellum buddies should do it? Freak doesn't have any family, and you're his best friend and business partner. Who other than you would do it?"

That made sense, even if I didn't like it. I definitely didn't like it. I looked at Larry Joe, "What about you? You're closer to being family than I am. Why don't you do it?"

"Not me, pardner. Ah'm just a little ole lawyer tryin' to get by in this tough ole world. Far as anybody needs to know, the boy's just another client with a checkbook."

Larry Joe wasn't little, nor was he just trying to get by in the world. But, if he didn't want the world to know he was Freak's godfather, I was fine with that. If he lived long enough, Freak might appreciate it, too.

"Okay, I'll do it." I said trying to sound like I didn't mind.

"Great," Randall said. "The funeral will be held at Forest Lawn on Hines. It'll be easy to have a surveillance team there and video of everybody who attends. Killers often like to go to their victim's funerals. We might pick up something helpful."

"That won't work. The funeral needs to be at Laurel Oaks in Mesquite. He already has a plot there. Doing it anyplace else will be suspicious."

Randall looked shocked, "Seriously, at his age, he has a plot already? We never even thought to check. That makes it more challenging. Mesquite PD doesn't always like to work with us, and I don't know the layout of that cemetery."

I stood up to take my leave, "Challenging or not, it won't work any other way. Why don't you check out the cemetery? I'll see what I can do about getting the Mesquite Police to cooperate."

Randall looked skeptical, but Blake and Larry Joe both nodded. Blake spoke, "He's right, Linda. Whatever issues you've had with the force out there don't matter, now. He'll get them to work with us. I promise."

She sighed, "Okay, I don't guess I have a better plan. Do you know where his plot is at Laurel Oaks?"

"Right beside Katherine Hightower's, of course. Where else would it be?"

I left without waiting for an answer. I had a fake obituary to write and a strong desire to make sure that it didn't become real. I also needed to get two police departments to work together. Then, I needed to find a killer. I was definitely going to need some help from my friends.

I knew which friends could help me complete the first two tasks without too much difficulty. I rightfully doubted that the third would be as easy.

24 Old Friends

I left Emily's car in the Thanksgiving Tower parking lot and walked over to my office. Larry Joe had already agreed to pay for my parking and he could easily afford the full-day rate. Once in the office, I called Emily's cell phone to check on her and let her know what was happening.

The call went through to voice mail, so I left a message and booted up the computer to see if Freak had kept notes that might bring me up to speed on our case. The phone rang before the computer even got to the log in screen. I looked at the caller i.d. and was surprised to see it was from Emily on our home phone.

"Hey honey, you got home quick. Have any trouble with the luggage?"

"Nothing I couldn't handle, and you know there are more important things to talk about than the luggage and how long it takes to get from DFW to Plano. Spill."

I did just that. After she was up-to-date, I asked, "You have any thoughts on how I go about writing a fake obituary for a man I've only really known for a year?"

"You don't, darling. I write the fake obituary. You make sure it doesn't become real."

"Of course I do. Should I mention that I don't know how to do that, either?"

"If you wish, but I don't know how to write the obituary, either. I'll figure it out, and so will you. Who all knows this is a ruse?"

"All I know for sure are Blake, Larry Joe, Detective Randall and us. I assume several people with the police and hospitals have to know, but I don't know who."

"I guess everybody Freak knows is a suspect, except us?"

"Yes, and the only reason I don't suspect you is because you were on the ship with me."

Emily laughed, "That's not the only reason, but I guess I'll cross you off my list of suspects, too. Get to work, darling. I'll call you when I finish writing the obituary."

Since I had the phone in my hand, I went ahead and made a call to Jack Cannelly, Mesquite's city manager. I gave his admin my name and started looking at Freak's notes on the computer. I was pleasantly surprised to see that there actually were some.

Jack came on the line sooner than I expected, "Hey Carl. How's the real estate business treating you?"

"You're never going to let me live that lie down, are you?"

"Of course not, what kind of friend would I be if I didn't razz you about that forever? Seriously, though what is going on?"

"Freak's been shot."

"I heard that, how's he doing?"

"Not good, that's why I called. His funeral is going to be in Mesquite and the Dallas Police Department wants to set up surveillance at the funeral in case the shooter shows up. I'd appreciate your help getting cooperation from the Mesquite Police Department."

"Oh, Jesus, I'm sorry, I didn't realize it was that serious. Nobody told me. Obviously our people will cooperate, why wouldn't they?"

"The detective on the case led me to believe there've been issues in the past. I didn't ask for details."

"I don't know of any, but I suppose it's possible. Egos often cause problems and cops often have egos. I'll make sure it doesn't happen this time. Who's the detective on the case?"

"Detective Randall," I told him.

"Okay. I'll make a few calls and have somebody from our force call him."

"Thanks; by the way, Detective Randall is a she. It might help things start better if your person knows that."

Jack laughed, "Yeah, I suppose it might. I'll make that clear. Anything else I can do?"

"No, that's all I can think of."

"Well, let me know if you think of anything else. Without you two, I'd probably be unemployed right now, not running for mayor."

He certainly overstated our role in his career, but I saw no reason to mention that to him. Instead I asked, "How's the campaign going?"

"Hell, I don't know. I've been in public service almost all my adult life and I still don't know the first thing about politics or running a campaign. Not that I'm actually running my campaign, but you know what I mean. Bethany says we're doing fine, but I don't know if she means it or is just trying to keep my morale up."

"Knowing Bethany, I'd assume both if I were you. Let me know if I can do anything to help the campaign and tell Bethany I said hello."

"I will, my friend, to both. Give our love to Emily when you see her, will you?"

I promised him I would and we said our goodbyes. As I hit the button on the answering machine to listen to our messages, it occurred to me that I hadn't mentioned to Jack that Emily and I were married. I probably should let him know. Bethany would be mad if she heard it second-hand, and with her grapevine she's bound to hear it sooner, rather than later.

We had four messages on the machine. Two were from April asking Freak to call her, which obviously wasn't going to happen. One was from somebody named Lisha and made very little sense. She sounded like she was trying to apologize for something, but she never said what it was she was trying to apologize for. She did leave a phone number which I wrote down on the pad by the phone. The last message was from Charlie Ray checking to see if Freak had made any progress finding his guitar.

Charlie's guitar had been found, but I was pretty sure the cops investigating Rick Taylor's murder weren't going to hand it over. I wasn't looking forward to telling Charlie Ray why he couldn't have it. Assuming that Detective Randall was right about the killings being related, finding the person who shot Rick would also find the person who blew up a city block and tried to shoot Freak.

I wasn't sure I believed it though. Serial killers generally don't use different weapons or methods, and the three attempts were as different on both those counts and several others. Besides, it's not like Freak never made any enemies before he became a detective. Still, it wouldn't hurt to look into Rick's shooting until or unless I could think of something to check related to Freak's shooting. I went to the computer and printed out Freak's notes on the case. The phone rang as the notes were printing.

"Pegasus Investigations," I answered in my professional voice.

"How is he?" asked an urgent voice in a deep baritone, which I recognized but couldn't quite place.

"How is who? And who's asking?"

"The Absolutely Incredible, et cetera or whatever he's calling himself these days. Has he recovered from his gunshot wound or hasn't he?"

He didn't answer my second question, but he didn't need to. As he spoke I recognized him. "The Reverend Ezekiel James, what a surprise to hear from you. I wouldn't have thought news of Freak's situation would be that big in Sin City. Or have you moved here to keep better tabs on him?"

"No, my calling is still saving those who sin in Las Vegas. I only keep tabs of Freak via the internet. Which is where I saw a report that says he was shot in broad daylight and lived, is it true?"

If I was going to have to lie to everybody about Freak, I was starting high. First, I lied to my good friend Jack; now I lied to a man of the cloth. "It was true yesterday, not today. Unfortunately, he didn't make it. We're working on funeral arrangements, now."

Ezekiel laughed, which was the last reaction I expected. "You're a good man and a good investigator, but you're a terrible liar. I'll presume whatever ruse you're trying to pull this time is as important as the one you pulled out here last year. I've already booked my flight to Dallas. Let me handle the service and the arrangements. At least that way, you won't have to lie to as many people."

He hung up before I had a chance to try to convince him I was telling the truth about Freak or talk him out of coming to Dallas to handle the funeral. Actually, I was pretty happy he was coming. The less people I had to deceive, the better the chances were that I could pull it off. Wednesday's edition of the paper contained an article saying that Freak had died from the gunshot wound he received.

I spent the morning at the office making the calls that I would make if Freak were really dead and trying to plan an investigation into his death. True to her word, Emily wrote the obituary without me. True to my word, I still had no plan for keeping Freak alive. I spent the afternoon and evening studying the notes on the case that Freak left, both online and on paper. I didn't have a plan; but I had some questions I wanted to ask, and I knew who I wanted to ask.

25   Guitar Hero

"I sure as Hell didn't kill him if that's what you're saying. I already told the police I had no reason. I don't believe the guitar y'all found is mine. We had matching guitars and cases from when he was in the band with me. I'm sure your friend made a mistake. Besides, Rick was my friend. He wouldn't do that."

Charlie Ray sat in one of my client chairs on Thursday morning. His dark gray eyes stared at me as if daring me to contradict him, so I did. "Of course, that's what you'd say if you had killed him, also. The guitar and the blue notebook we found in his apartment are still in an evidence locker. You want me to arrange for you to look at them?"

"Naw, what would that prove?"

It was a valid question, and I didn't have a good answer. In fact, I didn't have any answer at all. If Charlie Ray had killed Rick, he could have easily switched out the guitar and notebook when he did it. If he didn't kill him, the guitar and notebook probably had nothing to do with the murder.

"Bobbie Jo warned me you would likely just sit and stare at me when I talked to you. I asked you a question. I think I deserve an answer."

"Sorry, I like to think before I talk. Sometimes, my thinking is a little slow. I don't think it'll prove anything, but I'd still like to know. Since finding that guitar looks like the last case Freak's ever going to have, I'd like to know if he solved it before somebody shot him down."

Charlie Ray sighed, "I guess I do owe him that. I've been thinking about myself ever since the cops first questioned me. Hey, you don't think Freak's death had anything to with Rick, do you?"

"I haven't ruled it out. Actually, I haven't ruled anything out. Neither of the shootings makes any sense and as far as I can tell, the police don't have any real leads on either. They think they're related."

"I don't know why anybody thinks they're related, but you should get the idea out of your head that I shot either one of 'em, cause I didn't."

"I'm starting with Rick because it happened first," I lied, "For now, I'll presume you didn't shoot either of them. Why not give me some suggestions on who might have?"

Charlie Ray thought for a little before answering. I wondered if he was trying to decide what to tell me or really trying to think of a suspect.

Eventually he said, "I wish I could. I can't think of anybody who would want to hurt either one, let alone kill."

"Why don't you tell me about Rick Taylor? You knew him pretty well, right?"

"Sure I did, we was thick as thieves for awhile there. He's the best guitar player I've ever known. Of course, I never knew Stevie Ray, but Rick was right up there with him. He could play anything: ballads, metal, ska, you name it. If it could be played on a guitar, he could play it perfectly and make it sound like he was the only one who should be playing it. I swear I heard him play 'Stairway' at Bill's Records one day and everybody in the store drifted over to listen."

"Stairway, as in Stairway to Heaven," I asked. "Can't everybody who's ever picked up a guitar play that song?"

"Of course, man. That's my point. Everybody either plays it just like Zeppelin played it or they butcher it all to Hell. Rick takes the same song and makes it sound like something entirely fresh, like something only he should ever play. I don't know how to explain it so you'll understand, but he's just incredible. Or I guess I should say he was incredible."

I wasn't sure I understood, but I thought I might. "You mean like the way Hendrix recorded Dylan's 'All Along the Watchtower.'"

"Well, I'm not saying Rick was as good as Jimi, but that's exactly what I mean. He just owned every song he played."

"If he was that good, and you were such good friends, why'd he leave your band?"

"He left because he was that good and we both knew it. Would Hendrix have been happy playing lead guitar for a little old band like ours? Rick wanted to be a superstar, and he knew he never would be if he stayed with us. The Nothing Special Band is doing okay, but nothing like what Rick was trying to achieve."

"So why'd he stay in Dallas? Shouldn't he have moved to Nashville if he wanted to be famous?"

"I guess he could have, but Rick wanted to write his own songs. In Nashville, they'd have taken his good looks and guitar playing and made him record surefire hits that other people wrote. He wanted to be a star, but he didn't want to do it that way."

"So he wanted to be rich and famous without leaving Dallas or selling out to the industry. Isn't that the recipe for failure in the music business?"

"Maybe, but to be honest, I don't think the city or the industry is what kept Rick from becoming a star. Lots of artists from here have made it big without selling out, at least without selling out until after they made it."

His tone of voice made it clear that he had a particular person in mind, or maybe several particular people. I could probably have named who he meant if I got a couple of guesses. I also probably owned several of his, her or their CD's.

He didn't continue his line of thought, so I prompted. "What did keep Rick from becoming a star?"

"He just wasn't that good. I know it sounds mean after what happened, but if I'm going to help you, I need to be honest with you. Rick was a great guitar player, but his singing was average at best and he couldn't write a song worth a damn. That's the real reason he left our band. He wanted us to record some of his songs, and quite frankly, they sucked."

"So, if his songwriting was that bad, why are you so sure he wouldn't have stolen one of yours? It sounds like you just made the case for him doing it. I did explain that our associate caught him playing your chords and singing your lyrics at Poor David's, didn't I?"

"You did, but I don't think it means that much. You can't tour in this state as much as we do without seeing armadillos on the side of the road. If anything, I'm surprised there aren't more songs about them. Rick and I probably talked about them on a million drunken rides from gig to gig."

"Sure", I said skeptically. "Did you also discuss the chord progressions which should accompany a lyric about armadillos and the highway patrol?"

"No, but I don't believe that part, either. I don't think you really understand how good Rick was on the guitar. No matter how great your associate's ear for music is, he can't possibly compare what Rick actually plays to the chord progressions a hack like me jotted down in a notebook."

"When Rick plays the same progression, do his fingers touch different strings in a different order, or does he just do it so that it sounds better?"

"Sometimes both, but trust me, Rick can play the same song, touch the same strings in the same order I touch them and nobody but the music editor of Rolling Stone would ever know we'd played the same song. It's the difference between practiced skill and God-given talent. You'll never convince me that your associate has an ear good enough to make the connection."

I smiled. "No, you're right. My associate, or more accurately, Freak's associate certainly doesn't have that good an ear. Let me tell you about the Amazing Raymond and show you some things."

For the next forty-five minutes, Charlie Ray looked at the multicolor notebooks that The Amazing Raymond had given Freak. He whistled occasionally, sighed several times. After one of the sighs, he asked. "Do you have the sheets I emailed Freak that the guy made these notes from?"

"Sure," I said. I gave them to him.

For another thirty minutes, he looked back and forth from his notes to Raymond's notebooks. At 2:15, he looked at me and confirmed the one thing I already knew about the case.

"That dead son of a bitch stole my goddamned song."

26   Familiar Face

At four o'clock, I walked into the lobby of the Center for Community Cooperation. Freak's notes had mentioned a girl named Lisha that he met there while he and Detective Woodbury investigated the place where Charlie Ray's guitar was stolen. It was as good a place as any to start looking into the life and death of Rick Taylor, but mostly I wanted to know what Lisha had apologized for on our answering machine.

A petite, dark haired girl sat at the reception desk staring at her monitor and concentrating with great intensity. I approached and sat in one of the chairs in front of it. A nameplate reading Lisha suggested that she was indeed, the girl who had left an apology on our answering machine. I cleared my throat, and she turned her gaze from her monitor toward me.

"Sorry, I didn't hear you come in. Can I help you?" As she looked my way, I recognized something in her piercing green eyes. With her cupid bow lips and high cheekbones, she was definitely beautiful, and I felt sure I knew her from somewhere, but I couldn't quite place her.

I handed her my card. "I'm with Pegasus Investigations. I'm investigating the case of the guitar which appears to have been stolen during a songwriting workshop here. I believe my partner and the police have already been here."

"Sure, it was only a couple of weeks ago that he and Rick, I mean Detective Woodbury, came by to check out the facility. I feel terrible about what happened, even though I know it's not really my fault. How's he doing?"

I'd already become so used to lying about Freak's condition, that I was pretty much operating as if he had died. "He didn't make it, Lisha. He's dead."

She flinched like she'd been slapped. "He's what? No way! I mean, sure, he was freaked out at first, but he seemed to be doing better by the time they left. I only met him once, but I'm a good judge of people. There's no way he would do that; no way!"

Lisha was speaking in simple English. I was sure we were talking about the same person, but I had no idea what she was saying. I did what I always do in situations like that.

100

Lisha interrupted my silent attempt to figure out what she meant, "You're his partner, right? Surely, you know he wouldn't kill himself. He just wouldn't. He was sensitive, good-looking and considerate. I'll never believe he killed himself, never!"

"Lisha, I'm not sure what you're talking about, but nobody thinks he killed himself. He was shot from long distance by a sniper in broad daylight. Even Kevorkian wouldn't stage a suicide that elaborately."

She stared at me with wide, shocked eyes. Suddenly, I knew why she looked so familiar. I'd been looking at pictures of a girl who could be her twin since the first time Freak had hired me. The first two photos were to help me try to find her; later I saw more pictures of her at his house. More recently, several adorn the office Freak and I share.

I also knew now what she was talking about. "You're saying he reacted when he saw you?"

"Reacted is an understatement. He ran out of here like he'd seen a ghost. Which I guess is what he saw. Now, I feel the same way. Somebody really shot him? Who? Why?"

"I don't know. That's what I'm trying to find out. It may have had something to do with the case he was working on. Would it be possible for me to see the room he and Detective Woodbury viewed?"

"There's a group in there this afternoon." She looked back to her computer before continuing. "It'll be free tomorrow afternoon if you want to come back then."

I didn't have a set plan for tomorrow. I'd really come here mainly to talk to Lisha, but it wouldn't hurt to come back tomorrow and look at the room. Maybe I'd see something that Detective Woodbury and my partner had overlooked. More likely, I'd just waste some time, but wasting time is a large part of my business.

"Sure, I'll come by tomorrow afternoon to see it." I told Lisha.

"Can I ask you a question?" Lisha said as I stood up to leave.

I overcame the urge to tell her she just had. "Sure," I answered.

"Do I really look and sound just like her?"

"I don't know. I never met her. I've only seen pictures of her, but the likeness is very striking. She was a beautiful girl, like you."

Lisha blushed slightly. "Do you have any of her pictures? I'd like to see one."

I thought about it. "Are you sure that's a good idea? Seeing a ghost is hard enough without the ghost looking like your identical twin."

"Maybe so, but you said yourself that she's beautiful, right?"

"I did say that. She looks like you. You're both beautiful."

"See, that's just it. People say that to me sometimes, but I never believe it. At best, I think I'm kind of pretty. Maybe if I see her picture and think she's beautiful, I'll believe it if somebody ever tells me I'm beautiful again."

If looking in a mirror hadn't convinced Lisha she was beautiful, I doubted that a picture of a dead girl was likely to do it, but I couldn't think of any reason not to show her. It was almost a certainty that somebody would tell her she was beautiful again, so maybe if I showed her a picture of Katherine, she'd believe it next time.

"Okay, I'll bring one with me when I come to see the room."

"Thank you. I'll see you tomorrow, then."

I agreed and took my leave. As I started up my van, I wondered why so many beautiful people don't realize that they're beautiful, and so many people who aren't beautiful don't realize that they aren't. I didn't give it much thought once I got into traffic. From that point, I mostly thought about why the three mile drive from the Center on Live Oak to Poor David's Pub on Lamar took over twenty-five minutes.

Most people my age think Dallas had a better music scene when Poor David's was on Greenville Avenue and Bill's Records and Tapes was in Richardson. The two icons are now side by side on the south side of downtown and I guess there's nothing wrong with that. At least they're both still around.

That's more than can be said for many other iconic music venues in our fair city. If I didn't figure out who killed Rick Taylor and who tried twice to kill my partner, it might end up being more than can be said for the less iconic Pegasus Investigations.

27   Scorned Woman

"I damn sure didn't kill him if that's what you're suggesting."

I sat at the bar at Poor David's Pub with Nicole Lloyd who insisted I call her Nikki. She'd seemed happy to talk about Rick until she heard what I had to say. I'd expected that, which is why I wanted to have this conversation some place she couldn't just leave.

"I didn't say I thought you killed him. I only pointed out that you have a motive. I don't know if the cops know about your motive, but they'll eventually find out."

"I'm sure you just can't wait to tell them that I fucked the son of a bitch one time. Will that make you a real cop or something?"

"Honestly, I have no real desire to tell anybody anything about you, including the fact that you refer to the late Mr. Taylor as 'the son of a bitch'. What I do want to do is find out who killed him and my business partner."

"Killed? I heard he got shot, but I didn't know he died. That sucks. He seemed nice, even if he was full of crap."

"What do you mean?"

"Oh, he gave me this story about doing a background check on Rick for some cruise line gig he'd applied for. Even if he weren't such a bad liar, I'd have known better. Rick wouldn't work a cruise for all the money in Tennessee."

"You knew he was lying. Why'd you cooperate?"

"Like I said, he seemed nice. Besides, he bought me a nice lunch. I didn't kill him either, by the way."

"I believe you, but I still want to find out who did. Right now, I'm trying to learn more about Rick Taylor. What I know is that he was into music and girls. What else can you tell me?"

"That pretty much sums it up. He was obsessive about both, but he was only committed to music. Girls were just playthings for him. I knew that, but I still let him use me. Did you already know he was devastatingly good looking?"

"No, but I'll take your word for it. Was he a devastatingly good musician?"

"I'm not really an expert. I've spent too many nights listening to really loud music to judge good music, but I thought he was pretty good. I do know he never had much trouble getting gigs and I've heard people say he was good."

"You didn't just hook up with him one night; you must have talked about different things as he was hitting on you. Did he never mention any interests besides music?"

"No, he didn't. That's what eventually got me to go out with him. All he ever talked to me about was me. Even though I knew he was a player, I was flattered. I felt like an idiot later, but I didn't kill him over it."

It was the third time in fifteen minutes she had told me that she hadn't committed murder. Shakespeare's line 'methinks thou dost protest too much' came to mind. Of course, Shakespeare wasn't a professional investigator, and even if he was, protesting one's innocence doesn't prove guilt. Besides, I believed her.

"Okay, so if you didn't kill him, can you think of anybody who might have?"

She laughed, "Only about a thousand girls, and God only knows how many of their boyfriends and husbands."

"Can you name any of them?"

"Maybe, if I had a good reason. Right now I've got a bar to tend. We're about to open." She got off her stool and went behind the bar to get ready.

"Sure, I understand. Tell you what. If you'll make a list of names for me, I'll buy you a nice lunch any place you name."

She smiled, "You sure? I can name some pretty expensive places."

"I'll bet you can, but I'm sure. I'd really like those names."

A band started warming up loudly. Nikki didn't even try to answer loud enough for me to hear her over the music. Instead, she raised her right hand so her thumb touched her earlobe and her pinkie extended toward her mouth. I returned the signal and made my way through the incoming crowd toward the door. There wasn't a huge crowd, but most of it headed straight to the bar.

I made it out, happy again to be in the relative silence of my van. I parked the van in the underground garage on Ervay and walked to the office that used to double as my home. I was already inside before I remembered that having a partner in the hospital wasn't the only significant recent change in my life. I should have driven home to Plano as soon as I left Poor David's, but old habits die hard. I felt pretty guilty as I used the office phone to call my wife.

104

If Emily was mad, she didn't show it. She did, as always, insist on hearing all the details of the investigation. I told her everything about my conversations with Charlie Ray, Lisha and Nikki. Normally I filled her in on my cases in person, but this wasn't a normal situation.

"So, Charlie Ray and Nikki say they didn't kill anybody. That eliminates two suspects. All you have to do now is get everybody else who didn't do it to say so, and you'll have your killer."

"Sarcasm doesn't become you, but you're right. Just because I believe them doesn't make it so. I'll keep an open mind. You have any other thoughts on the investigation I should think about before I finish up here and head home?"

"Maybe; nobody as good looking and talented as Rick Taylor supposedly was could possibly be that easily defined. He must have had some hobby or passion other than just music and attractive girls. Maybe if he was bad or unlucky at both, he might be that obsessively focused. But, I don't believe he could be even moderately successful in both arenas and not have some other hobby or interest."

"Makes sense to me, but why is there no hint of it? If he had another hobby, wouldn't somebody who knew him know about it?"

"Depends on the hobby darling, some people have interests they don't share with anybody."

"Possibly, so all I have to do is find his secret interest and I'll find his killer. I love how you make it so easy for me. Any suggestions on what his hidden hobby might be?"

"Nope! I'm a simple old married lady with no knowledge of the secret hobbies of the young and devastatingly good looking. But if he had one, maybe it involved something someone in Freak's old circle might know about."

One reason I always share my cases with Emily is because it makes her happy to be involved in my work. Another reason is that she frequently thinks of things that I completely overlook. Freak's old circle was involved in a multitude of things that people might not want to share with their friends and family. Bobbie Jo's spiders bothered me the most, but that was because of my arachnophobia.

Some of the other performers and groupies associated with his 'Absolutely Incredible Completely Unbelievable Freak Show and Burlesque Revue' certainly were more offensive to the moral majority and family values society. If Rick was into some of them while still hoping to be a big Nashville star, he certainly would have kept it a secret.

I was thinking about which freak show fetish might have interested Rick, when Emily said, "Even now that we're married, I get the silent thinker act. Keep thinking darling, I love you."

"I love you, too. I'm sorry our honeymoon isn't going as planned. I should be home in an hour or so."

"Darling, I knew what I was getting into when I married you. Shouldn't you spend another night at the office so you can get an earlier start tomorrow? Driving home to watch me sleep isn't going to help you solve the case. I didn't marry Nick Charles expecting to live like a typical housewife."

I started to tell her I didn't know I had married Myrna Loy, but I decided I'd told enough lies for one day. After I agreed with her and we finished saying goodbye and I love you, I spent some time updating my notes and comparing them to Freak's. After reviewing the notes, I felt I knew less about who shot Freak than I knew when April called.

Before I turned in, I took some time to more thoroughly read the local press accounts of the two shootings. According to the Morning News, Freak and Rick had both been killed for no reason at all. Neither of them had an enemy in the world. I couldn't really blame the paper for inaccurately reporting that Freak was dead. After all, I had helped fabricate the story they were reporting.

However, even in an attempt not to speak ill of the dead, some degree of honesty should be in place. Rick had at least one enemy. I had interviewed her today. Even though I didn't think she killed him, she definitely qualified as an enemy. She had suggested that he may have many others, and I believed her about that, too.

Freak also has enemies. I don't know how many, and I don't know how many of them are capable of committing murder, but I know at least one is. I wasn't shocked the papers didn't mention it, but I wondered why Detective Randall hadn't said anything about the lunatic who killed Freak's fiancée last year and tried to kill Freak and me. I decided to find out first thing in the morning.

28   Convicted Killer

At 9 o'clock Friday morning, I called the police homicide number and asked to speak to Detective Randall. I got transferred three times and waited on hold for a total of thirty-seven minutes, before she finally came on the line. I asked her if the lunatic who killed Freak's fiancée was considered a suspect and told her what I was thinking.

She wasn't impressed, "Generally, we look for shooters among the population which is not currently incarcerated. You do realize that the prison is a long way from Downtown Dallas, don't you?"

"I'm not an expert on prisons, but I do watch TV occasionally. Isn't it possible for an inmate to exert influence on the outside world?"

"Possible? Yes, it's possible, but it happens more on television than it does in the real world. Besides, what motive would there be for Rick Taylor's death?"

"You're convinced there's only one shooter, I'm not. I'm not a profiler, but don't serial killers generally use the same method."

"Not as much as they once did. Thanks to television and the internet, they've become more flexible. Besides, we're not calling this a serial killing. We think somebody wanted Freak and Rick dead and made it happen by whatever means were available. Your incarcerated killer may still want Freak dead, but there's no link to Rick Taylor at all."

"I still don't know why you want so badly to think they're related. I see different weapons and different styles of attack. I also see nothing that links the two victims but a stupid guitar that nobody would kill over."

"Nothing is so stupid that nobody would kill over it, and we're not convinced they're related, but we have reasons to suspect they are. You know, there may be one or two bits of evidence that we haven't released to the general public. I probably shouldn't even be telling you this, but there's more evidence linking the two than the stupid guitar your partner was allegedly trying to find."

I thought about that. The police often withhold evidence when they feel it might jeopardize the case to release it. It may be a violation of some part of the freedom of information act, but it is sometimes necessary to help justice be served. If too much information is released, the cops could spend all their time dealing with crackpots confessing to crimes they didn't commit.

"So you're keeping a few secrets from the general public, I'm okay with that. I'm not the general public, though. Why don't you tell me the secret that makes you think the two killings are related?"

Randall laughed, "One reason is that I don't want to tell you. Another is that you might be the next suspect."

"I might be a suspect? I was on a boat in the middle of God knows where. You must be getting desperate for suspects."

"Weren't you just telling me that you thought an inmate could have arranged a shooting? Surely a clever man like you could do the same from a boat if you tried, especially with a little help from your friends."

"Touché, I'll accept that you aren't going to tell me any secrets. Will you at least arrange a prison visit for me? Maybe, I'll find some previously overlooked connection."

"I doubt it, but it can't hurt. In fact, I'll do even better than that. I'll get you a visit and I'll pull the prison visitor files to see if anybody on the list might be capable of orchestrating a murder attempt or two."

"Thanks. I really appreciate that." I told her honestly.

"Good luck. See you tomorrow."

"You will?"

"At the funeral, you didn't forget that we're going to be there doing surveillance, did you?"

Actually, I had forgotten about the fake funeral altogether. After Emily and Ezekiel started planning it, I'd put it out of my mind. I saw no reason to let Detective Randall know that I'd forgotten something that important, so I answered carefully.

"No, I didn't forget about the surveillance, but I presumed it would be so discreet I wouldn't see you."

"Oh, you won't see me. I'll see you, though, along with all the other suspects." She could barely keep from laughing as she said it, so I kept any response I might have had to myself. I had a prisoner to visit, so I hung up without comment.

At one-thirty, thanks to Randall's help, I sat across the glass from Katherine Elizabeth's killer with a phone in my hand. In addition to arranging the visit, Randall had discovered that I was the first visitor since the conviction. That didn't surprise me very much.

A thousand lawyers and loved ones had held conversations on these hand-held phones with the rightly or wrongly convicted. I was neither a lawyer nor a loved one. The only thing wrong with this killer's conviction is that it didn't carry the death penalty.

The killer stared at me with cold, dark eyes for several minutes before saying, "I didn't have to come and talk to you, you know."

"No, you didn't. I guess you didn't have anything better to do, since there aren't any children inside for you to kill."

If I expected a reaction, I didn't get it. The killer simply smiled at me. "I assume you're here to try to frame me for the killing of that son of Satan, Freak. Maybe nobody told you, but we don't get passes to leave here and shoot people, not even people who should have been executed a long time ago."

The glass is there mostly to protect the visitors from the inmates, but at the moment, it was protecting the inmate from the visitor.

"No, I know you didn't shoot him. Even if you weren't here where you belong, you were never good enough to kill somebody like Freak. You pretty much reached your limit with the children that you did kill. Hell, you had me tied up and helpless and you couldn't even kill me. If you were any good at killing adults, we wouldn't be having this conversation. Remember, you had Freak's death and mine all planned out last year, but you fucked it up. That's why you're going to miss the funeral. I bet that just pisses you off to no end, doesn't it?"

"There's a difference between a killing and an exorcism, and there's a difference between an adult and a demon. There is a God, and vengeance will always be His!" The lunatic jumped up in mid-tirade. "I don't know why He waited until now to send Freak to Hell, but I hope you're next. I'll suffer my unjust imprisonment just as Peter suffered his, but your smugness I don't have to accept."

I found myself sitting at the window staring at an empty chair with a phone handset hanging by it. The only thing I'd learned was that Katherine Elizabeth's killer was still insane. It wasn't exactly breaking news, but at least it was true.

I still didn't completely believe the cop's theory that the same person who shot Rick Taylor had tried twice to kill Freak. I was sure though, that neither shooting had anything to do with the coward whom I just interviewed.

Friday afternoon traffic is never good around Dallas, but coming in from the south isn't as bad as most trips. With no traffic, it should take a little over an hour to get from the prison to my office. Today, it took a little over three. That put me in downtown at straight up five o'clock. At that time of day, the drive to our apartment in Plano takes hours and would give Gandhi road rage.

On the drive, I called Emily and brought her up to date on my progress, or lack thereof, on the case. As always, she was supportive and encouraging. I can always use support and encouragement, but what I really needed was a clue. Maybe, there'd be one at the funeral, if I was smart enough to recognize it.

29   Amazing Grace

At eleven thirty-seven, Emily and I entered the vestibule of a chapel on Galloway in Mesquite. As we entered, a young lady in a black pantsuit handed each of us a pen and pointed us to a table with a white cloth draped over it and two men in black suits sitting behind it. There we signed the memorial book, placed the pens in a black tray and entered the chapel.

If it's true what they say about the size of one's funeral depending more on the weather than how many friends or how much money you have, I'll be interested to see how many people show up for Freak's next funeral if the weather is nicer. This Saturday morning was as bleak as I could remember a May morning in Dallas being, and the cascading rain and high winds made it downright miserable.

Despite the weather, over a hundred people were in the chapel waiting for Ezekiel to start the eulogy. To call it a diverse crowd would be an understatement of Biblical proportions. As agreed, Emily and I stayed in the back of the chapel so I could check out the attendees.

The back pews on the left were occupied by a group of men and women wearing leather jackets, boots and jeans. It didn't take a great detective to know this was the group that owned the Harleys which were outside the chapel getting soaked. Even without the jackets, they weren't really dressed for a funeral. I presumed these were some of Freak's friends from Reno's Chop Shop, and perhaps some of Deep Ellum's other biker bars.

Directly in front of the bikers sat three rows of people I mostly recognized as having been part of the Absolutely Incredible Freak Show Revue. The only two people on those rows I hadn't seen before were a petite redhead sitting by Bobbie Jo and a taller brunette sitting between Bobbie Jo and Raymond. That group was mostly dressed appropriately for a funeral, although that doesn't mean they blended. Even in conservative attire, multi-colored Mohawk haircuts, pierced eyes and tattooed faces stand out. Sam The Man sat with this group and even at seven foot tall, he seemed ordinary compared to several of them.

In the front rows on both sides of the chapel, dressed in black suits and dresses were most of Mesquite's political elite, including

Jack and Bethany Cannelly and the current mayor and her husband. I couldn't help but wonder how many were there to pay their respects and how many were there because they knew Jack might become the next mayor.

In the rows on the right behind the Mesquite politburo sat April, her managers at The Rodeo Bar and several other faces I recognized from the bar. One was Chris, the cocky young waiter. The rest were customers, including the high maintenance guy who won't let anybody but April serve him.

I'm usually good with names, but I never remember his. I didn't think Freak had that many friends at Walt's, but since April was there, I wasn't surprised. I figured most of them were there to support her more than to pay respects to him. Maybe with April not being at the bar, they had no place else to go.

Behind that group sat Larry Joe, Blake, with his wife Jade, and several other lawyers and law enforcement types, including several Freak thought hated him. I hoped Freak would survive, just so I could tell him how popular he was with the cops when they thought he died.

The back rows on the right were filled with men and women in suits trying to pretend they were mourners and not cops on a mission. If I hadn't known they'd be here, they might have fooled me, so it was possible they'd fooled the shooter.

Charlie Ray and his band stood by a wall on the right hand side of the chapel. All of them looked exhausted and uncomfortable in the suits they were wearing. They obviously wanted to be together, and as true southern boys, they'd never dream of sitting while a lady might have to stand.

They'd probably bought the suits for Rick Taylor's funeral. I'm sure none of them expected to need it again so soon. That is, unless one of them was a killer. As I thought of that, I scanned the rest of the crowd, trying to think the way Detective Randall would be thinking from wherever she was.

Killers often attend the funerals of their victims. Of course, so do friends and loved ones. I was still looking over the crowd, hoping I might get a clue as to who here was a killer when Emily squeezed my hand and directed my gaze to the podium at the front. Behind it to the left was a casket which only a few of us knew to be empty. Ezekiel started his eulogy in a deep voice that rendered the microphone unnecessary.

"Today we are not here to grieve for a man who has died. Instead, we are here to celebrate the many lives of a man that we all know will live forever. That his time on this earth has been for such a short time and he still has made an impact on the lives of so many people in so many different ways is a testament to the legacy that he will one day leave behind."

"As with so many who live many lives, he did not live them all using a single name. I call the man, Freak, because that is the name he used when I first met him. Many of his friends that I see here also know him by that name. He has been called by many other names, and I won't be surprised if he is called by even more in the future."

"Long ago, a carpenter named Jesus of Nazareth became a teacher called Lord. Later, His names included Lamb of God and Messiah. Today, two thousand years after His funeral, He is called Christ the Savior. Even some who don't believe call him Savior, and many use that name of His to describe anybody who offers hope to the hopeless."

"Some say the man for whom we are here to pay respects saw himself as a real-life Superman. Many of the people he fought to protect from attack and save from danger certainly saw him that way. Like Jesus, Superman had many names. He was called Kal-El, Clark Kent, The Last Son of Krypton and The Man of Steel just to name a few. Eventually, the word Superhero was coined to describe others like him."

"The titles Savior and Superhero aren't names that are bestowed just because they are deserved. One often receives the title only after the world finally realizes what should have been obvious from the first. When it's all said and done, Freak may be called neither or he may be called both, but that does not matter at this time."

"What matters now, is that we all remember to celebrate his impact on our lives more than we keen and wail about losing him too soon. He may not have been more powerful than a locomotive or able to leap tall buildings in a single bound. He may not been able to turn water into wine or rise again three days after his funeral. However, he tried to save lives, prevent attacks and fight for truth and justice every chance that he got. In the process, he has always been a caring, loving man who would run through a wall of fire to help a friend."

"Freak has been many things in this life; a lover, a fighter, a hero, an entertainer, a life-saver, a crime-stopper, a business man and many others. What's more important is that he has always been a friend to those who need a friend. I would ask that we add one more name to the list of names he has been called: Inspiration."

"I urge everybody who knew him to live their lives a little bit more like he lived. When you see somebody being bullied, stop the bully. When you see somebody who needs an encouraging word, say an encouraging word. When you see somebody needing assistance, assist them. If he inspires us all to do these things, then we will inspire others to do the same. Before I turn the podium over to any of his friends who would like to share their memories and feelings about Freak, I'd like everyone to help me sing Amazing Grace."

Ezekiel paused for effect before singing.

I realized his eulogy was as moving as his sermons and his baritone voice was as commanding when he sang as when he preached. As we sang, the tears were flowing throughout the chapel. Emily and I knew that Freak wasn't in a coffin yet, but we were moved, nonetheless. I even think I saw Blake wipe away a tear or two, but I was behind him so I can't be sure.

When the singing ended, Ezekiel spoke in soft voice that carried as if he were yelling, "Grace is always amazing, but the love I feel being shared in this room full of so many wonderful people with so many different backgrounds and lifestyles reaffirms my belief that with God's grace anything is possible."

"Anything is possible," he repeated his voice rising slightly.

He paused and looked across the chapel as if daring anybody to disagree. His baritone was still louder when he said, "The virgin Mary gave birth to a Son. Man walked on the moon."

He paused for emphasis before repeating. "Anything is possible."

I was starting to believe him, and as I looked around the chapel, it appeared I wasn't alone.

Ezekiel's crescendo continued, "Jesus of Nazareth rose from His grave. The Red Sox won the World Series."

Another pause, then he repeated, "Anything is possible."

114

His commanding voice and scattershot delivery made me want to believe him. I definitely believed that with his voice, faith, passion and ability to command a room, he could be a famous televangelist. I wanted to believe and the Reverend James was very convincing.

He walked into the crowd reached out for Bobbie Jo's hand and escorted her back to the podium. When I first met Ezekiel, he agreed to meet me only if I made sure 'the harlot' as he called Bobbie Jo would not be present. The second time I met him, she and I conspired to trick him into revealing his darkest secret. Now he was holding her hand and comforting her. Maybe, anything is possible.

Ezekiel spoke to Bobbie Jo in a soft voice we only heard because of the microphone, "You knew Freak better than anybody; he once told me you were his most trusted friend. He wanted you to be his best man at his wedding. He would want you to be the first to speak at his funeral."

Bobbie Jo spoke softly into the microphone, "The Right Reverend Ezekiel James just asked me to follow one of his sermons." She glanced at Ezekiel. "You're right, Reverend. Anything is possible."

I looked around the chapel and saw many heads nodding. I wasn't the only one starting to believe that anything was possible. Little did I know that before I left the chapel, I wouldn't just believe it, I'd be certain of it.

30   Unusual Suspects

Bobbie Jo was crying as she started speaking, but she managed to get enough control to be heard, "He was the first real friend, maybe the only real friend I had after I came out. My parents all but disowned me. The friends I thought I had made suddenly quit calling. Even my brother acted at first like I no longer existed."

She didn't look at Charlie Ray as she mentioned him, but I did. The look on his face made it obvious that she was telling the truth. It also made it clear that he was not proud of it. Bobbie Jo started to lose control again, but she clinched her hands into fists on the podium and continued.

"Freak never wavered, never let me be alone for one second if I wasn't up to it. The man hated telephones more than anybody I've ever met, but he spent hours talking to me on the phone. Any time I needed somebody to talk to, he was there for me. I always knew he was going to die young, but I never thought it would be this soon. His girl…"

She paused briefly. She looked around the room until she found April's contingent, and then started back. "Our friend, Sunflower of the thousand names used to tell us that God doesn't give us problems He hasn't given us the strength to handle. I never really believed it, and I still don't. But I do thank God that Freak lived long enough to be there for me when I most needed him."

Bobbie Jo started crying again, and this time she didn't control it. As soon as it was obvious that she wasn't going to get control, Charlie Ray appeared at her side. He wiped at her tears with a bandanna and hugged her. Because they were standing by the microphone, we all heard the conversation. "I'm so sorry, B.J. I should have been there for you; I should have protected you from everything, and I fucking bailed on you. Can you ever forgive me?"

Bobbie Jo's reply was muffled by her crying, "I do… I did… I forgave you a long time ago. I love you, Charlie Ray. I always have…. Don't make me go through that again. Please don't."

"Won't happen, girl, not again. I love you, too. So do Mom and Dad."

Charlie Ray walked her back to her seat, so the rest of their conversation wasn't broadcast, but it was obvious that any rift between the siblings that once existed was gone forever. Ezekiel

116

stood again at the podium and waited patiently. As Charlie Ray started back toward his band, Ezekiel spoke, "Charlie Ray, since you're up, why don't you come say a few words?"

Charlie Ray hesitated, but eventually went to the podium. "I hadn't planned to say anything today, but I guess I can. I guess I don't need to mention that Freak was there for my sister when I should have been. I should have thanked him for that, but I don't think I ever did. Lately, I'm learning that I didn't do a lot of things I should have done."

"It's too late for me to change the past, but like the Reverend said, it's not too late to do things differently from now on. Freak was there for my sister and me every time we needed him. Hell, he was always there for everybody pretty much all his life. Maybe I never thanked him or repaid him like I should have. Maybe none of us did. I can't repay him now, maybe I never could have, but I can thank him."

Charlie Ray turned toward the casket, "Thank you, Freak. Thank you for being our friend. Thank you for being you. Thank you for everything. I miss you, you crazy son of a bitch. I always will."

He ambled over and rapped his knuckles on the casket and walked back to his band. I continued looking around the crowd, hoping, but not expecting, to see anything that might be a clue. Mostly I saw sad people with their heads bowed, either crying or trying not to cry. I realized that some of the bowed heads were actually looking at their phones either sending or receiving text messages.

I wished that shocked me more than it did, but it didn't. Freak's friends were mostly people his age, and people his age text constantly. I knew that well enough to know it wasn't a sign of disrespect, more a sign of the times. I decided long ago not to become the old guy who criticizes everything young people do, so I just kept looking for something that might be a clue.

I was still looking for a clue when April followed Charlie Ray. "I didn't know Freak as long as most of you did, but I'll miss him forever just the same. I've only met a few men in my life that I trusted immediately and not all of them proved worthy of that trust. Freak always deserved it. He is famous and infamous for so many unbelievable things, but I'll always remember him for two simple things. Every word he ever told me was the truth and every promise he ever made, he kept."

April was crying and stepped back from the podium to compose herself. I looked over at her co-workers and the rest of the contingent from Walt's. The way they were watching her confirmed my theory that most were there supporting her at least as much as they were mourning Freak.

When April got herself back together she said, "The preacher suggested that we should all follow Freak's examples. If we only follow one example, I hope it's that one. Almost nobody tells the truth or keeps promises in this world. Maybe, we can change that."

April walked back to her seat and Sam The Man followed her to the podium. "When I first escaped to this country, I always felt like a freak. I was different than everybody else and it bothered me. I was taller, darker and fatter than anybody I knew, and nobody could understand me when I tried to speak English. It bothered me to be a freak and I never made friends easily."

"When I met Freak, that changed completely. I'm still taller, darker and bigger than anybody, but it doesn't bother me like it once did. He taught me how awesome it is to be a freak. He's the only person in Deep Ellum who learned how to pronounce my real name, but he also gave me my new name. He made sure I understood that Sam The Man was my proper name and that I spoke it and wrote it with pride."

"He did more for me in the first few months I knew him than anybody else I ever met. I think everybody he knows feels the same way. That's how he lived; that's how he was. I've heard hundreds of people called one of a kind even though they were all pretty much the same. Freak truly was one of a kind. I miss him. I'll always miss him."

Sam The Man didn't cry, but it was clear that he was on the verge of it throughout his talk. The chapel was full of tears; even most of the people who knew the deceased wasn't actually deceased were tearing up at various times. Before it was over, more than twenty people said nice things about my partner and talked about how much they missed him. If any of them shot him, I didn't hear anything in their words to suggest it.

If any of those present who didn't say anything about Freak shot him, I also didn't notice anything to suggest it. Mostly what I

118

noticed was that everybody was sad; everybody had a cell phone, and everybody under twenty-five received at least two text messages an hour no matter where they were. As planned, Ezekiel asked me last to come say a few words about my partner.

As I walked toward the podium, I noticed that even Blake wasn't immune to the texting phenomenon. As I passed his aisle, he stood up and grabbed my shoulder. I turned toward him and he embraced me in the first hug we had shared during our friendship. I wasn't sure if he was caught up in emotion or just trying to play his role as grieving friend.

I figured it out when I heard him whisper, "Make it fast! He's out of the coma, and we have a plane to catch."

I walked to the podium and said into the microphone, "Anything is possible." Emily and I had prepared some words for me to say, but I skipped most of them to make it fast. I didn't think anybody would notice; I'm not exactly known for being wordy. Besides, anything is possible.

31   Wrong Question

"Ah should've figured that sumbitch would wake up during his own damn funeral." Larry Joe said it once when he first saw me at the airport. He repeated it when Blake arrived. By the time the three of us boarded his plane he had repeated it six more times.

Getting to the airport while making sure I wasn't followed or observed took longer than the flight to Houston. Larry Joe had moved his private plane to the east side freight area of Love Field. We were certain that only the pilot Oscar knew the three of us were on a plane to Houston. Oscar had worked for Larry Joe for a long time. He wouldn't tell anybody we were going to visit the man whose funeral we just attended even if he knew, which he didn't.

McCoy's Cessna Skylane 182T seats four comfortably, as long as all four are average sized or smaller. Since only Oscar fit that description, three of us felt a little cramped on the flight. The only conversation during the 90 minute flight was Oscar telling us all that the wind was in our favor and we were making good time and Larry Joe occasionally repeating what had become his mantra for the flight.

"Ah should've figured that sumbitch would wake up during his own damn funeral."

I didn't mind the relative silence or the occasional repeating of the same sentence. The cramped quarters and the effects even the slightest turbulence has on a small plane bothered me, though. Blake didn't seem to be enjoying the flight, either. For awhile, I wondered if he was going to need an air-sickness bag, but he made do without one.

I resisted the urge to kiss the ground when we deplaned at 7:30. Traffic in Houston is every bit as bad as Dallas, maybe even worse. That's why the 15 mile trip up 610 to LBJ General took almost 45 minutes even that late. For once, I was happy not to be driving. At ten minutes to nine, we arrived, and I again resisted the urge to kiss the ground.

After showing our driver's licenses to two of Houston's finest, we entered Freak's hospital room. It was almost eight hours since I'd learned he was awake and I had no better idea what I wanted to ask him or tell him than I did when Blake told me at the funeral that he was awake. I don't normally mind awkward silence, but I was expecting more than the usual amount this evening. At first, I appeared to be wrong.

"Ah should've figured a sumbitch like you would wake up during your own damn funeral."

Freak was propped up on the bed with several tubes running out from under the blanket. "And I should have known you'd try to bury me before I actually died."

Larry Joe crossed to the bed and grasped Freak's right hand. The awkward silence I'd been expecting only lasted about three minutes. When Larry Joe broke it, his fake accent was gone. "We're just trying to keep you alive, like I promised your old man I would. Until we learn who's trying to kill you, it will be better if he thinks he succeeded."

"Or she," Detective Randall interjected from the chair in the corner where she'd been sitting when we entered.

Larry Joe turned as if he'd just noticed she was there. He probably had. He took off his hat, and nodded to her. "Of course, ma'am; we can't rule out half the suspects based on the errant perception that the fairer sex is too genteel to attempt murder." He turned back to Freak. "Until we catch him or her, it would be best if he or she still thinks the job is done."

"Now that the political correctness mandate has been satisfied, can we get down to business?" Blake asked, looking directly at Detective Randall. He turned to Freak. "How much do you know about the situation?"

Randall answered for him, tersely. "I briefed him on the situation as thoroughly as a victim should be briefed. I'm grateful for your help, but it's not a missing person case. I respect you and your desire to be involved, but you have to let me manage my case if you expect me to let you continue to be involved."

Blake straightened up like he'd been slapped. "Of course, Detective, I appreciate your understanding. I didn't mean to usurp your jurisdiction."

Randall snapped, "Maybe you didn't mean to, but you did!"

Blake bit his lip and walked to the door. He turned back only after he had opened it. "Try to find the shooter before he kills again! Make that before she kills again. I'll be in Dallas pretending you have things under control if you need my help."

The silence I'd expected earlier followed that exchange and gave new meaning to the phrase awkward silence. I thought about going after him, but decided against it. Freak looked at me with the half-smile he always has when other people and their pettiness amuse the hell out of him. I tried to remember if the tension between Blake and Detective Randall had been there earlier in Larry Joe's office.

I didn't know who would break the silence, but I knew it wouldn't be me. All four of us had been trained at one time or another not to be the one to break the silence during a negotiation. This wasn't a negotiation, but it had the same feel. I might expect Freak to say something first, since I'd only recently begun training him, but I suspected he wouldn't want to disappoint his mentor. Besides, these things entertain him even more than they do me.

Fortunately or unfortunately depending on one's perspective, a nurse entered the room and broke the silence for us. "Everybody get out. I have to attend to the patient."

Like most people in a hospital, we obeyed the nurse as if she were the highest authority in the land. If cops or teachers commanded the instant obedience that nurses do, there's no telling how much less crime there might be. For that matter, it might help if parents still commanded that level of cooperation.

Once we were out in the hall, Randall spoke, "I'm going to find Blake and see if I can learn what's bothering him." She was out of sight before I had time to decide if it was prudent to mention that it was pretty obvious that she was what was bothering him.

Larry Joe looked at me and smiled, "Ain't that hard to reckon why Mesquite PD don't always wanna pardner up with her, is it? Reckon it's a good thing you and the city manager are thick as thieves."

"We ain't... I mean we aren't that close, but I see what you mean. If she's always more worried about being in charge than she is about solving cases, I'm amazed anybody cooperates with her."

The nurse came out in time to save me from another of Larry Joe's colloquialisms and let us back in the room. "Visiting hour is over at ten. Don't plan to stay too much longer."

"Yes, Ma'am," we said in unison as we went back into Freak's room.

122

"I'm not staying here, and I will not talk to her again!" Freak said with the tone he uses when he's decided something, which he doesn't consider open for debate. When I first met him, that tone always sounded petulant. Lately, he's been better at making it sound defiant. Today, it simply sounded final.

"Good to know you've been working on your William Wallace impression, but you have to talk to the cop investigating your shooting, and you are here for your own protection."

"She's not investigating my shooting. She's trying to frame me for Rick Taylor's murder. She's in-fucking-sane!"

Larry Joe answered without using his faux accent, "She thinks the two shootings are related. She isn't trying to pin anything on you, Son."

"Really? Then why did she ask me where I got the guitar that April planted in his apartment?"

I had no answer to that question, but I suspected it had something to do with the rift between Blake and Detective Randall. Obviously, her view of the case differed dramatically from what we discussed in Larry Joe's office. I really wanted to know why, and the only person who might know and be willing to tell me was on his way back to Dallas.

I told Freak, "Okay, I guess you're right. I'm going to figure out what's going on. Promise me you won't do anything rash until you hear from me, okay?"

Freak sighed, "Okay, but make it fast. I'm going crazy in this hospital. It was bad enough last time when I had visitors. This is torture. By the way, do you have a couple of dollar bills on you? I've got a new magic trick to show you."

I looked in my wallet and was pleasantly surprised to discover a ten and a single. I handed them to him and he showed off his trick. It wasn't the best trick I'd ever seen him perform, but I pretended to be impressed in the hopes that it would help his morale.

Larry Joe and I took turns shaking hands with Freak and left the room just as the nurse returned to tell us visiting hours were over. I should have known Freak's definition of rash would differ dramatically from mine. I also should have known he kept my eleven dollars. I was destined to learn both of those facts in a matter of days.

32   Conspiracy Theories

"Damned if I know." Blake obviously hadn't calmed down much and my asking why he thought DPD had cut him out of the investigation got him wound up again. "I spent all day making calls and trying to pull in favors. Everybody keeps finding different ways to tell me politely that it's not a missing person case and I need to stay out of the way."

"You'd think they'd want more help, not less. I did at least learn from a friend at the D.A's office that no arrest warrants have been requested. If they don't know who did it, and Freak is one of the damn suspects, you'd think they'd be looking for help. I know I would."

Blake and I were at our usual table at Walt's for Monday happy hour. I got there about three beers before Blake did. April wasn't working, but Chris did a good job of making sure we always had a beer in front of us. Of course, with April not there, the crowd was smaller and the regulars were a little less demanding, but Chris was still doing well.

I didn't ask Blake how he got back to Dallas and he didn't volunteer any details. I hadn't mentioned how much roomier McCoy's plane had seemed with one less passenger, either. Mostly, we'd been discussing what we'd learned about the case, which was basically nothing. Honestly, mostly we'd been drinking, but our conversation had mostly been about the case.

"Sure you would, Blake. But, you only want to solve cases and find people. You don't have grand ambitions which can only be achieved by solving everything alone or making sure nothing gets solved at all like most cops."

"That's not a fair assessment of most cops and you know it." Blake took a quaff of beer before continuing. "But in this case, it appears to be correct. I don't know what her problem is; she's always been a standup, team-first cop before. Maybe, she just thinks this is the high-profile case that will advance her career."

"Somebody shoots Freak and a barely famous guitar player and that makes for a high-profile case?" I asked, "How so?"

"It's not about who got shot, it's about where and how. Don't forget Freak was shot with a high powered rifle by a sniper in broad daylight in Downtown Dallas."

124

"So?"

"You ever hear of anybody else being shot in downtown Dallas from long distance by a sniper?"

I didn't mean to laugh, but I couldn't help it. "You're not kidding, are you? You're seriously suggesting that Freak's murder is a high profile case because Kennedy got himself assassinated here."

"I'm not actually suggesting it, I'm just repeating it." Blake shook his head slowly. "I wasn't raised here like you were, but I've been here long enough to know the city still isn't over it. At least, law enforcement in this city isn't over it."

"Okay sure, but as my old boss used to tell me every time we had too much time on our hands and too little detective work to do, 'Kennedy pissed off the Mafia, the Klan, the FBI, the Communists, the CIA and everybody else who knew how to use a gun, except possibly John Wayne. Somebody was bound to shoot him, some time and some place. It just happened to occur in Dallas, just like the Grand Canyon just happens to be in New Mexico.'"

"The Grand Canyon isn't in New Mexico."

I smiled, "I know that and you know that. My old boss knew two things; how to solve cases and everything about anything that ever happened in the state of Texas. Everything else, he knew nothing about and cared nothing about. The only thing that surprised me was that he only missed it by one state."

"You miss him, don't you?" Blake could always tell when I was getting melancholy. Most people, I could fool, but Blake and Emily always knew.

"Yeah, this is the first case I've had since he died that I really could have used his help, and he's not around to take my call or bitch at me for interrupting his retirement."

Blake took another drink, "And how often did you call him after he retired?"

"Almost never, but I always knew I could."

"And now you can't call him. I understand. At least he lived long enough to see you put the agency back on the map. You always told me that was one of your goals."

"It was. Believe me, it comforts me greatly. Still, when I don't know what to do, I miss him. Right now, I don't know what to do."

Blake nodded, "Me either, but we'll think of something. We always do."

I returned my attention to my beer, and nothing was said while I tried to think about what the old man would have thought about this case and what he might have suggested. I presume Blake also returned to his beer, but I didn't watch him, I just reflected. My eyes were open, but I wasn't seeing anything.

I'm not sure how long we sat quietly, but for a change, I broke the silence, "Actually, the old man knew one more thing. He knew that if people aren't acting like they normally act, there's usually a reason for it. Maybe Freak's shooting has one more thing in common with Kennedy's."

Blake looked at me quizzically, "What are you suggesting?"

"Maybe our friends at DPD are relating this to the Kennedy assassination because they're planning to cover up certain facts again." I said it as if I was joking, but I wasn't.

"Oh God! You're not about to turn into Oliver Stone on me again, are you?"

"You don't have to be a crackpot director to recognize that when the facts don't add up, then you haven't been given all the facts. Has anybody told you anything that conclusively ties Rick Taylor's murder to Freak's shooting?"

"Conclusively? No, not conclusively, but there is a connection, you know."

"Sure, I know there's a connection. I also know that Oswald was up in that book depository. That doesn't make it fait accompli that he just decided to shoot a president and all of the other suspects are as innocent as a newborn child."

Blake rolled his eyes. He rolls them the same way every time we discuss Kennedy. "I've got a suggestion. Why don't you just tell me your conspiracy theory regarding Freak's shooting without comparing it to what your old boss told you about the Kennedy Assassination? It will help me focus, and tremendously improve my chance of taking you seriously."

"Okay, a week ago we sat in Larry Joe's office and Detective Randall told us she believed the two shootings were related. She didn't give us a good reason for that belief, and we didn't press her."

Blake stopped himself from actually rolling his eyes, but he asked, "So how does that make it a conspiracy?"

"It doesn't, but Friday after you left, Freak told me she accused him of shooting Rick Taylor and asked him where he got the guitar that April planted at his apartment. You and I know Freak didn't shoot him, and April didn't plant that guitar. Hell, anybody with a brain knows April didn't plant a guitar. If something isn't fishy, tell me why Detective Randall is suggesting that she did."

Blake stared at me. There was no doubt he was taking me seriously. "I don't know. Maybe she was doing some kind of good cop, bad cop routine to get an answer from him. He's not as reticent as you, but he will refuse to answer questions."

"Sure, he will. Most citizens and all good detectives know their constitutional rights. If she was doing a good cop, bad cop thing, where was the good cop?"

"I don't know, but I still don't see what you're getting at."

"I want to know what happened in one week that changed the official position from 'we think the two shootings are related and we want to protect the surviving victim' to 'we know the two shootings are related and the second victim is a suspect.' Something happened. If it was real evidence, why would they freeze you out? If it's some kind of cover up, that would explain it. They'd know you'd never agree to be a part of it."

"I don't know. I'm not saying you're right, but your question is valid." He signaled to Chris for the check. "Jade's expecting me home soon, and you only discuss assassination theories when you're at or over your limit, so you should either walk back to your office or call Emily to come get you. Tomorrow morning, I'll start asking different questions and see what I can turn up."

I watched Blake leave as I finished my beer. Then I took his advice and headed toward my office. On the walk, I thought of all the possible ways I might be able to gain access to whatever the police weren't sharing about Freak's shooting. The Freedom of Information Act is a tough card to play while a case is still being investigated, but I could try it. I pretty much figured that if Blake didn't have an inside source who would talk, I certainly didn't.

I decided to call Larry Joe in the morning and tell him my theory and see if he knew of any way to get more information. As it turned out, I might as well have spent the ten minutes it took to walk to my office counting sidewalk cracks or reminiscing about my honeymoon.

33   Surprise Visit

As I mounted the stairs to the office, I heard somebody pacing in the waiting room; no small feat when you consider that the entire length of the room is less than ten feet. As I entered, I saw it was Lisha. Since she's barely five foot tall, pacing in a small room is easier for her than it is for me at six-nine. She looked up at me as I entered, "I thought you were coming by to see the room on Friday."

"Sorry, I got busy and things have been kind of hectic." I told her truthfully. "I would have brought you the pictures of Katherine Elizabeth. You didn't need to come by and wait for me."

I opened the door to the office lobby and invited her in. She sat in the client chair while I went into Freak's office to get a picture or two. Lisha called out to me as I did so, "Actually, that's not why I'm here."

I was already in his office, so I grabbed one of the pictures off his desk and went back to the lobby. I sat the picture face down on the desk so she wouldn't see it if she'd changed her mind. "Okay, what does bring you here?"

She was holding a few strands of her hair in her mouth and was absent-mindedly chewing it. There's something slightly disgusting about chewing hair, but when she did it, it looked cute. Thankfully, she took the hair out of her mouth and brushed it back before answering.

"Rick wants to see you."

Rick would be Detective Woodbury. I hadn't had enough beer at Walt's to not remember that Lisha's conversation about him when I talked to her before suggested that they knew each other pretty well. "If Detective Woodbury wants to talk to me, why are you here instead of him?"

"He wants it be a secret, of course. He didn't tell me what about or why it's such a secret. He did tell me to tell you that he'll get fired if anybody finds out about it."

I had a few reasons not to trust anything I heard from DPD these days. I had many reasons not to trust Woodbury, one of which was that he and his partner had tried to frame Freak a few years ago. But, I also had a strong desire to know what was going on behind the scenes at city hall, and Woodbury just might have decided to tell me.

"Did he tell you where and when he wanted to talk with me in secret?"

"He said he'd meet you any time you wanted, but he suggested meeting at my apartment."

I asked, "Why your apartment?"

Lisha blushed. "He already knows how to get there without being seen. Besides, if he is seen…"

She didn't finish the sentence. Instead, she started crying. She looked around until she saw the ladies room and went to it. She came out three and a half minutes later, completely composed. "You must think I'm a total slut or a complete idiot."

"No, I don't." I told her honestly since I'd never given her morality or intelligence much thought in the four days since I met her. "I do think you're a brave and beautiful girl, which gives you two things in common with the love of my late partner's life."

I hadn't planned on showing her Katherine Elizabeth's picture unless she asked, but it seemed like the right thing to do. I turned it over and she first glanced at it, then took it from me and looked at it intently. I let her take her time. After seven minutes, she took it over to the mirror which hung on the east wall and held the picture so she could see it and her own face side by side.

When she sat back down she surprised me by asking, "What makes you think I'm brave?"

"Well, you know my partner was murdered. You know I'm a private eye and Rick is a cop, and you're willing to arrange a meeting in your apartment. What if the killer follows one of us there?"

"Rick won't be followed. Like I said, he knows how to do it. He's kept his wife from finding out about it. Surely, he can keep a simple killer from finding it."

I suspected there had to be a flaw in that logic somewhere, but I had no desire and was in no condition to try to analyze it. I wanted to meet with Woodbury and debating Introduction to Logic 101 with Lisha after drinking a few too many beers at Walt's could be counter-productive to that goal.

I decided to reassure her, "I'm sure he won't be followed. He knows what he's doing. I won't be followed either. I don't have a jealous wife to dodge, but I know how to make sure I'm not being followed. Why don't you let him know I'll meet him at ten tomorrow morning?"

"Okay," she said as she pulled her phone out of her purse and started texting. It took less than thirty seconds for her to look back up. "He says ten is fine."

"Ten it is, I'll just need your address."

She gave me the information on her apartment, which was on Southwestern Blvd in the Villages Apartment community. I wondered if she knew Rick Taylor. I couldn't picture her shooting him, but Woodbury would certainly be capable of putting a bullet right between the eyes of a handsome, young musician if the musician had something going on with his girlfriend. Cheating husbands are just as jealous as faithful men, sometimes more jealous and more likely to be violent.

Lisha reached into her purse and pulled out a key. "Here, when you get there, just let yourself in. That way if Rick's not there yet, you won't have to stand around on the landing waiting for him."

She put the key on my desk and took her leave.

As soon as Lisha left, I called Emily. She answered on the first ring, "Hello, darling. Did you and Blake solve the case, yet?"

"No, we came closer to finishing a case of Walt's beer than we came to solving any cases."

Emily laughed, "I suppose now that we're married, I'm supposed to nag you about not drinking, but you come up with some of your best ideas when you're drunk, so I'll pass."

"You're only saying that because you still think you're Myrna Loy."

"No, I'm only saying that because you were drunk the first time you asked me out. Other than getting drunk and leaving April too big a tip, have you accomplished anything since we last talked."

"Actually, April wasn't there, but when I got to the office a beautiful girl was waiting for me and she left me a key to her apartment before she left."

"Of course, that happens to married men all the time, dear. Did you show her your wedding ring to remind her that you were committed only to me?"

This time, I laughed. "I don't think that would have worked. Apparently, not all women are repulsed by older married men. Maybe, I should tell you about it."

130

She didn't laugh, but I could hear her smile in her voice. Both were beautiful. "Maybe, you should."

I did. I included my conversation with Blake at Walt's and my curiosity about Lisha and Rick Taylor. If Emily was impressed with my theory, she didn't show it.

"Tomorrow is date night, darling. I won't accept your drinking, our marriage, or this case as an excuse to skip it."

Emily and I had agreed to make Tuesday night date night over five years ago to make sure her busy schedule and my unpredictable job didn't interfere with our relationship. Hospital stays, incarceration, 70 hour work weeks at JC Penney and other barriers had occasionally made it a challenge, but we've stuck to it with very few exceptions.

I had no intention of letting tomorrow be one of those exceptions. "Of course not, my love. I plan to have both cases solved by mid-afternoon tomorrow. Then I'll pick you up at your office and we'll paint the town red."

Emily sighed, "Well, one out of three's not bad. I'll expect you to pick me up at five-thirty. I don't expect you to solve the cases that quickly, and I know we won't paint the town red, whatever that really means. I love you, and you need to sleep if you're going to be up in time to meet Woodbury at ten."

"I love you, too." I said expecting her to repeat it a few times before hanging up.

Instead she asked, "Do you know why April wasn't working tonight?"

"No, I never gave it any thought."

"Maybe you should have. She always works Mondays, that's one of the reasons you two go there so often on Mondays."

There was no reason to deny it, even though I never realized that Blake and I tended to go to Walt's on Mondays. If Emily had ever been jealous of April, she wasn't any more. Maybe, it's because she trusts me completely. Maybe, it's because without April's help we'd never have put Katherine Elizabeth's killer behind bars.

Emily and I said 'I love you' a few more times; then I took her advice and went to bed. I spent more time than I should have wondering why April hadn't been at Walt's today. When I finally got to sleep I dreamed about Walt's. In the dreams, April wasn't there, and all the regulars who went there mostly to see her just stood around looking lost like the nameless extras in an old cowboy shoot-em-up film.

Fortunately, I'm not psychic, so my dreams don't always mean anything. Unfortunately, sometimes they do. Some dreams are the subconscious trying to prod the conscious mind to notice something important that's being overlooked. Other dreams are just meaningless fantasies. Unfortunately, I'm not always smart enough to know which ones are which. I should have realized that any dream that didn't involve Emily or the Rangers playing in the World Series wasn't one of those fantasy dreams.

34   Secret Meeting

The alarm clock went off at 7:45 interrupting a fantastic dream featuring Emily, myself and a vacation in the Australian outback. I felt sure that wasn't one of the dreams that my subconscious uses to prod my conscious mind. I'm not a morning person, but I managed to only hit the snooze button a couple of times before I got my day started. I decided quickly that breakfast at Tootsies restaurant was going to be the best way to get going, so I got dressed and walked to it.

After a hearty breakfast of crispy bacon and scrambled eggs, I got my van from the garage and drove to Lisha's apartment. I circled downtown a couple of times to make sure I wasn't followed. Just to be sure, I took a detour through the Target parking lot at Medallion Center before taking Skillman over to Southwestern Blvd. I knew I wasn't followed by the time I got to her apartment complex. I'd also turned a twelve minute trip into a twenty-five minute journey, so it was nearly ten when I arrived.

As Lisha had promised, the main security gate was wide open. I've always wondered how much security an open gate really provides, but even residents of gated complexes seem to prefer convenience over security during the day. I did find it amusingly ironic that an apartment complex called The Gate kept its gate open, but I didn't mind the convenience either.

At five minutes before ten, I walked up the stairs toward Lisha's apartment. Detective Woodbury opened the door before I even reached the landing. He ushered me in, and I followed him into her living room. It was tastefully decorated, although not really for somebody with my tastes. I could tell Emily would like it, though. I wondered briefly how much Lisha made at the Center for Community Cooperation.

I might have wondered longer or studied the décor more, but Woodbury asked, "Are you sure you weren't followed?"

"Did you know there used to be a store called Medallion in the Medallion Center?"

"What are you talking about?" Woodbury's face reddened, but he kept his voice calm. "I asked you a question."

"Yes you did." I replied gently. "Then, I asked you a question. The difference is that my question was simply immaterial.

Yours was completely out of line. If you didn't like my question any better than I liked yours, maybe we should just move forward."

He moved into a small kitchenette and I followed. "I didn't like your question or not like it. It made no sense at all. I don't know what was so out of line about mine, but I'll assume you weren't followed." He sat at a quaint little table and pointed to a chair opposite his. "Have a seat."

Her quaint little table came with four old-fashioned chairs made of brass and wicker which aren't really great for tall men with bad knees, but I managed it. "I'm normally not a big fan of assumptions, but I think that's one you should have made before you invited me to your paramour's home."

"I suppose you're right. I brought you here to level with you, so I won't even deny that Lisha and I are more than just friends. You're not a blabbermouth, so I'll trust my assumption that you won't tell anybody about that without even asking for a promise. I see why the earlier question pissed you off. I apologize. I know how good you are; otherwise, I wouldn't have wanted this meeting."

"Apology accepted. You didn't need to flatter me. So why are we sitting at this little table in an apartment I presume you normally visit only for more enjoyable, if no less clandestine reasons?"

Woodbury laughed. "Don't take this the wrong way, but is it possible you've spent a little too much time with Daniel Leeds? I'm starting to have as much trouble understanding you as I do him."

Woodbury clearly wasn't trying to insult me and being compared to the best attorney I've ever known can't really be an insult anyway. "Thank you. Enough with the flattery; these chairs aren't that comfortable for a man of my height. Perhaps, you might tell me what you brought me here to tell me."

Woodbury fidgeted. Watching children fidget isn't much fun if they aren't your children. Watching an adult fidget isn't any fun at all unless you're trying to make them fidget to pry loose some detail or another. This didn't really count since I wasn't even remotely aware of what he might have to tell me. I didn't think he brought me here for me to watch him fidget so I waited patiently.

Four patient minutes later, Rick asked me another question. "How much do you know about the two shootings?"

"Only what I've read in the Morning News and what Detective Randall told me. Considering both sources, I think that means I know nothing at all."

"Cynical. I should have known you'd be cynical. It's probably a job requirement. This time you're right to be cynical, though. Do you even know that your partner isn't really dead?"

If I'd reacted quicker, I could have pretended to be shocked by his comment, but I didn't. That probably was a good thing, since pretending not to be shocked is more in my dramatic range. Besides, acting shocked would make Woodbury think I believed him and I didn't see any advantage in that. Instead, I asked, "Really? The Morning News seemed pretty clear on that point. Besides, I attended his funeral on Saturday. Aren't those only held for dead people?"

"Usually, but stupid people do stupid things. Unfortunately, some stupid people are cops with too much ambition and too much influence."

I smiled at Woodbury. "Since you aren't stupid and have more ambition than influence, at least for now, I presume you're talking about a different cop. Detective Randall, I presume?"

He nodded, but he didn't say anything. At least he wasn't fidgeting now. I settled back as comfortably as I could in Lisha's kitchen chair waiting for him to tell me something helpful. Two minutes later he obliged. "I know I insulted you, and I'm sorry. I don't want to insult you again, but I need you to promise you won't tell anybody, and I mean anybody, what I'm about to tell you."

"Why? I keep secrets pretty well."

"I know you do, but you keep promises even better. I think somebody in your circle of friends might be a murderer and more importantly, the people investigating these shootings are absolutely convinced of it."

I had already decided on the not acting shocked approach to whatever Woodbury had to say. Since Freak had already told me he was sure he was a suspect, I didn't have be Nicolas Cage to pull it off. "So, which of my friends is a killer? Blake? Emily? Go ahead and tell me. I can take it."

"Don't joke about this. I'm serious. I can't tell you what I want to tell you unless I know you won't tell anybody. When I say anybody, I mean anybody. I know you trust your friends, who doesn't? This isn't the time for trust. I hope I'm wrong, especially since that would mean Randall is wrong, which might cause her to fall on her face. But if I'm not, and I tell you and you tell somebody, I'll lose my job and a serial killer might walk."

He at least had the professionalism to pretend he thought a serial killer walking would be almost as bad as him losing his job, but he wasn't very convincing. I thought about it. I really wanted to know what Woodbury knew. I had no other way of learning it. His asking price for the information was my promise not to tell anybody. That didn't seem like too much to ask.

Of course, the promise that caused me to spend a week in jail a while back hadn't seemed like too much to ask at the time I gave it. I decided to try a little negotiation. "How about if I promise not to tell anybody unless they throw me in jail for not telling?"

Woodbury laughed, "I guess that'll work. You getting thrown in jail isn't what I'm worried about. Do you promise?"

"Yes, I promise. What is going on?"

He stood up. "Let's go talk in the living room. These chairs aren't all that comfortable for me either."

I gladly followed him back to the living room where we both found more comfortable places to sit. Once we were both comfortable, he said, "I'm sure you know more than you're letting on, but I also know you won't tell me what you know. I won't even ask. Feel free to tell me to skip past anything you already know."

I smiled, "Assume I know nothing."

"Sure, I'll assume it, but I don't believe it. Anyway, homicide is convinced that Rick Taylor's murder and your partner's shooting are directly related. You probably know that. The theory is that your partner was shot by somebody who blamed him for Taylor's death. Are you with me so far?"

"Amazingly, I'm keeping up so far. Go on."

"The homicide department, or more accurately, Randall is convinced that the second shooter is correct to blame him for Taylor's murder."

He looked at me like he expected me to be impressed by this revelation. I couldn't even pretend convincingly that I was impressed, so I just smiled pleasantly. I had time to waste if I needed to waste it, and I still hoped he had something important to tell me. Waiting is one thing I'm good at, and this was definitely a good time to do so.

35   Serious Allegations

Woodbury broke the silence. "Your silent act is more famous than you are, but don't you have anything to say about Randall's theory?"

"Sure, she apparently plans to give the sniper a medal instead of making an arrest if she finds him or her. I haven't seen anything to suggest that she'll ever figure out who fired the shot, so what does it matter?"

"Good point, but I think it's worse than that. I think she's planning to give the shooter another chance to finish the job."

This time I didn't have to pretend to be impressed, "Why would you say that?"

"It's not really what I meant to tell you, but I guess I might as well. One of my buddies from my days on the beat was assigned to guard his room. He called me Sunday night and told me he thinks he's guarding an empty room."

"Did he tell you where the room is?"

"No, but it's not in Dallas. He called me hoping I could pull some strings to get him off the detail so he could get home to be with his wife and children."

Any comments I could have made about cops actually missing their wives seemed counter-productive to my objective. I kept them to myself and asked Woodbury, "What do you think that means?"

"I don't know, but if he was in a hospital room with a police guard, and she moved him somewhere without a guard, it means the shooter might have a chance to finish what he started."

"Or it could mean she didn't trust the guards and moved him someplace safer. Did you pull strings to get your friend out of there?"

"I no longer have any pull at all on this, maybe I never did. If I still had any, I might not be talking to you right now." Woodbury shook his head and continued, "But I don't, and I am. Maybe you're right; maybe she moved him someplace safer. But it's also possible she moved him some place less safe."

"Or maybe he got tired of being guarded and decided to leave," I suggested.

"Not likely. Even if he woke up, the guards' assignment was as much to keep him in as to keep anybody out. Call it hospital arrest if you'd like."

I couldn't think any reason to like using two words I'd recently come to dislike in one phrase, so I just waited for Woodbury to continue.

He obliged quickly, "I might as well tell you the other bad news. Your friend April Rose is going to be arrested this week. Randall interrogated her last night for several hours. Apparently, she didn't like April's answers."

"For what? Are they hoping to hold her as a material witness or something? Rumor has it Kenth once said he wouldn't try to convict her of murder if he had eleven eyewitnesses on the jury."

Woodbury laughed, "Maybe little Dougie is smarter than I thought. Doesn't matter though, his boss is prosecuting this one. They're going over the paperwork with a fine toothed comb before going to a judge, but the plan is to charge her with accessory to murder; accessory after the fact; leaving the scene of a crime; obstruction of justice and tampering with evidence."

"I didn't know elected officials got their hands dirty with simple prosecutions. Do you think they expect to get a conviction on any of that without first convicting somebody of murder?"

"This elected official does, especially since he thinks it might help him get elected again. I don't see why he thinks this one will, but stranger things have happened. Maybe he thinks she'll confess or give them some information they can use."

This time I laughed. "Have any of Larry Joe McCoy's clients ever confessed?"

"I doubt it. I didn't realize she could afford McCoy's fees. The D.A. probably doesn't know that, either. Can she?"

I knew how flexible McCoy's fees could be for people he or his godson liked, but I didn't see any reason to share that with Woodbury and risk ruining McCoy's hard earned reputation as an expensive and ruthless attorney. "If she can't, I can."

"And you will? How will your new bride feel about you paying outrageous legal fees for the hottest bartender in Dallas County?"

"She'd be more likely to divorce me if I didn't than if I did. April is hot, but she and Emily are thick as thieves. If it weren't for April, Emily might not be my wife."

"I'd love to hear that story some day, but this isn't the time." Woodbury got back to the issue at hand. "It won't matter who her lawyer is. He's hell-bent to make an arrest and he either thinks he knows exactly what happened, or…"

Woodbury trailed off, so I finished the sentence for him. "…or he has a plan to make a jury believe his version of what happened."

"You said that, I didn't. But, you usually don't start making arrests until you have a scenario that you're either sure about, or are sure you can convince a jury to believe. You arrest a gangbanger for killing another gangbanger, you don't have to be sure, since you figure the jury will be sure anyway. But when you start arresting charming and beautiful young ladies, you better have real solid evidence."

"I understand that. Isn't that why Kenth didn't want her charged?"

"Probably, but here's the problem. As far as I can tell, they've got a wild assed theory and no real evidence to support it."

"What's the theory?"

"It's actually Randall's theory, but apparently they're going forward with it. They think Freak and April conspired to murder Rick Taylor in order to steal a song for Charlie Ray Nothing."

"And then Rick came back from the dead and shot Freak? Sounds like a great theory, do they have any evidence?"

"It's not funny. They think Charlie Ray felt guilty and told Rick's brother about it. Rick's brother was a sniper in Desert Storm, so they think he shot Freak."

"Means and motive; I presume opportunity is there. I know that's not what happened, but it's no worse than some other theories I've seen them put forth to get warrants. What makes you think they aren't seriously convinced that's how it happened?"

"Don't forget you promised not to repeat any of this! Apparently, their coup de grace evidence is that Freak and Rick both wore matching dog tags when they were shot. I'm not sure why they think that proves anything, but I know they're keeping that under wraps."

He paused, so I nodded to confirm my promise.

"The thing is I spent an entire afternoon with Freak ten days before he was shot and he wasn't wearing a dog-tag. I saw Rick Taylor's body at the crime scene and he wasn't wearing a dog tag, either. It was right after I mentioned that to Randall and the D.A. that they froze me out of the case. Maybe, it's a coincidence, but I'm having trouble believing it."

"Do you always notice people's dog tags?"

He pulled a chain out from under his shirt and showed me his dog tag, I couldn't see it well enough to read it, but I didn't need to read it. He said, "37th Armored Division at Desert Storm; 100 hours that changed us all forever. I've been noticing dog tags for the last fifteen years. Neither of the victims wore them regularly; nobody I've talked to has suggested otherwise. I've never known anybody who sometimes wears one. You either wear one or you don't. I don't know what it means, but I don't like it. Besides, neither of them was ever in the military."

I tried to remember if I'd ever seen Freak wearing a dog tag. I'd seen him wear just about every possible thing in every possible way, including necklaces, bracelets, handcuffs (as decoration), nipple rings, earrings and rings in other places, but I couldn't remember seeing him wear a dog tag. I knew he'd been in ROTC in high school, but that probably didn't really count as military.

On the other hand, a dog tag deflecting the bullet supposedly saved his life. That is, unless Randall had lied about that. I didn't trust Randall any more, if I ever had. Of course, I didn't really trust Woodbury either. I was beginning to feel like Mel Gibson in Conspiracy Theory. Except nothing made any sense to me no matter which conspiracy theory I chose to believe.

Woodbury stood up. "I've told you what I wanted to tell you. God knows I don't know what to make of it, but I hope you can figure something out. I've got to get back to work."

I stood up and we walked out of Lisha's apartment. As we went down the stairs, I asked him one more question. "Why did you decide to tell me this?"

Woodbury said, "Partly because I like you and your partner, and I know you're good. Partly because I feel guilty about what happened before. Mostly, though because I think something is really messed up. I can't do anything about it, so I guess I'm hoping you can."

"I hope so, too. Honestly though, even if I can, I don't see how that's going to help you. They won't promote you if I solve anything, and I won't even be able to give you credit since you shouldn't have told me this."

"You forget. I've seen corruption first hand before. I should have stopped my ex-partner from framing people as soon as I realized what he was doing, but I didn't. I swore if it happened again, I wouldn't hesitate. I don't know if it's happening again, but it might be. If you find something that proves it, it won't matter what I told you. I'll take care of it."

I didn't know what I might find out, but I didn't expect to need Woodbury's help when I found it. Of course, Santa Ana didn't expect a little nap at San Jacinto would hurt anything, either.

36   Bible Verses

I wasn't worried much about being followed back downtown, so the twelve minute trip back only took about fifteen minutes. I exhibited enough of the cynicism or paranoia required by my trade to keep an eye on the rearview mirror and circle one block just east of downtown to see if I was followed, but the effort mostly kept me in practice and wasted three minutes.

Once I'd parked the van in the Republic garage and started walking south toward the office, I started thinking more about what Woodbury had told me, and trying to decide if he'd actually told me anything helpful. Walking through downtown at lunch hour is similar to walking in a mall around Christmas. If you're in a hurry, you can probably fight through the crowd and get where you're going, but you can't do it without making some people mad.

I wasn't in a hurry since I had no real plan of action, so I just fell in step with the crowd and stood patiently waiting for the light to change. An elderly black man was reading aloud from a Bible in front of the liquor store at Elm and Ervay. He spoke loudly enough to be heard over the din of conversation, but with far less volume and passion than most street preachers I'd heard.

I listened as he recited, "Do you not know that your bodies are members of Christ? Shall I then take the members of Christ and make them members of a prostitute? Never! Or do you not know that he who is joined to a prostitute becomes one body with her? For, as it is written the two will become one flesh."

The light changed to green and the do not walk sign was replaced by the walk sign. The crowd slowly began to surge forward, and I continued toward my office expecting the preacher's voice to fade.

Instead I heard him reading, "But he who is joined to the Lord becomes one spirit with him. Flee from sexual immorality. Every other sin a person commits is outside the body, but the sexually immoral person sins against his own body. Or do you not know that your body is a temple of the Holy Spirit within you, whom you have from God? You are not your own, for you were bought with a price. So glorify God in your body."

I turned slightly and saw that he was right behind me. He walked with a slight limp and he was slumped over so badly that I

142

couldn't be sure how tall he was, but from my vantage point, I could see his white curly hair hadn't been washed recently and his clothes weren't much younger than he was. For some reason, he had decided today to preach to me, and I saw no reason to try to stop him. I kept walking and he kept reading from his Bible as he followed me.

"I want you to be free from anxieties. The unmarried man is anxious about the things of the Lord, how to please the Lord. But the married man is anxious about worldly things, how to please his wife and his interests are divided. And the unmarried or betrothed woman is anxious about the things of the Lord, how to be holy in body and spirit. But the married woman is anxious about worldly things, how to please her husband. I say this for your own benefit, not to lay any restraint upon you, but to promote good order and to secure your undivided devotion to the Lord."

The further south we walked the more the crowd thinned, and by the time we were across the street from my office and the library, I was alone except for the preacher who was still reading from his Bible. Now that we were alone, I could smell the unmistakable smell of really cheap wine, but I didn't see a bottle anywhere. The library is still a popular spot for the homeless; so I figured we'd be parting ways when I crossed toward my office. The light changed to walk, and I started toward the office

He reached for my arm as I did so. His grip was frail, and he quivered a little as he did so. "The good Lord told me I should read to a tall, white gentleman today. You is surely white, and even taller than 'ary an angel. I sure enough do hope you'd be kind enough to let me finish this here reading."

As he spoke he sounded like somebody from the Amos and Andy radio show, but when he'd been reading he sounded a lot like Ezekiel. I decided a little more preaching couldn't hurt me, so I stopped to let him finish.

"If anyone thinks that he is not behaving properly toward his betrothed, if his passions are strong, and it has to be, let him do as he wishes: let them marry—it is no sin. But whoever is firmly established in his heart, being under no necessity but having his desire under control, and has determined this in his heart, to keep her as his betrothed, he will do well. So then he who marries his betrothed does well, and he who refrains from marriage will do even better."

The old man closed his Bible when he finished that and looked up at me expectantly. His wrinkled face matched his white hair and he appeared to be in his sixties, but his eyes had a gleam to them that belied his age. Maybe his faith was keeping part of him young despite his hardships, or maybe I was imagining things.

I presumed he wasn't expecting me to comment on the Bible verses he'd been reading and only expected some money. I pulled a five out of my wallet and handed it to him. Like most of the street beggars I've tried to help, he took the money with as much pride and dignity as he could manage, and then had it pocketed out of sight in less than three seconds.

He looked up at me gratefully. "The Lord does provide, I sure won't doubt that again. The Lord may be mysterious, but He sure enough is constant. He wants you to have this, my young friend."

With that he handed me his Bible and slowly made his way down Young Street past the library. I watched him slowly shuffle along until he turned right on Ackard and was out of sight. I'd heard of people giving Bibles away, but I'd never seen a street preacher do it before. Maybe he thought I needed more spiritual help than he could give me in one reading.

I realized I'd been standing on the same corner for seven light changes. As soon as it changed again, I crossed the street and walked up to my office. I sat the Bible on the desk and turned on the computer to check email and update my notes on the case. I spent five minutes deleting email I didn't even need to read; three minutes replying to the few that I did need to read and ten minutes updating the notes on the case. I didn't include anything Woodbury had asked me to keep secret in the notes.

When I finished I had two hours to kill before going to pick up Emily for date night. If I were Nero Wolfe, I'd probably drink a beer, read a book, then purse my lips and solve both shootings. If I were Sherlock Holmes, I'd probably light my pipe and tell Watson how elementary the case actually was. Unfortunately, I'm just me, so I turned off the computer and paced for twenty-one minutes.

At two-twenty, I sat down at the desk and looked at the Bible I'd recently been given. It looked like most of the Bibles I've seen. It was textured black with gold embossed printing on the cover, which read:

The
Holy
Bible

ESV

The only thing out of the ordinary about it was the ESV where I was used to seeing King James or American Standard. I was curious enough to open the cover to see what version the initials ESV indicated. What I found was far more interesting; a stamp on the inside cover which read:

Donated by Good News Publishers
To LBJ General Hospital
Houston, TX

Instantly, I no longer cared about Bible versions or the initials ESV. I'm sure there are many people who would steal a Bible from a hospital, but I doubted that many of them would be preaching from it and then giving it to a complete stranger over 200 miles away. Freak's probably capable of stealing a Bible from a hospital if he has a reason to do so.

He also has a network of friends and former co-stars who would do anything for him. I didn't remember any wrinkled, white-haired black men in any of his shows, but I hadn't attended that many of his shows. It didn't matter much; I know how his mind works well enough to know this was his way of letting me know that he had left the hospital.

That likely meant I'd be seeing him or hearing from him shortly. He had no way of knowing that Woodbury had already told me that he had left the hospital, and I had no way of telling him that he may have left the hospital because Detective Randall hoped his shooter would get another chance at him.

That meant I needed to do the one thing a private detective should never do unless he has a client paying all expenses. I needed to hire a private detective.

37   Changed Plans

I called an agency I'd used before and asked, "How soon can you start 24/7 surveillance on a house?"

"Depends on where the house is, and how good a man you need on the first couple of shifts." I knew Pat didn't typically ask his clients how good an agent was needed, but we'd worked together on enough cases recently to be honest with each other.

"The house is on Adolph. I just want to be called if anybody goes in or out. Pretty much anybody who can find the house and remember my number will do."

Pat laughed, "I'm sure all my ops can handle that. Give me the address and I'll have somebody there in twenty minutes."

I gave him the address and we discussed the logistics of the assignment for a few minutes. Pat's agency is a good one. I had no doubt the surveillance would be handled professionally. Next, I called Emily's cell phone.

She answered on the second ring, "Hello Darling, please tell me you're not calling to cancel our date."

"No, I'm not canceling, but we do need to change plans slightly. Things may start to happen fast. I don't want to be too far from the office tonight. Anything Uptown or around here you feel like doing tonight?"

"As long as we're together, any place is what I feel like doing tonight. You think of something and I'll think of something. When I pick you up, we'll decide."

Since I was sure Emily would think of something fun, I didn't spend much time thinking of something to do. We hadn't been Uptown to West Village in a couple of months, so I decided to suggest that. There are enough nightclubs around there that it'd be impossible not to find something to do. Plus, unlike Victory Plaza, you can self-park in some of their lots. If Freak showed up at his house, I wasn't going to want to rely on a valet attendant to retrieve my van.

At 3:05, my cell phone rang. I answered it as if it were my office phone, "Pegasus Investigations."

"This is Jeff with Secure Investigation. Pat said I should call you to let you know I'm in position."

It's always a pleasure to work with real professionals. I told Jeff, "Wasn't necessary, but thanks, anyway."

"No problem. That's how we do things at Dallas' premiere detective agency."

Okay, maybe it isn't always a pleasure to work with real professionals. "Pat did tell me you'd be in position by 2:55. Is Dallas premiere detective agency always ten minutes late?"

"Of course we're not. I was delayed because somebody else is watching the target, and I had to abandon my vehicle to find a more hidden, though less comfortable viewing position."

I didn't want the smug little bastard to know I was impressed. "Well, better late than never, I suppose. If somebody else is still watching the house, you're probably there soon enough. Is the other watcher official or private?"

"The car looks private, but the jarhead haircut in it looks like a rookie cop. Should I go ask?"

I gave Jeff a courtesy laugh. "No, it's probably official. However, the owner of that house was shot by a sniper with a military weapon. Your jarhead may be an ex-Marine who doesn't understand he isn't allowed to shoot people any more."

"So it is his house? Pat thought it might be. If you don't mind me asking, is this assignment business or personal?"

"What do you mean?"

"I want to know if I'm staking out a dead man's house because a client is paying you to have me do it or because you want to know if the bastard that shot him shows up at his house."

"There's no client, but don't worry, I can afford to pay your agency for your time. Did you get the plates off the other watcher's car?"

"Of course, you can. Of course, I did. We're both professionals, aren't we?"

"Of course, we are. Did you have Pat run the plates?"

"No, I figured this was personal. Knowing Pat, he'd probably bill you for the time he spent running them. I thought I'd save you a few bucks by letting you do that yourself. By the way, this first shift is on me. I'll tell Pat not to clock me in on this one."

"Thanks, but you don't need to do that."

"Yes, I do. He may have been your partner, but he was my friend. I owe him this much, at least. By the way, I thought your words at the funeral summed him up perfectly. I never thought you had it in you to be an orator, but I was impressed."

"Thanks, again. Give me the plate number. I'll run it and call you back to let you know who your company is."

He gave me the number and we hung up. I called Blake's office and was pleasantly surprised when Ana Marie told me he was in his office and connected me.

He answered gruffly, "I'll help if I can, but I'm so out of the loop I may be the last person you should call."

"I don't need inside information. Frankly, I'm rapidly losing interest in the official investigation. I'm just hoping you can run a license plate for me and tell me if it's official or private."

"I can. Should I?"

"It's parked outside Freak's house with a guy with a crew cut sitting behind the wheel."

"Yeah, I suppose that should be run. Give me the number."

I did, and he promised to call back as soon as he had an answer. The phone rang a few minutes later. "Pegasus Investigations", I answered.

Pat's voice was accusatory. "Why didn't you tell me this was about Freak and not for a client? We'll bill expenses only on this, and we can provide more help than simple surveillance if you need it."

"Thanks, I guess. Is my office close enough to the homeless shelter for your charitable contribution to be deductible?"

"It's not charity, dummy. It's business. Having detectives gunned down in broad daylight is bad for business. Catching the fucking killer is good for business. I'd like my agency to be a part of the catching. Hell, maybe I'll get lucky and get a chance to kill the bastard myself."

"It's always good to have a dream. I'll keep you in mind when I find out who the bastard, or bitch (we can't rule out the fairer sex), who shot him is."

"You do that. While you're at it, don't forget that we're here to help."

I promised him I wouldn't. After we hung up, I worked on updating my case notes while I waited for Blake to call. I was barely started when the phone rang at 3:55.

"Pegasus Investigations," I answered.

"It's me", Blake said. "The car is official. It's DPD. I couldn't get much info on it, since I'm currently persona non grata with the department. It's definitely a cop, though. Why do you think it's sitting there, and for that matter how do you know it is?"

"I know it is because one of Pat's guys saw it sitting there. Why it's there is another question entirely. Let's do lunch tomorrow and discuss the possibilities."

"Sounds good, Walt's at eleven?"

"Sure."

I called Jeff to let him know his jarhead was a cop and returned to working on my notes. I expected the next call to be Emily telling me she had a new plan for date night. At, 5:20, she met my expectations. "Is Mockingbird Station close enough to the office for our date?"

"I suppose so; do we often spend our dates at shopping centers?"

She laughed, "Not often enough, but I was thinking we could go to the Pocket Sandwich Theatre across the street. That way, if you have to rush off to solve a crime, I can take the Dart Rail back to your office to get my car without you having to lose time dropping me someplace."

"Great idea, dear. Plus, I'll have popcorn to throw at the suspects once I catch them."

"Unless you've already thrown it all at the stage before you get the bat signal. Is 6:30 okay to meet you at the office?"

I assured her 6:30 would be fine, knowing full well she'd be at least 20 minutes late. The Pocket Sandwich Theatre doesn't always have shows on Tuesdays, but I didn't ask her about that. I know her well enough to know she had already checked.

I also knew there'd be plenty of popcorn since throwing popcorn at the stage is one of the reasons the place advertises itself as the most fun you can have in a Dallas theatre. I bet some fans of the Rocky Horror Picture show might disagree. Personally, I prefer the Pocket Sandwich Theatre since most of the girls wearing fishnet stockings on its stage are actually girls.

I was hard at work reviewing and revising the notes on the case when the phone rang again at 5:50. Even though it wasn't officially office hours, I answered professionally, "Pegasus Investigations."

An urgent, male voice said, "I can't talk long, but if you're hiding anything or anybody at your office you need to get it out of there and soon!"

About halfway through the warning, I realized it was Woodbury. I thanked him for the tip and assured him I wasn't hiding anything or anybody and had nothing to worry about. If I'd been hiding something or somebody, I probably would have said the same thing, but since I wasn't, I said it without feeling guilty. He hung up with no further comment.

I figured his warning meant Freak really had left the hospital without the cops' permission, and they thought he might be hiding at the office. I was sure he wasn't, since I hadn't seen him since I left Houston. I was also sure the cops weren't going to find anything suspicious at the office. Of course, being sure and being right are two completely different things.

38   Search Warrant

My caution in not leaving central Dallas for date night, and Emily's brilliance in finding a place on the Dart Rail proved to be unnecessary, as nothing happened related to the case. Much laughter at the theatre and a delicious post-show dinner at the original Campisi's just east of the theatre preceded a night of marital bliss at the office I used to call home and seemed to be calling home again.

Emily left for work at six-fifty. By eight-fifteen, I had the office converted back to looking like an office, instead of a newlywed's den. I looked out the north window toward Neiman-Marcus. The street preacher who'd given me the Bible yesterday was reading from a Bible to nobody in particular this morning.

I briefly considered going down to talk to him, but decided against it. I knew why he'd given me the Bible; I also knew that discussing it in public wouldn't be a great idea. I also considered the idea of going to Tootsie's for breakfast, decided against that, too. Since I was meeting Blake for lunch at 11, I figured I could wait for a delicious chicken fried steak at Walt Garrison's Rodeo Bar.

Instead, I had a couple of slices of toast and wasted a few hours pretending if I studied the case notes long enough, I'd suddenly solve the case or cases. At ten-fifty, I locked up my office and headed for the Rodeo Bar. The street preacher was on the steps of the library nibbling on what was left of a sandwich I suspected he'd been given or found. I decided to give him more than five dollars the next time I saw him.

As I walked down Commerce Street, I knew I was being tailed, but I didn't bother to lose it. My shadow followed the police academy instruction for a tail so thoroughly that I knew he was DPD, and I had no reason to hide that I was going to lunch with Blake. Besides, even if I did want to hide it, The Rodeo Bar would be the first place they looked for me if I shook the tail.

The bar wasn't open when I got there, but Chris Austin saw me and unlocked the door to let me in. "How you holding up, big guy? I could tell at the funeral you're taking it hard."

"As well as can be expected, I guess. Losing a friend is never easy."

He walked me to the corner table that Blake and I usually take and I took a seat. For the first time ever, Chris sat down at the table with me.

"Can I ask you a question?"

I couldn't resist with Chris, "You just did, but if you want, you can ask another one."

Chris didn't react, "April's taking it pretty hard, were the two of them together?"

"When he got shot? No, I don't think so. There's nothing in the police report to suggest that she was there."

"No, I mean, were they a couple? She's taking it really hard, and I like her. If they were together I don't want to be her rebound guy. But if they weren't, I don't want to wait too long to make my move. Girls like her don't stay on the market long, you know."

I resisted the urge to tell him my personal opinion of boys who use the word girl and market in the same sentence. I thought about telling him that bragging to his buddies about having already tagged a girl isn't likely to help his chances of ever really having her.

I decided not to because I thought it might be best if he didn't know I could overhear his conversations at other tables in case he ever said something important or interesting. I was still trying to find a polite way to end the conversation when Blake arrived and saved me the trouble. Chris hustled behind the bar as soon as April walked toward the door to open it for Blake.

April brought over two glasses of iced tea. "I presume you're both working this morning, so I don't need the manager to bring out more beer."

I smiled, "Correct. You won't need to call a cab for either of us today. How are you holding up?

"I'm okay. It's not like I've never lost a friend before. How are you doing?"

"Right now, I'm trying to find the shooter. If I have to grieve, I'll do it after that's done."

April never misses a thing, "If? Why wouldn't you have to grieve?"

Blake saved me from having to get out of it. "If he gets killed looking for the shooter, then he won't need to grieve."

"Don't get killed, baby. I'm holding up for now, but I don't think I could handle losing both of you. Besides, I know Emily can't."

The bar was open now, and the regulars were starting to come in. April took our orders and hustled back to the bar to greet the regulars. Blake and I both hate talking business over lunch, so I wasn't surprised when he asked, "Did you catch the Ranger game last night?"

"No, Emily and I went to the Pocket Sandwich Theater. I saw the final, was it as bad as it looked?

"Pretty much; I hoped the three game winning streak might be the start of something, but I guess not."

"Maybe not," I agreed. "But, losing to the Yankees doesn't always mean there's no hope."

"True, but Young's not hitting; nobody's hitting with runners in scoring position and we still can't pitch. It doesn't look good. When Sammy Sosa's the lone bright spot, there's not much to look forward to."

"This is Dallas, Blake. There's always something to look forward to."

"Really, what?" he asked.

I smiled, "Football season."

"Sure, too bad the Cowboys don't seem any more able to win a playoff game than the Rangers."

We were saved from further discussion of the depressing local sports scene by April bringing us our food. We dug in, and as usual, the chicken fried steak was delicious.

Blake had just finished and I had only a couple of bites left when Detective Randall strolled into the bar. She carried a stack of official looking envelopes and sat down looking as smug as Boss Hogg counting his money.

"Having a nice lunch, gentleman?"

Blake answered, "I was."

She turned toward me, "How about you, Marlowe?"

My friends don't call me Marlowe, but it was pretty obvious that she wasn't my friend at the moment. She probably never had been. "A delightful lunch with delightful company interrupted only by an uninvited guest."

I pointed at the envelopes. "Are those search warrants or arrest warrants?"

"What makes you so sure they're warrants, guilty conscience?"

"Not at all; process serving is a big part of the detective business. I recognize the envelopes." I didn't bother mentioning that I'd been delivering them as a bike courier long before I had the detective agency functioning well enough to only need the one source of income. I also didn't mention that Woodbury had warned me that this was coming. "Are you going to answer the question?"

"Both, we'll start with the search warrant and see how it goes."

"Well, if you're here to search Walt's, you don't need to be wasting time with me."

"Actually, we will be searching Walt Garrison's Rodeo Bar. I'm talking to you though, because I have a warrant to search your office. You'd be well advised to cooperate."

I reached for my cell phone. "I always cooperate with the police, unless my attorney advises me against it. I'll just call Mr. McCoy and see what he says."

As I dialed, Randall said, "Do that if you wish, but we're executing these warrants whether you're there to let us in or not."

Blake started to laugh, but held it back. Adriana answered on the second ring.

"Is Mr. McCoy available? I think it's important."

"I know it's important, let me see if he's available."

While I waited, Randall continued. "That son of a bitch is hiding somewhere and we're going to find him. McCoy's office is going to be searched at the same time we search your office, your home, his house, this bar and several in Deep Ellum where he might hide. We're going to find him."

April appeared behind her with the check. "Who are you going to find, Officer?"

Larry Joe came on the line with little trace of his Texas accent, "The police appear to be trying to fish every lake simultaneously, Pardner. I'm going to be busy protecting my own rights, here. Think you'll be alright on your own?"

"Sure I will, aren't I always? Are there any fish in those lakes?"

154

"Some fish don't need to live in water; they're wasting time and making fools of themselves. Don't do anything rash, and everything will work out."

While I was talking to Larry Joe, Randall had paid our tab. I presumed that was to get rid of April, not out of friendship, but I thanked her anyway. My phone rang. I looked at the caller I.D. and saw it was Emily. "Hello Darling, I trust your lunch is accompanied by the same sort of delightful people with whom I am enjoying mine."

"Of course, it is darling, except I'm not as used to being escorted to my home by the police. They have a warrant to search the house, what should I do?"

"You might want to warn them about your lacy pink jungle paradise. Other than that, just hang around and make a note of anything they damage or steal."

"Is everything okay?" For one of the few times since I'd known her she sounded worried.

"It will be. I promise."

That satisfied her. "Okay I'll warn him about what he's about to endure. By the way, last night was wonderful."

"Yes it was, my love, Tonight will be wonderful, too."

When I hung up, Randall asked, "Any more calls you want to make or take to delay the inevitable? Your office is being watched. If he's there, he isn't getting out."

I dialed one more number on my phone while I answered her. "I'm not delaying anything. I'm simply exercising my rights as an American citizen to use the telephone when I choose to do so. Surely, you haven't been with DPD so long you've forgotten about Constitutional rights, have you? By the way, how many of your convictions have been overturned this year?"

It was a low blow and I knew it. But any cop who works in the city that leads the nation in convictions overturned based on DNA evidence or proof of evidence tampering should be used to hearing it. Apparently Randall wasn't. She slapped me so hard I almost dropped the phone just as Daniel Leeds answered.

39   Old Friends

At one forty-five, I saw Daniel park his Lincoln Town Car in the pay lot across the street from my office. I'd been standing outside with three police officers for thirty minutes waiting for him. For the first ten minutes, two of the cops took turns threatening to break in or physically take my key from me.

Eventually, Officer Childress, who was clearly in charge said, "Knock it off guys. If he wants to wait for his lawyer, we'll wait for his lawyer."

I guess Childress realized that threatening to violate my rights while we were waiting for a lawyer wasn't smart. I kept looking around for the street preacher, but saw no sign of him. A little preaching might have hit the spot, but I guess street preachers are like cops: never around when you need one. Daniel walked leisurely from the car to the office. I knew him well enough to know he never wanted the opponent to think he was in a hurry.

"Greetings, my young associate," he said as he shook my hand. "I presume these gentlemen desire to invade your domicile."

I saw no reason to mention that it wasn't my home anymore. Daniel turned to the officer with the envelope, "I shall peruse your documentation in advance of such an event."

"What?"

Childress hadn't said anything in the half hour I'd known him that caused me to think he was a genius, but he wasn't the only person around who sometimes needed help translating Daniel's version of English.

"He wants to read the warrants, Officer." I told him politely,

"Well, you could have just said so," he said to Daniel as he handed him the warrants.

"In point of fact, I did, my dear sir. However, no benefit to a quibble over miniscule technicalities is foreseeable."

Childress surprised me by saying nothing while Daniel read over the warrant. I'm not sure how many times Daniel read it, but it had to be several times. Finally, he looked at me, "Cessation of my retirement was indeed warranted, pardon my pun. This document specifies the parameters of this quixotic quest in totality."

He handed the warrant back to Childress. "My client and I will adjourn to his home to confer briefly. When we permit you

156

access, you'll be expected to abide by that document precisely. Failure to abide will breach it, actionably."

"We'll come in with you." Childress stated it as a fact, not a suggestion.

Daniel stared at them. "You will not. That document neither implies nor expresses that you must. Insist and you will be denied entry and I'll commence litigation."

Childress walked away and pulled out his cell phone. He talked to somebody for three minutes, then walked back. "We'll give you five minutes."

"You will 'give' us nothing. However, five minutes is sufficient. Again, I'll not wrangle over the inconsequential."

Daniel and I entered the office. "Why do we need to confer?" I asked as I picked up the remote to the panel which covers the hidden window and put it in my pocket.

"We have no such necessity. I considered it most likely you'd wish to maintain some secrecy regarding this edifice's more unusual features. Your actions confirm my rationale. Additionally, I desired to flex some legal muscle. In my retirement, I've missed the pleasure." He smiled before continuing. "Invite your guests at your earliest convenience."

I opened the door and invited the cops to enter. They entered and searched thoroughly, but professionally for an hour and twenty-two minutes. The only conversation was the officers talking among themselves as they worked until Childress came out of the room Emily and I had spent last night in.

"The Murphy bed appears to have been used recently."

"Sure it has, but if you want details regarding the sex life of my wife and me, you'll have to wait for the memoir."

"I don't. I assume she'll confirm that. Of course, if you're both lying, your stories will match."

Daniel cleared his throat and Childress held up his hand. "I'm not accusing your client of anything, just idly discussing the nature of police work with a professional colleague."

"Indubitably, although it might be interesting to ascertain if a panel of six or twelve peers would garner substantial comprehension regarding the subtle difference."

Childress smiled, "Indubitably, it might also be interesting to be able to understand more than half of what you say."

Daniel laughed and Childress rejoined his team to complete the search. When they were leaving, I asked, "Find anything interesting?"

"If we did, we'll report it to our bosses, not to you."

When they were gone, Daniel asked the shortest question I'd ever heard him ask, "Your wife?" I suspected it was the shortest sentence he was capable of using.

"I guess we have some catching up to do. Let me call Emily, then we can talk."

The search at the house went about like the search of the office without the legal posturing and witty repartee. Emily survived unharmed and was back at work. Daniel and I chatted for a little while. On his way out, he told me to keep him involved and informed. Retirement was boring him, so he was glad to be back in action. Of course, he used more and bigger words to say it, but I've learned to understand him most of the time.

Daniel left at just before five, so I decided to let traffic clear before heading home. I hit the switch to slide the panels away from the window and called Emily to let her know. Then, I made myself a sandwich and ate it while I took turns staring at the case notes and staring out the window. Both activities only passed the time.

At five-thirty, I watched a wino cross the street toward the office. He fell once, but the backpack he was carrying like a papoose broke the fall. Somehow he managed to keep the bottle he had in a paper sack from hitting the concrete as he fell. Once he righted himself, he looked in the sack and celebrated by taking a long pull.

It took him over a minute to negotiate his way up the steps to my waiting room, but he made it. He sat the backpack and bottle in the corner and lay down on the floor. I couldn't think of any good reason to shoo him away, so I just let him take his nap. He looked younger than most winos, and his long black hair looked a little cleaner than most. I guessed he'd been to the Y or a homeless center within the last couple of days. I wondered if he'd eaten recently and thought about making him a sandwich.

I decided against it and went back to studying the case notes. At six-thirty, I heard a knocking on the door. I presumed correctly it was the wino and reluctantly went to answer it. I opened it, and he surprised me by crawling into the office before I could stop him. He scurried toward the kitchenette on hands and knees with surprising speed. Apparently, his nap had sobered him up, even though I could smell cheap wine from across the room.

"Hey, Archie Goodwin, aren't you going to greet an old friend."

"I don't have any friends …"

He joined me for the conclusion, 'who call me Archie Goodwin."

It finally dawned on me who he was, "Freak, what in the Hell are you doing here?"

He went behind the desk and hit the switch to slide the protective panels back over the window before answering. "We've got a case to solve, Archie. Feel free to call me Mr. Wolfe, or Nero, if you prefer."

"Despite the fact that you aren't making any sense, and smell like a winery, I presume you're sober. You shouldn't be here."

"On the contrary, this is exactly where I should be. If somebody is still trying to kill me, where would I be safer? Since the police just searched the place and found no sign of me, it will be almost impossible for them to get a warrant to do it again. We just need to get me back here unobserved, so I can stay here in peace."

"And I suppose you have a plan to make that happen?"

"Of course, I do. I've had plenty of time to come up with one when I haven't been giving stolen Bibles to heathen detectives and hanging out at liquor stores and homeless shelters. Oh, by the way this is for Emily."

He handed me the paper sack, which contained an unopened bottle of her favorite Merlot. "For her, I thank you. Tell me what you've been doing, and what your plan is."

"We'll go over the plan for now, partner. Traffic should be clearing soon and you need to go. I'll fill you in on what I've been doing once we've got me safely stashed at the office."

He told me his plan. I offered a couple of improvements and we agreed to implement it on Saturday morning. After he stumbled out of the office and down the stairs, I called Emily to tell her I was on my way home.

"See you soon, darling. Let's make tonight as wonderful as last night."

"Yes let's do. By the way, Saturday, I need you to pick up a couple of Mexicans."

40   Mexican Sweat

"Tell me again why I'm picking up four Mexicans tomorrow morning in this beautiful Chevy Silverado pickup truck?" Emily was concentrating on driving while we talked. It had been a long time since she'd driven a stick and she was trying to get comfortable with it again.

It was Friday night and we were driving home from Keller's on Harry Hines. Since I'd borrowed a pickup truck from Jessie, I couldn't resist tailgating with a greasy hamburger, tater tots and a long-neck bottle of Miller Lite. Since Emily was driving, I also couldn't resist following the beer with several others. Emily passed on the burger and the beer; opting instead for chicken strips, tater tots and a milkshake so thick she needed the spoon the carhop brought with it.

For the last three days, I'd been pretending to investigate the two shootings while trying to think of any reason why Freak's plan wouldn't work. I hadn't made any progress on the shootings, but I'd come up with about a thousand reasons why his plan might not work. Fortunately, or unfortunately, for every reason I came up with that the plan wouldn't work, I came up with a reason why we should try it, anyway.

None of which mattered, since I'd already promised him we'd try it. Freak had it well thought out. Spending almost a week in a hospital had given him plenty of time to think things out. The worst thing that could happen would be both of us going to jail or him dying a painful death by suffocation. We'd both been to jail before, and most likely would go again. Besides, a painful death wouldn't actually be painful for him.

Emily lightly punched my arm. "Answer the question, Silent Bob." It was one of her favorite nicknames for me. It also was one of the most apropos.

"Sorry, you're driving this pickup because tomorrow when you turn from Royal Lane onto Dennis, the day laborers there will flock to you, so you won't have to recruit. You're getting four because the freezer they're going to carry upstairs weighs about two hundred pounds more than a normal freezer and I don't want anyone watching to see them struggle."

"You're choosing Mexicans because even most of the ones who are here legally and have papers to prove it know others who aren't. This causes them to be very much disinclined to answer questions from police. In fact, most of them don't speak English well enough to even answer police questions at all."

"If they don't speak English, how am I going to hire them?"

"Don't worry. At least one will speak English well enough for you to hire them. It's only around law enforcement types that their command of the English language fades."

"If you're such an expert on hiring day laborers, why am I hiring them instead of you?"

"Well, Mrs. Charles," I said using one of my favorite nicknames for her. "I thought you married a detective so you could experience the fun and glamour of detective work."

"Of course I did. Is this the fun part? Are we having fun, yet?"

We both laughed at her referencing an old movie, which is usually what I do. While we were laughing, she figured it out. "Of course not, I'm not hiring the laborers because it's the fun and glamorous part. I'm doing it because it's the safe part. If this goes wrong and you two get arrested, I won't be implicated. I'm just a simple woman hiring some cheap help for her frugal husband."

"I think they call it plausible deniability, my love. Freak and I both know we can survive in jail if it happens. It would kill us both to think we put you in there in the process."

"And if you asked Blake or Jessie to help you carry him upstairs, you'd be putting them at risk. So we hire some people who can help without being at risk. I don't guess I'll complain about you spending our retirement fund on day laborers. How much will they ask for, by the way?"

"Not as much as they're worth, but we'll pay them more. Our retirement fund can take it, and I can't stand to pay them less."

She parked the truck in the driveway and opened the garage door. We walked inside holding hands. She kissed me as we entered. Her eyes twinkled like they always do when she's about to do or say something she thinks will shock me.

"I think you're just afraid I'm a repressed lesbian and you might never win me back if I spend enough time in jail to discover my true self."

I laughed, "Maybe we should ask Bobbie Jo to help us with the risky parts."

"Maybe you should be sure she didn't shoot anybody first. I know you hate thinking of your friends as suspects, but people in your circle are getting shot. I don't think you can rule anybody out."

"No, you're right. The sad thing is, all of my friends who are suspects are capable of killing. That may be one reason they're my friends."

"Even April," she asked playfully.

"Well she's my friend because she brings me beer and chicken fried steak any time I want. But, there's more to her than meets the eye. She's taken pretty quickly to detective work for a part-time model, full-time bartender. You know she took a gun on her 'date' with Rick Taylor."

Emily laughed. "If I looked like her, I'd carry a gun to church. Every girl dreams of being irresistible, but it probably comes with as many drawbacks as benefits."

"You should know, since you're completely irresistible." I held her tight and kissed her.

"And since this might be your last night as a free man, you'd better make sure your irresistible wife has a night she'll remember you by while you serve your time."

I hoped it wouldn't be my last night as a free man, but I did what I could to follow her suggestion. I was still worn out when I woke up in the morning, but that didn't matter much. Freak and Emily had the challenging parts of our plan. All I had to do was drive my van two blocks from the parking garage to the office and open the door.

I drove the truck from the house to the DART rail station on Parker Road. I circled Collin Creek Mall and zigzagged through a couple of other side streets to make sure we weren't followed. I didn't think the Plano police would still be interested in the case after finding nothing earlier in the week, but I wanted to be sure.

Dallas Police would be a different matter, but that's why we had planned this so carefully. I took the red line downtown, while Emily went to pick up some day laborers. I loitered around the Plaza of the Americas Building waiting for her to text me. At eleven fifteen, I got her text message. I walked over to Republic Tower and went downstairs to where my friend, Gus still lets me keep the van at no charge. I opened the back door. As I did I heard the soft sound of a freezer door closing.

Freak was in the freezer and had enough air for the trip. I took the roll of Kenmore tape that Freak had provided and sealed the cardboard box so it looked straight from the factory. It took three minutes to get from the garage to the office. As planned, Emily was already there with four day laborers. Jessie's truck was parked in the lot across from the office. I parked the van illegally on the street at the bottom of the stairs.

I opened the back door to the van and the laborers wasted no time getting the freezer out of the van. As soon as they got the box out of the van, Emily got in and moved it to a legal parking place. If the additional weight bothered them, it wasn't noticeable as they followed me upstairs. By the time I had the inner office unlocked, they were in the waiting area with the box.

Five minutes after I'd parked the van, the freezer box sat in the office and I was outside paying four day laborers far more than they usually make for one hour, but hopefully not so much that they'd want to tell everybody about the generous gringo. Emily drove them back to Royal Lane while I went in to get Freak out of the freezer.

By my calculations, Freak had been trapped in a closed freezer for less than twenty minutes. He had assured me that he knew he'd be fine in the freezer for at least an hour, but I didn't trust him. By the time I got back upstairs and cut through the tape on the box and opened the freezer, I was sweating more than the guys who'd carried it upstairs.

41   Escape Artist

"Before I forget, here's the eleven dollars I borrowed from you."

Freak was sitting behind the desk in the office lobby and I was sitting in one of the client chairs. He'd watched me unpack the freezer, move it in place and plug it in without comment. Without him in it, the freezer didn't weigh as much as it had when the guys brought it in, but it still weighed enough to be hard to move around by myself.

"I don't remember you borrowing eleven dollars, but I'd have let you keep it, if you'd have helped me with the freezer."

"I couldn't, we had to know for sure that you could unpack it yourself, since I'm not supposed to be here to help you. It'd be a real shame if you got convicted of aiding and abetting because Kenth proved you couldn't unpack a freezer by yourself."

"Sure it would, but since you didn't kill Rick Taylor, I'm not guilty of aiding and abetting, anyway. When did you borrow eleven dollars from me?"

"At the hospital, when I did the magic trick."

I picked up the eleven dollars from the desk and put it in my wallet. "Not your greatest trick, by the way."

"I know, but I knew I was going to need money to get back to Dallas. It's the only trick that came to mind that uses paper money."

"How exactly did you get back here on eleven dollars?"

"I invested wisely and caught a greyhound bus."

"By which you mean you scammed some innocent people out of their hard-earned money."

"You've been a detective for how many years and you still believe in the existence of innocent people? Besides, I didn't scam anybody. I simply placed a few wagers in a few local establishments regarding the limits of human endurance and the actions of certain playing cards. Fortunately, some cards behave less randomly than others, and some humans have more endurance than others."

"Of course, and what kind of dividend did your investments yield?"

"Enough. I wasn't sure how much I might need, so I kept finding new bars and raising the stakes until I had a couple grand."

"You turned eleven dollars into two thousand in three days? Why the Hell did you ever run that Freak Show Revue? For that matter, why are you a partner in a piss-ant detective agency?"

"Actually I made the money the night I slipped away. But, where's the job satisfaction in winning money from drunks? It's too easy."

"Of course, it is. That can't be nearly as fulfilling as having lapel pins stuck on every part of your body. While I'm on the subject of dangerous stunts, are you sure it's safe for you to not still be hospitalized? You did get shot in the heart recently didn't you?"

"No, miraculously, the bullet missed everything and mostly left flesh wounds. The first doctor I saw there told me I was only being kept as a precaution. After I heard precaution from the third different physician within earshot of two Houston cops, I realized that by precaution, they meant custody. I'm fine."

"You weren't in a coma when you got to LBJ?"

"No, they gave me something at Parkland so I'd sleep on the Care-Flite helicopter, but I was awake when we got to Houston. Why do you ask?"

"Just another thing Detective Randall wasn't honest about. So you've been awake for days, and you're fine medically. Be interesting to hear how Larry Joe wants to treat the dishonesty when this is all over. DPD hasn't won too many lawsuits lately."

"It might be interesting, but let's hope it doesn't come to that. I'm fine, but if we don't clear things up in a couple of weeks, we'll have to figure out a way to sneak me out of here to see my doctor just to be sure."

"You got out of the hospital despite being in police custody, and we got you in here. We'll figure out a way to get you out, if and when we must. Maybe sneaking him in here will be easier."

"Probably, but unless you sneak an X-ray machine in with her, it won't do any good. She has to check my organs to make sure there's nothing pain should be warning me about, not just check my blood pressure."

"Of course, I should have realized that. By the way, how'd you slip away from the hospital, anyway?"

"Sunday afternoon, right after the nurses changed shifts; I started complaining of massive stomach pains. They rolled me down to X-ray. The guards followed, of course, but they waited outside in the hall. When the nurse left me there to wait for the technician, I followed him through the lab, borrowed some scrubs that I found and strolled out of the hospital."

"So you walked into a bar with eleven dollars wearing scrubs and started gambling?"

"No I walked into a thrift store, bought a pair of shorts, sneakers and a tee shirt. Then, I scouted around until it was late enough that bar patrons would be drunk. That's when I walked into a bar and turned the remaining six dollars into enough cash to get home."

Monday morning, I went to a costume shop, and bought everything else I'd need. When I got on the bus, the cops were there checking out every young, white male. Fortunately, they never batted an eye at the older African-Americans who boarded."

"You disguised yourself as an old black man? I don't believe it."

"Why don't you? You believed I was one when I gave you the Bible, but you shouldn't assume I was disguised as a man. I am a performer, you know?"

It finally dawned on me that he hadn't given the Bible to a street preacher to give me. He'd been the street preacher who gave it to me. "I guess I do now, why didn't the hospital know you don't feel pain? Isn't it part of your medical history?"

"Sure it is, but Larry Joe, as my next of kin, is the guardian of my medical history and chooses only to share that which he deems advisable. The file he gave LBJ contained no mention of it. I guess he figured they were monitoring every thing anyway, no reason to burden them with extra details."

"Maybe, but he might have given them a different file if he'd known you weren't in a coma."

Freak laughed, "Possibly, another reason we should thank her for her lies, not sue her. But he probably wouldn't have. Larry Joe knows like I do that doctors get squeamish about things they don't understand. Pain is something medical science doesn't really understand. It's best with a new doctor not to confuse them with details they don't think they can control."

"Doctors don't understand pain? I thought they specialized in it."

"No, they specialize in disease and injury. Their mindset is that pain is both a byproduct and a warning sign relating to one or the other. People like me who feel no pain don't fit into their paradigm. It's the same with fibromyalgia sufferers who feel pain even when there is no detectable injury or disease. Many doctors won't even accept either one as patients."

"So doctors hate the unknown, huh? I'll remember that. Good thing they aren't detectives, I guess."

"In a way they are. The difference is that when somebody dies unexpectedly on our case, we get to react and look for the killer. When that happens to doctors, they often get sued or lose their license or both."

"And this would be a good time for us start looking for Rick Taylor's killer, especially if we don't want to lose our license."

Freak smiled, "I kind of assumed that's what you were doing since I got shot. It sure as Hell was what I was doing until I got shot. If you haven't been looking for a killer, what have you been doing?"

It was damn good question. As usual when I'm I asked a damn good question, I would have liked to have a damn good answer. This time unfortunately, I most certainly didn't. It was time to change that, immediately.

42   Legal Manuevers

"Listen to this from the Morning Snooze Website."

Freak was sitting at the computer in the office lobby and I was in the kitchenette trying to make sense out of about thirty articles I had downloaded by Googling Charlie Ray Nothing and Rick Taylor. I wanted to know more about their relationship. Charlie wasn't saying very much about it, and Rick wasn't saying anything.

"Go ahead."

'Entertainer Not Dead; local entertainer The Absolutely Incredible Freak Show is not dead, according to a press release issued by the Dallas Police Department. The release states that the gunshot wound appeared to be critical, but the victim recovered in a Houston Hospital and craftily slipped away from monitoring police officers with his superior cunning and intellect."

"That's not what it says, Freak."

"It would if that paper ever printed the truth. I did craftily evade the cops, remember?"

"Sure, I believed that part. I just know the only person who still calls you the Absolutely Incredible Freak Show is you."

"Not true," he replied indignantly. "Sam The Man and Bobbie Jo sometimes do. But, you're right, the article uses my real name, only slightly misspelled."

"What'd you expect? Is anything in the article of interest? Blake already emailed us the press release. We knew it was coming."

"No, it's what we expected; no mention of police involvement in the 'mix-up.' It's like they expect people to believe I accidentally faked my own death."

The phone rang before I could tell him that nobody believes anything they read in the paper anyway, "Pegasus Investigations."

Larry Joe spoke without accent, "Good, you're there. Don't leave. I'm on my way."

"Okay, but if it's about the press release, I've seen it."

"It's not, Blake copied me on his email; I knew you'd seen it. Stay there."

Eight minutes later at eleven a.m., Freak was safely in the room that once had been my bedroom, then had been my office and

168

now was his office. We'd switched offices so he would have the one with the private bath. I watched Larry Joe ascend the stairs and opened the door for him before he got to it. When I had it closed again, I went and knocked on the office door to let Freak know the coast was clear.

"I talked to your doctor this morning. She says you need to come in."

Freak laughed, "Sure, I also need to get some fresh air and hang out with my buddies in Deep Ellum, but this isn't the time."

"She thinks it is. She says you have an impressive ability to sense when something is wrong with your body in spite of your condition. However, you've never been shot like this before. She's very worried."

"Probably not, she probably just misses me. You know women find me irresistible. She's not immune to my charms."

Larry Joe shook his head, "This also is not the time for jokes. I explained the situation to her, and she's agreed to see you after hours; way after hours if needed."

Freak sighed, "Okay, she's probably right. What's your plan to sneak me out of here into her office, back out and here again?"

Larry Joe's accent returned instantly, "I reckon we ain't fixin' to need one."

"How do you figure that?" Freak asked.

"Your doctor lady gave me some plumb interesting details about medical liability litigation."

I interrupted. "I thought you were the world's second greatest lawyer. Why did she need to teach you?"

"I'll ignore that second greatest crack, since I heard Daniel was practicing again and I know how fond you are of him." He said with no hint of accent. "My specialty has never been ambulance chasing. But, even the best ambulance chaser could probably learn something from Doctor Tinnin.

"She specializes in pain disorders such as you. Most fall on the opposite end of the scale and treatment most often is limited to minimizing the victim's pain. That means addictive drugs such as morphine or oxycodone eventually are required. It also means that treatment is almost never 100% successful. Also pain and depression are linked, so suicide is always a risk. Bereaved relatives never want to believe the doctors did everything possible, so lawsuits are inevitable."

Larry Joe was clearly just getting started on the subject. Fortunately, Freak interrupted. "So you're going to sue my doctor? How will that help?"

"We're not actually hoping to sue anybody. But I plan to file actions contingent upon developments against the Dallas Police Department, Parkland Hospital, LBJ General, and the cities of Dallas, Mesquite and Houston, Detective Randall, Blake and everybody else involved. As we speak, three paralegals and six admins are finishing up the paperwork."

"Out of curiosity, what is the basis for these lawsuits you don't plan to ever file?" I asked.

"They think Freak's alive. They also think I know where he is, but they don't know either for sure. I'm pressing the action as if we think he's either dead or will be. If he's murdered, then the police were negligent to let him slip away. If he dies as a result of the gunshot, then the police and both hospitals should have prevented it."

"How does that get me to see the doctor?"

"Ain't you learned yet that scared money folds fastest?"

I answered for him, "I know it, but sometimes scared money is too scared to fold. Aren't you a little worried that they've dug themselves in so deep that they can't afford to fold?"

"I never worry; that's why I never have to fold. I'll admit Randall and Kenth may be in this too deep to back down. But it won't matter; that's why one paralegal is working specifically on suits against the Chief of Police himself."

I looked from Larry Joe to Freak and back while Freak was looking from Larry Joe to me and back. Larry Joe was just looking pleased with himself. At one-fifteen, Larry Joe left the office promising that something good would happen soon.

For the next twenty-three hours, I worked on the case, ate dinner, worked on the case, drove home, slept, drove back to the office, worked on the case and waited to hear from Larry Joe. Every bit of it was a waste of time except for the part about waiting for Larry Joe to make good on his promise.

"Pegasus Investigations," I answered when the phone rang just after noon.

"Ah told you scared money would fold. We've done got ourselves an invite to powwow with the Chief of Police as soon as we can get there."

"I can be there in ten minutes."

"Reckon I could too, but I ain't plannin' on it. Scared money don't get less scared as the little hands go tick-tock. Let's mosey over there around two o'clock. Invite Counselor Leeds, if he ain't busy."

At two o'clock, Larry Joe, Daniel and I were standing on Lamar Street outside the Jack Evans Police Headquarters building. Larry Joe had reminded me twice that we held all the cards, so we strolled in leisurely and each handed a business card to the admin. She invited us to sit while she notified the Chief that we were there.

Three minutes after we sat down, Detective Randall and Dougie Kenth walked past us. The admin quickly ushered them into the chief's office. Four minutes later, she got to repeat the action. This time she ushered in a heavy-set Hispanic man in a very expensive suit. I didn't recognize him, so I looked a question toward Larry Joe.

"That's Hector Jimenez, the new Homicide Commander." He had barely finished talking when the admin told us to go on in.

The chief wasted no time getting down to business, "I should warn you, Larry Joe, or should I say Lawrence, I'm not intimidated by your legal maneuvering. I presume you had a reason for naming me specifically in these." As he said that he slapped a small sheaf of the reams of documentation on the desk against his other hand. "I'd like to know what you were thinking."

"I was thinking you look so good on television when you don't squirm as you explain another department snafu, that it might be fun to see you not squirm in person. If you're interested, I think I was right."

"You're not funny, and I don't have time to waste. Give me a good reason why I don't tell the mayor that all of these dead trees are simply a desperate act by a desperate man trying to harbor a fugitive by threatening to sue for more than any jury has ever awarded."

"Honestly, I'll admit some of the damages I plan to seek are a little out of line. Really, how much is the life of one little performance artist worth? Sure, he was working as a detective when he was shot, but are detectives really worth more than performance artists? It's not like he was ever going to be mayor or chief of police or even an ambulance chasing attorney."

"Enough, you've made your point about the money. What are you trying to accomplish?"

Detective Randall became the first person in the group other than Larry Joe and the chief to speak. "He's trying to halt the investigation, Sir."

The chief looked at Randall briefly and sharply, and then turned to McCoy. "Is that right?"

"Stop the investigation? I don't think an investigation is in progress. A man was shot in broad daylight in Downtown Dallas. So far, all I've seen is police duplicity, lies and the media printing those lies as facts. It's no damn wonder there used to be a conspiracy museum in this town. Chief, I know you. You're an honest man. Can you sit here and tell me that the shooting of my client has been thoroughly investigated by anybody who isn't trying to tie it into Rick Taylor's murder?"

"My department does its job, McCoy. If they're investigating the two cases as if they're connected, there's a reason. I promise you that."

"I believe you, but that wasn't the question. The question is why is the victim the only person being investigated in the case?"

If the chief had an answer for that question, he declined to share it. Instead, he asked the three of us to wait out in the lobby. I wasn't sure if that was good news or bad news, but Larry Joe seemed very pleased about it.

43   Liars' Poker

"You look pretty smug for somebody who's just been told to go away."

Larry Joe smiled, "We ain't been told to go away. We've been told to wait which is a horse of a completely different color. The chief wants to count his chips before he decides if he wants to call our bluff."

We had barely sat down when the chief came out of his office. "McCoy, about this medical condition you're claiming he has, is that real?"

"Try me, you'll find his Doctor very convincing. Even if you don't, I promise you a jury will."

"Can you stop posturing for a second and answer the question?"

"I reckon I just answered that one, chief. Do you have a different one?"

Leeds spoke softly, "My dear sir, permit me to suggest that an inquiry with fewer actionable integrants might be expedient."

The chief sighed, "Let me rephrase the question. In general, not relating to your client at all; is it your opinion that congenital analgesia is a real disease or is it a way to get better drugs and a handicap parking sticker?"

Larry Joe laughed. "I'll acknowledge for the record that your question probably is not actionable. I can't answer it in general, but I'll gladly answer it regarding my client. He doesn't drive, so he needs no handicap space. He also is not being prescribed any medication for the disease. He did, however, lose both his parents to the disease while he was in high school."

"Sorry, I didn't realize." The chief was obviously sincere.

Larry Joe waved him off dismissively. "Don't worry about it, you couldn't have known. If it will help, I can get his medical file sent over from the office."

"Please do that." The chief went back in his office after telling his admin, "As soon as that file gets here, bring them and it in."

Larry Joe called his office to have the file sent over. I went outside and called the office to let Freak know how things were progressing. Of course, I called him by a different name and pretended I was discussing an old movie I had rented from Blockbuster in case the phone was bugged and the chief ended up calling our bluff.

I had just hung up the phone when I heard a female voice call to me, "Hey, Troy Aikman, why aren't you inside with the boss."

I turned and saw Larry Joe's admin, Adriana, walking toward me. I don't have any friends who call me Troy Aikman, but Adriana and I get along better now than we once did. In fact, if I could get her to quit calling me Troy Aikman, we might actually be friends.

She handed me an envelope and hugged me. "Don't let my boss tick off the chief too bad, okay."

"I'll do what I can." I said.

As instructed, the admin escorted us back into the office as soon as I got back with the file. I handed it to Larry Joe as we entered. Randall had the impossible to mistake and almost impossible to fake look of somebody who had just been severely reprimanded. Kenth, as always, looked like a short, depressed chipmunk with a terrible comb-over. Jimenez' suit was still so impressive, I couldn't really tell much about how he'd been doing, but I suspected it wasn't well. If Randall had been chewed out, her direct superior couldn't have emerged unscathed.

Larry Joe handed the folder to the chief. "Anything in particular you're looking to find?"

The chief was already skimming it. "I'll know it if I see it. I have a question for you. Why was this file not given to the staff at LBJ General?"

"Because Detective Randall dishonestly told me he was in a coma. That fact will be germane to the legal actions should it get to that. Issues related to pain tolerance don't apply to coma victims."

Randall had enough, "But you didn't turn it over after you talked to him, either. You can't pretend you still thought he was in a coma."

"I don't have to pretend anything, Ma'am. By that time, I realized what you were. My son's enemies deserve no information from me, and deserve to battle me when they battle him."

Larry Joe stood up and glared at her. "You have been battling him when you should have been helping him. You may have already killed him. You may be killing him while we sit here. If so, know that you will battle me for it."

"The money the city loses will make a nice article in the Dallas Observer, but I'll want more than that in exchange for his life. If that boy dies because of your dishonesty, you should probably kill me if you can. But I warn you, I am not so easily killed. I have a huge advantage over the boy."

The little color that was left in Randall's face after McCoy stood up was gone. She managed to reply, "And that advantage is?"

"I can feel pain, and when I feel it, I respond. I promise you that I will respond. You won't like it if that happens."

Jimenez stepped between them. "Are you threatening a Dallas Police Officer, McCoy?"

Daniel put a hand on Larry Joe's shoulder and guided him back to his seat. As he did so, he told Jimenez, "Threatening a peace officer is a severe transgression. An untenable accusation of such malfeasance could be of greater consequence. I'd advise you to confirm that the officer felt sufficient duress to pursue a complaint prior to articulating such an accusation with witnesses present."

Randall responded angrily, "Maybe I do plan to file. He threatened me in front of witnesses. Maybe he should be accused in front of witnesses."

I said, "Sure he did, Randall, if you call telling the truth in front of your co-workers threatening you in front of witnesses. File charges if you want. By the way, how many witnesses do you think saw you physically assault me at The Rodeo Bar?"

"That wasn't an assault. I barely slapped you."

The chief's voice wasn't loud, but it carried more force than a shout, "Shut up, Teresa!. Don't say anything else unless I ask you a direct question."

He picked up the medical report from the desk, "It says here that he should see a doctor familiar with the syndrome at least once a month for a full checkup since he won't feel the pain that normally warns a patient that medical treatment is needed. Does anybody know when he last saw his doctor?"

Nobody answered. He pointed at the large stack of possible lawsuits on his desk. "What would you say if I told you I think these lawsuits are being pressed only because you want to clear a path for him to see his doctor?"

Larry Joe smiled, "If you were to say that, and I acknowledge that you didn't, I would tell you that my client probably doesn't need to see a doctor if he's already been murdered, or is about to be murdered because your department failed to serve and protect."

"Do you really think he may be dead?"

"I know he's not in the hospital where your officers foolishly transported him. He's not in jail unless somebody's lying about that, too. I'm his legal guardian and his oldest friend. He'd have called me by now if he was alive and he hasn't."

Kenth smirked, "According to you? Why should we believe you?"

"I can't think of any reason you should or any reason you must. It's possible the wiretap on my phone was put there by the FBI or CIA and not by a homicide cop with an agenda. But just in case it's local, maybe Randall will tell you if he called me."

Kenth exploded, "How did you know?" He realized he shouldn't be saying anything and went silent.

Larry Joe grinned, "I didn't until you asked the wrong question."

The chief looked at Randall, "Well?"

"We don't believe the suspect has called him. That doesn't prove anything, though. He could have…"

"Stop", again the chief's voice was soft but commanding and Randall stopped in mid-sentence. He stared at Randall and pointed at Kenth, "You two can go now. We'll talk later."

Randall was very relieved to go, and Kenth followed her like a whipped puppy. As soon as they left, the chief continued, "I know I'm not going to help our chance of winning a lawsuit by saying this, but you've made some valid points. It's possible that we've mishandled certain aspects of this case from the beginning. I'm going to remove all the warrants on your client and reassign the case. If he shot Rick Taylor, we will catch him and convict him of it. If he didn't, we will learn that, also."

He turned to Jimenez, "All charges dropped, all related warrants dismissed immediately. A new investigation starts now with no presupposed persons of interest. Tomorrow morning on my desk, I want a list of officers you think can handle this case. If Randall's name is on it, put your resignation beside it. Is that clear?"

Jimenez stopped just short of bowing as he answered, "Yes, sir."

"Good; you can go."

Jimenez left the office. The chief addressed me. "I know your partner didn't shoot himself, and there's not enough evidence to suggest he shot Rick Taylor to justify Randall's actions. She's a good cop, but for some reason, she didn't handle this one right. On behalf of the department, I apologize."

Larry Joe picked up the stack of lawsuit papers from the Chief's desk and dropped them in a waste basket. "We accept your apology."

The chief smiled, "Good, tell your client to be careful. Who ever shot him probably knows by now that he survived."

"If and when I see him, I'll be sure to mention that."

The chief looked directly at me, "You might want to tell him not to spend too much time hiding in freezers. It can't be healthy. As far as I'm concerned, this meeting is over; any questions."

Daniel and Larry Joe shook their heads no. I couldn't resist, "I have one. Do you like your gig?"

The chief laughed, but barely. "That's not the question, and you aren't as funny as you think you are."

I doubted that, since I didn't think I was all that funny. But I saw no reason to argue the point, so I got up to leave. For a change, Larry Joe and Daniel also got up without responding and we left the office together without talking. When we were back on Lamar Street, Larry Joe looked at me, "Do you like your job? What kind of question is that?"

Another good question; this time I had a good answer, but I chose not to waste it on Larry Joe. Only Blake would appreciate its humor, so I decided to save it for him. Larry Joe walked north toward his office in Thanksgiving Tower.

Daniel and I walked east toward my less pretentious, but better fortified office. A few days ago, Daniel had asked me the shortest question I thought he could ask. He proved me wrong when he looked at the departing figure of Larry Joe McCoy and asked, "Son?"

Part 3 – Final Showdown

"Look up and around you, baby
Get up off the floor.
You've just been surviving, baby
What you living for?"

Emmeline
'Apathetic'

44 Office Space

I don't pace. My partner, Carl paces, but he's about forty, so it's okay. I'm still young, so I don't pace. Instead, I text or MySpace or play Grand Theft Auto to kill time when I'm nervous. Unfortunately, a person on the lam from the police shouldn't text or MySpace, and it had never occurred to me that we might need a PlayStation or Wii for the office. I couldn't even surf the net, since nobody was supposed to be in the office and an internet address is extremely easy to trace.

That's why I was walking around the office, going from one window to another, grateful for the one-way see through glass that allowed me to at least look out of my self-imposed prison when the phone rang around 3 o'clock. Even though I knew I couldn't answer it, and knew I could hear any message being left from anywhere in the office, I still walked over and stood by the answering machine.

The machine seemed to take forever with the outgoing message before the caller's voice finally came on, "Hey, it's me. I just watched the first part of a great movie on AMC Classics. It was sort of like The Fugitive only with better acting and more realistic dialogue. I don't remember the name, but the cops in it were really confused, and the bad guys were really the good guys. Eventually, they all got together to talk about what was going on. I think cooperation is always better than confrontation. Anyway, I'm going to watch the second part soon, and I think it's going to turn out fine."

It was Carl, and I knew he wasn't talking about a movie. He was talking about the meeting with the chief of police. He sounded optimistic, but I couldn't be sure if he was just trying to keep my spirits up or if things really were going well. I went back to looking out the windows.

In front of the library, the cop watching the office looked as bored as he had ninety minutes earlier when he got there. If he was trying to go unnoticed, he wasn't very good at it. Of course, he didn't look homeless, so he couldn't exactly blend. The guy he replaced had at least made some effort. He'd moved from spot to spot and occasionally pretended to read the newspaper or talk on his cell phone.

When I got tired of watching the cop, I walked to the north window and looked out toward Neiman-Marcus. I didn't see any homeless people there or any cops watching the office. I walked back into the office I'd been staying in, the one without windows which had been my partner's office until we decided I should stay in it, since it has the private bath.

I walked from the door to the back wall. It took seven steps, leaving me just under a foot from the wall. I turned around and walked from the wall back to the door. Again it took seven steps. I went back to the other office and glanced out the window to watch the cop watching the office. Entertaining yourself when you're stuck in an office requires creativity. I'm a performer; being creative comes naturally to me.

I walked to the door leading to this office again and walked to the wall. It only took six steps. I turned around and walked it the other direction. Again, it took six steps. I made a note to ask the Great Detective why he didn't tell me when we converted his home office to our shared office that he was giving me the smaller office. I didn't mind since I liked having the window and didn't care that his had the private bathroom, but it's not like him to be anything less than completely honest and open.

I glanced out the window and saw the cop talking on his cell phone. I wondered briefly if he was finally trying to hide the fact that he was watching our office. Then I noticed his red face and clinched fist. He was obviously mad. It's possible to fake that, but he wouldn't put forth the effort. While I wondered what had him so fired up, he slammed the phone closed and walked away.

As I looked around trying to find his replacement, I saw Daniel Leeds and Carl walking past Neiman's. I wasn't sure why he hadn't called to warn me to hide, but I wasted no time making sure there was no evidence of my presence in the lobby and locking myself in the office.

Less than five minutes later, I heard him yell. "Come on out! Larry Joe was right about scared money."

"He usually is." I said as I sauntered out to the lobby. "So, what's the 411?"

He smiled, "The 411 is that you're free to check your MySpace page, surf the net or run naked through city hall if you wish. You can also move your stuff back into your office and spend the rest of the day sending text messages. Except, of course, for the little matter of us still not knowing who shot you and why."

"Yeah, that little mystery still needs to be addressed." I decided this was as good a time as any to ask him about the room sizes. "Speaking of moving my stuff, tell me again why you gave me that office."

"I don't know. Did we ever discuss it? I don't remember giving it much thought. If you want to change, I'm fine with it. Have you spent your entire time cooped up here wishing you had the other office?"

"No, I just noticed that mine is smaller and wondered why I ended up with it." It occurred to me that I was being petty, but if he minded he didn't show it.

"Is it really? I thought they were the same size. I know they're the same width. The other walls are shared. Are you sure?"

For the next five minutes we took turns measuring our offices and he finally admitted that mine was in fact smaller.

"Honestly, I didn't know. Apparently, the entire office isn't an exact square. I guess the office that used to be part of this building jutted part way into this one. If you want to trade offices, let's do it."

For the first time since we'd started measuring the offices Daniel spoke, "You postulate a ludicrous, albeit commensurably irrelevant explanation for a moderately unanticipated revelation regarding this singular edifice. Lacking any rational supposition that it relates to the contemporaneous vexations, I recommend concentration on matters of greater consequence for the foreseeable future."

"Good idea," I answered, hoping I really understood what he meant. "Let's try to find the shooters without getting ourselves killed in the process. Once that's done we can try to figure out what other secrets this office might be hiding. How sure are we that it's not a trick?"

"What do you mean?"

"I don't want to sound paranoid, but I wouldn't put it past Randall to tell you the warrants were dropped just to get me to show my face."

"I wouldn't put that past her either, but she's off the case. The chief made that clear. He's not happy with how she handled

182

things. He said the charges were dropped. I heard him say it. He's a man of his word."

I couldn't help but laugh. "My friend and partner, the king of conspiracy theories trusts the chief of police completely. I never thought I'd live to see the day."

"My friends don't call me the king of conspiracy theories, and you almost didn't live long enough. Let's find a shooter before he gets a chance to make sure you don't live long enough to see the day when I prove my theories are correct."

"Nobody is going to live that long." I told him confidently.

"Maybe not, but that won't prove I'm wrong. Now that you're free to investigate your own shooting, do you have a plan?"

"I do. I'm going to spend the weekend hanging out with Sam The Man in Deep Ellum and see if anybody confesses."

He laughed, "Think it will work?"

"Probably not," I admitted. "But maybe somebody will try again and Sam will put an end to that part of the investigation."

"I guess that could happen. Want me to come along just in case Sam needs a little help?"

"I think your weekend would be better spent with your bride. She did get her honeymoon cut short because I decided to add dancing with bullets to my performance art portfolio. She may pretend it didn't bother her, but even amazing women like her are still women."

"I suppose you're right. Don't have too much fun shocking the suburban kids in Deep Ellum."

I promised him I wouldn't. I thought about Katherine and how much fun she and I used to have doing just that, and I knew it would be an easy promise to keep. After he left, I considered not even going. However, if I went home I'd probably just spend the weekend staring at Katherine's pictures. I damn sure wasn't going to stay here or do that. I quickly realized I didn't have any place better to go. Once I decided, I sent a text to Sam The Man, and locked down the fortress we call our office.

45   Detective Work

"How was the King of Deep Ellum's weekend back among his people?" asked the Great Detective as he came in the office Monday morning at nine.

"Nobody calls me the King of Deep Ellum these days, partner." I answered without mentioning that to the best of my knowledge nobody ever had. "I've abdicated the throne since the tragic passing of my queen. But to answer the question, it was strangely cathartic."

"Cathartic, have you been taking English lessons from Daniel?"

I laughed. "I'd have to learn more of his version of English to take lessons from him. All I'm saying is seeing everybody again in these circumstances kind of helps with the closure."

"What do you mean?" he asked, obviously genuinely interested.

"It's hard to explain. I guess this time it seemed everybody walked around on eggshells because I got shot recently, and they attended my funeral. Before, the awkwardness was always about Katherine. Does that make any sense?"

"Sure, it does. This time the elephant in the room wasn't the one that keeps you up at night and causes you to spend more nights in this office than at your home."

"Exactly... wait a minute. What makes you think I sleep here that often?"

"I didn't say anything about sleep. I think you spend more nights pacing the floor here than you do at home. In addition to being a great detective, I'm also a cheapskate with a very observant wife. When she pointed out that the carpet needs replaced I noticed there was more wear and tear in the circle from window to window than in front of the desk where I do my pacing."

"I hate when you do that Sherlock Holmes stuff. Besides, I don't pace."

"Of course, you don't. You never get petulant either. Now that you've regained your Deep Ellum throne without getting killed and I've restored marital bliss to our Plano Palace, let's decide how to catch a killer and an attempted killer or two."

We discussed it and quickly decided to investigate the two murders separately. If it turned out that they were related, catching the killer of either would reveal the relationship. We also agreed easily that we should work independently, sharing information as we go.

We argued briefly about who should take which case, but he convinced me that I should work on Rick Taylor's murder while he worked on my shooting. He had several reasons, but the one that finally convinced me was that I'd already spent time on the case. I suspect his real reason was that he thought it might be hard for me to investigate my own murder, but I know I could have handled it.

With that decided, we started discussing Rick Taylor's murder. Nothing much had happened on the case since I'd been shot which he considered to be an interesting fact. "The police clearly targeted Charlie Ray and April in their investigation. Neither one has been charged. That tells us something."

"Sure it does," I said. "What exactly does it tell us?"

"Nothing exact, but it does tell us they found no smoking gun on either suspect. Most homicides are solved within 48 hours. Sometimes it takes longer to gather the evidence. But if they don't know who did it by now, or at least think they do, it means it's probably not a simple murder."

"I thought they did think they knew who did it? Didn't you tell me Woodbury said they thought Charlie Ray did it?"

"He did, but since Charlie hasn't been arrested and Randall's been taken off the case, I'm sure they have no supporting evidence."

"Right and we know he didn't have anything to do with it, anyway."

"We do, how do we know?"

"He was shot before we had a chance to tell him about the guitar."

"True, unless the whole guitar story was a scam intended to get us to create additional suspects and remove suspicion."

The Great Detective has loved a good conspiracy theory ever since I've known him. Normally, I mock him for it, but this time he might have a point. I'd talked myself into thinking it was a real case, but paying a detective to find an ordinary guitar doesn't make good business sense. Of course, musicians aren't famous for business sense.

"Say it was, do you think Bobbie Jo was in on it?"

I got the long silence he's perfected. I presumed he was thinking, not posturing. I decided to think, too. Bobbie Jo wouldn't set me up that way, not even for her brother. She might kill for him, in fact I'm sure she would, but she wouldn't be party to that kind of scenario. I didn't like the idea of Bobbie Jo shooting Rick Taylor and tried to put it out of my mind. Fortunately, Carl ended the silence soon after the thought occurred to me.

"No, it's not her style. If she were involved, Rick would have died from a tarantula bite." He visibly shuddered as he said it.

"Even you know that tarantulas, at least the ones Bobbie Jo trains, can't kill a person. You're right though, she'd find a spider that can, which would be easy for her and nobody would ever know it was murder."

The Great Detective is a former college athlete who stands almost seven feet tall. He once saved my life by carrying my unconscious, two-hundred pound body half a mile from a burning forest to safety even though he was almost dead himself. Maybe that's why I always enjoy watching him quiver like a little schoolgirl at the mere mention of spiders.

He pulled himself together and asked, "Would Charlie Ray kill without asking Bobbie Jo to help? They're pretty tight."

"Probably, in fact, I'd say it would be more likely. If he were going to take that kind of chance, he wouldn't want to put her at risk."

He smiled, "Okay, so he didn't do it either. We've only been working together on this for ten minutes and we've already ruled out two suspects."

"How did you decide he's innocent?"

"She's involved. She talked to you about the case before he hired you. He wouldn't involve her; she's involved; ergo, he didn't set Rick Taylor up to kill him."

He looked so smug as he said it that I wanted to argue. I couldn't though, since he was obviously right. "Okay, two down, the rest of the planet to go. What about April?"

"Well, she had means and opportunity. If we think Mr. Taylor could forget that no means no, then we have a possible motive. I'm not sure we can eliminate her quickly."

186

"I don't like that as a motive. There's no evidence that he would attempt date rape. In fact, when I gave Nikki every chance to suggest he was capable of it, she declined. If a woman who hates him won't accuse him of it, I tend to think it's not his nature."

"Probably, but Nikki suspected you were conning her and April is April. I don't believe she shot him, but I believe she might have had motive. Believe me, April can cause men to behave in uncharacteristic fashion."

I thought back to my reaction to the kiss she gave me at the bar and said nothing. I was still saying nothing when the phone rang.

The Great Detective answered like he usually does, "Pegasus Investigations."

After a short silence, he said. "Hold on, I'll check."

He put the caller on hold and turned to me. "It's Detective Woodbury and he sounds giddy. Are you here?"

I thought about it. I was out of hiding, investigating a murder and a citizen in good standing of the City of Dallas. I couldn't think of any good reason not to talk to a police detective who might have information on our case. I held my hand out for the phone and answered, "Why not?"

As he handed me the phone, he said, "You're still asking the wrong question."

46   Different Emotions

"I've got good news and better news for you, which do you want first?"

I thought Carl was kidding when he told me Detective Woodbury sounded giddy, but I was wrong; Woodbury definitely sounded like a sophomore girl who'd just been invited to the senior prom.

"Start me off with the good news."

"I'm in charge of the investigation. I don't know how y'all got Randall removed, but thank you."

"I think she got herself removed. What makes this good news?"

"For one thing, when I solve it, it will help my career. For another, it means we can cooperate on the case."

"Apparently, I asked the wrong question again. My partner's trying to teach me not to do that. What I mean is what makes that good news for me?"

He laughed, "It sounds like your partner's taught you the cynicism part, too. You must like that the detective in charge of the case now doesn't think you killed Rick Taylor."

"I guess so," I admitted. "Give me the better news. Maybe, I'll like that even more."

"I've got a witness for you to question who may have seen the son of a bitch shoot you."

I thought about that. Woodbury had suggested cooperation, but for a cop to turn a witness over to a private investigator made no sense at all. As I was thinking about that, I realized what the Great Detective meant when he handed me the phone. "Why?" I asked Woodbury.

"I told you, I'm in charge now. We're going to cooperate on this."

"I heard you. Are you going to answer the question, now?"

"Fine, the witness won't talk to us. We've had him at Lew Sterrett since last night and he won't tell us anything. He's a homeless guy who's been busted for panhandling a few times this year. He won't talk to us, but he might talk to you. As private citizens, you may have methods of persuasion that we're not allowed to use."

"Possibly," I answered wondering if we were thinking of the same method. "If he won't talk, what makes you think he saw anything?"

"The patrolman who saw the SUV also remembered seeing this guy on the corner. We checked into it and it's been his regular corner for months now. If the shooter got out of the SUV for any reason, he'd have seen him and tried to get money from him."

"Okay, we'll try it. When are you releasing him, and how do we recognize him?"

"At one o'clock; Be at the jail and I'll point him out.

It seemed like a good plan, so I agreed to it. After I hung up, I relayed the conversation. Carl liked the plan, but he wanted to meet Woodbury instead of me because my shooting was supposed to be his case. We eventually compromised by agreeing to both meet Woodbury at Lew Sterrett.

At fifteen minutes to one, the Great Detective and I were in his van outside the Lew Sterrett Correctional Facility. When I saw Woodbury's Mustang pull into the parking lot, we got out so he'd see us. He parked beside the van and got out and we shook hands.

"Let's sit in my car. It's too hot to stand out here."

Out of respect for the Great Detective's height and his status as senior partner, I crawled into the back of Woodbury's Mustang and let him ride shotgun. When we were settled into the car, Woodbury put the a/c on max and turned to me.

"So Freak, you got a plan for Mr. Lamont Washington when they release him?"

"Of course, I do. If he walks somewhere, I'm going to follow him. If he gets a ride, the Great Detective there is going to follow him. Once we know where he is and he's been out of jail long enough not to blame us for being there in the first place, we're going to make him an offer he can't refuse."

"A financial offer, I presume? Some of the guys hoped you'd take a more aggressive approach. I guess working with Silent Bob here has taken all the starch and vinegar out of you. I remember a day when every thug in Deep Ellum was scared to talk bad about you, let alone take you on."

I laughed, "Don't worry; they're still scared of me. I just have principles, you know. This guy's not a thug. In fact, as far as I know the only thing he's done wrong is not answering questions for the cops. Hell, Woodbury, you're the only one in this car who hasn't done that."

Woodbury smiled, "You don't know if I have or haven't, but I get your point. There he is."

Woodbury pointed at the door where a middle aged black man wearing blue jean shorts and a gray tee shirt that was probably white once had just exited. He carried a trash bag over his shoulder like Santa's bag of presents. I knew it contained all his worldly possessions and I wondered what kind of person would hope we'd use physical force against him.

I expected him to walk and he did. He ambled up Industrial Boulevard slowly. It didn't appear that he had any trouble walking, but he was taking his time. It had probably been a long time since he'd had anywhere to be, so he'd gotten used to walking slowly. That wouldn't make it any easier to follow him, but it wouldn't make it any harder either.

I followed him from the jail on Lew Sterrett back into the heart of downtown. The half mile walk took over an hour and a half partially because he walked so slowly, but mainly because he stopped at every trash can to look for not quite empty wine bottles. He finally found one at Main and Houston. For some reason, I felt very happy for him.

As we walked toward his corner, I realized I was walking the exact path I was walking when I got shot. I should have expected that, since the reason I was following him was that his corner sat close enough to it that somebody could shoot me from it. Foolishly, I looked around as if somebody might try again, since I was here. Nobody did and if they did, I doubted paying attention would have helped. That's basically the concept regarding sniper rifles.

When he was almost to the exact spot where the shooter parked his stolen car, he stashed the trash bag in an alcove behind a newspaper stand. He lay down beside it and appeared to take a nap. He laid there about an hour, then got up and started panhandling at a few minutes before four. His timing was perfect because many business people were getting off work around then. I watched him ply his craft for the next three and a half hours.

He was consistent in that he asked for a handout from everybody who walked within range, but he wasn't persistent. He accepted each 'no' with a smile and a nod. Occasionally, his targets would say "God Bless You' or something similar when they gave him nothing, and he'd bow his head and tap his forehead once and chest three times.

When foot traffic began to slow around seven-fifteen, he retrieved his trash bag and walked to the store and bought a bottle of wine and two packs of jerky. He ate one stick of jerky on the way back and took several pulls from the wine. At nine o'clock when the bar crowds started showing up, he stashed the rest of the wine and the other beef jerky with his trash bag and continued panhandling.

At ten-thirty, he retrieved his trash bag and walked to the First Presbyterian Church at Young and Canton. There, he found a cardboard pallet to sleep on, along with several dozen other homeless people. He used the trash bag as a pillow and was asleep before midnight.

I wondered briefly if he might wake up in time to be on the streets when the bars closed. I dismissed the idea because the people who leave bars at two in the morning are more dangerous than generous, and he clearly had been in this game long enough to know that. I used my cell phone to call the Great Detective.

He answered on the first ring, "Don't tell me you lost him."

"Of course not, he's sleeping on a pallet at the church two blocks from the office. He'll be up early though, want me to pick him up in the morning?"

"No, I'll do it. It's my case, remember? What makes you think he'll be up early?"

I detailed his activities for the day, emphasizing how our witness made sure he was at the corner during peak traffic times. I also offered again to resume the tail tomorrow since I know how much he hates mornings.

"No, I'll do it. I'll be there at six-thirty just in case. It's good news really."

"Why?" I asked.

"You were shot during lunch hour. If he's always at his corner during peak hours, he was there."

He was right, of course. Maybe that's why I call him the Great Detective. We ended the call and I walked to the office. As I approached the stairs, I wondered briefly if I was going upstairs to sleep or to walk the floor. Instead, I did neither.

47   Material Witness

I slept, in my own bed, for the first time since Katherine Elizabeth's body had been found; I really slept. I don't know why it took this long. I also don't know why I slept here this time, but I did. It's too big a bed for one person, but I'd never noticed that before I'd shared it with her.

My cell phone woke me up. Technically, the song 'Welcome to the Black Parade' by My Chemical Romance woke me up. Since that's my current ringtone, I figured out it was my cell phone fairly quickly. Finding the phone and answering it took a little bit longer.

"Hello," I barely managed to say when I finally answered.

"Good morning, sleepyhead." Carl's sarcastic voice greeted me.

"What makes you think I was sleeping?"

"Freak, I'm an expert on the subject of sleep. I know a sleepy voice when I hear one. You got some sleep, congratulations. I know you're not at the office. Where are you?"

"At home, what time is it?"

"Nine-fifteen," he answered. "How soon can you be at the office ready to work?"

"Ten, maybe fifteen minutes; how soon do I need to be there?"

"Not that soon. As you noticed yesterday, Mr. Washington is committed to his trade. He won't leave his post earlier than nine-thirty. Why don't you meet me at the office at ten?"

"Okay."

"Don't worry about breakfast. I'll have it here when you get here."

At nine-forty five, I left my house and walked to the office. I'd showered and shaved and put on jeans and a tee shirt. I wasn't sure how presentable I needed to be to interview a homeless man who may have seen me get shot, but I doubted if it mattered much. If the Great Detective thought I'd need a certain look, he'd have mentioned it.

As promised, breakfast was provided. Our kitchenette was loaded with scrambled eggs, bacon, hash browns and buns. I'd known my partner well enough to know that he'd picked up the breakfast at Tootsie's. He was behind the desk quietly eating bacon.

192

Washington was in a guest chair with two paper plates loaded with food and two emptied plates off to the side.

In spite of the amount of food he was eating, Washington ate deliberately. This is not typical of the homeless, who often go too long between meals and gorge themselves when the opportunity presents. His eyes followed me as I filled my plate and sat beside him in the other client chair.

He sat his fork down and stared straight at me. "Sucks, don't it?"

"Actually, it tastes pretty good to me. Maybe crispy bacon and scrambled eggs are an acquired taste."

When he laughed, he showed all his teeth. It wasn't a pretty sight and did nothing to improve the taste of the breakfast. "Not the breakfast; getting shot."

"Yeah, I guess it did. I haven't really thought about it. I've been thinking more about finding the shooter. You know anything about him?"

"That's what the cops asked me about a thousand times. I told them no a thousand times, too. How come you guys think I do, and what makes you think a little breakfast will make me tell you?"

I glanced at my partner who, as usual, wasn't saying anything. Obviously, Mr. Washington hadn't told the cops what he saw, and he hadn't told the Great Detective, either. I couldn't think of any reason why he might tell me, so I ate another piece of bacon. Washington took that as an invitation and went back to eating.

When he finished everything on both his plates, he looked at me again, "How come you ain't dead?"

"Luck, I guess. My time just hasn't come, yet."

"Bullshit, your time done came. I saw it. That cracker shot you with one serious piece of artillery."

"It might as well be a water pistol if it doesn't hit the target. So, you know something about artillery, do you?"

"I know enough to know how bad it sucks to get shot. I got shot during Desert Storm. And I saw you fall. It hit the target. Tell me for real why you ain't dead and maybe I'll tell you what I saw."

"The bullet hit the dog tag I was wearing and deflected through my chest cavity without hitting anything vital."

Washington looked at me with a new respect. "Dog tag, huh? What branch?"

It took me about two seconds to decide to lie to the man, but quite a bit longer to figure out a way to pull it off convincingly. I was pretty happy when the Great Detective saved me the trouble.

"My partner doesn't like to discuss his time in the military. It brings back too many bad memories."

"I can dig that. Hell, if it weren't for getting shot in Desert Storm, I wouldn't be living on the street."

"How so?" I tried to sound sympathetic when I asked it. Since I was sympathetic, I think I succeeded.

"Because I fired back and got dishonorably discharged."

"For firing back, isn't that what you're supposed to do?"

"Not really, I was too drunk to realize I was shooting back at our own MPs."

I wanted to know more, but I didn't ask. While he was in a talkative mood, I wanted to talk about the shooting he saw. "What can you tell me about the dude you saw shoot me."

"Not much. He was white, drove a big SUV and had a really big gun."

"I already know about the SUV and the gun. I'm more interested in the shooter. I figured he was white since you called him a cracker."

"I didn't look him over real close; once I saw the gun I mostly wanted him not to see me. I saw he was white, but he looked pretty much just like an ordinary white guy."

"Sure he did, and I'll bet he smelled like a wet puppy, too. I get it, he was white. We don't really all look alike, you know."

"Sorry about the cracker comment. I know you don't all look alike. I'm just saying that he did. I didn't see a damn thing about him that would distinguish him from anybody else."

"Don't worry about it. What about his clothes," I asked. "What was he wearing?"

He pointed at the Great Detective, "preppy like him, but he had on a cap and frames. The frames looked expensive, but they could have been knock-offs. I can't tell the difference without looking real close."

"How did you see the gun? Did he park right by you?"

"No, when I see an expensive car like that one, I always try to mosey toward it." He looked a little ashamed as he continued.

"Just in case, you know? Rich folks don't really help me more than regular folks, but I keep hoping."

I couldn't really blame him for that. Any hope is better than no hope at all, and it's hard to have much hope in his situation. "That's why you noticed the expensive sunglasses. You were sizing him up as a prospect."

"Exactly, but when I saw the gun, I moseyed on past without looking any closer."

I couldn't blame him for that either. We questioned him for another half-hour and he seemed to be trying to help. He knew the exact make and model of the SUV. He also recognized the gun as a sniper rifle, but he'd never seen one exactly like it before.

He suggested it might be Russian, but I didn't put any stock in that. He'd admitted he didn't get a good look at it, and that he'd done too much drinking during his service time. I couldn't be mad that he didn't recognize the gun that shot me. I just wish he could describe the man who did it better.

At ten-forty, we gave up. I gave him forty bucks and Carl offered to drop him off anywhere he wanted to go. It surprised nobody when he asked to be driven to Andrews Fine Beverages on Ross Avenue. As they went downstairs to the van, I briefly wished I'd asked for more details on his discharge and the events that led up to it.

I just knew there had to be a good story in it, and I'd probably never get another chance to ask him. A half hour later, I no longer cared about Washington's discharge.

48   Another Victim

The office phone rang just after eleven. I answered, "Pegasus Investigations."

April didn't waste time with a greeting. "Can you come down to the bar? There's something here you need to see."

April sounded tense, like when we'd first met with Larry Joe. I figured that meant it was important. "I'll be right there."

It normally takes about ten minutes to walk from our office to the bar. Today it took less than five. Even though it was after eleven, all three doors were locked and the closed signs were still out. April let me in and locked the door behind me. As she led me toward the kitchen, my nose told me that what she wanted me to see was going to be bad, very bad. Death's odor is unmistakable. I wasn't sure whose body I was going to see, but I knew it was going to be a body.

She opened the door, and I saw Chris Austin on his back with the handle of a steak knife sticking out of his ribcage and blood all around. I'd seen a few dead bodies over the years, but I was still shook by this scene. I looked at April. If she was shook at all, it didn't show.

"Are you okay?"

"I've seen worse, much worse. Besides, he was a prick."

I didn't ask where she could have possibly seen worse. April always deflected any conversation away from her past. Occasionally I had thoughts about pressing for details, but I'd never pursued it. This certainly wasn't the time to delve into it. If she'd seen anything worse than just this, then I understood why she never talked about it.

I asked, "Enough of a prick to deserve a knife to the heart?"

"Somebody apparently thought so. It wasn't me, if that's what you're thinking."

It may have been what I was thinking, but I saw no reason to let April know that. "No, but when the cops get here, they'll be thinking it. You should call Larry Joe."

"I guess I should."

She grabbed her cell phone and started dialing. While she did, I leaned down and grabbed Chris's right wrist to feel for a pulse I knew I wouldn't find. I knew it was a wasted effort, but it had to be done.

196

April's conversation with Larry Joe was brief. Her end of it consisted of telling him Chris Austin was dead on the kitchen floor of the bar, then saying okay a couple of times. When she hung up, she put her phone back in her purse. "He says you need to call the police. I'm too distraught over the death of a dear friend and co-worker to make the call."

"Of course, you are. I'll do it."

Woodbury must have been in a meeting because it took more than ten minutes to get him on the line. "This better be important, Freak."

"I wouldn't have told your admin three times it was important if it wasn't important. Since you're in charge of the homicides that keep occurring to people I know, such as myself, I thought you should be the first to know there's been another."

I had his attention "Now who?" he asked.

"A bartender at The Rodeo Bar named Chris Austin; he took a steak knife in the heart and wasn't as lucky as I was."

"Nobody's as lucky as you are. Are you there, now?"

"I am. April and I are guarding the body like true professionals."

"I'll bet you are, don't go anywhere, we'll be right there."

I didn't get a chance to ask him where he thought I might go because he hung up too soon.

The first cops arrived in minutes and secured the area and started asking us questions we mostly declined to answer. The crime scene team got there about a quarter to noon and went to work in the kitchen. They didn't want April or me to be there, so the beat cops ushered us back into the bar.

Woodbury arrived a few minutes later and sat at the table with April and me. He looked at April. "Tell me what happened."

"My lawyer suggested that I shouldn't answer questions until I'm less distraught."

"Of course, he did." He looked at me, "Are you also too distraught to answer any questions?

I asked, "Without a lawyer present, officer?"

Woodbury smiled. He looked at the beat cop who was hovering nearby. "Jackson, have you secured the perimeter?"

"Yes, Sir! We did that when we got here, Sir."

"Do it again, now!"

As soon as the beat cop moved on, Woodbury turned back to me. "I told you yesterday that I don't think you killed anybody. I meant it and I still do. I don't know what's going on, but I don't believe you or your associates are killing anybody."

He nodded at April when he said the word associates. "The Chief agrees. That's why I'm on the case now instead of Randall. I thought we were going to cooperate."

"Okay, I'll cooperate. I'll tell you everything I know. Chris Austin got stabbed and died."

Woodbury smiled again, "Well you know more than you sometimes do on your cases. April, do you know anything more than that?"

April looked at me. "Do I?"

I sometimes do impressions. I thought about impersonating Larry Joe, but decided to do Daniel Leeds instead. "With the caveat that Miss Rose's rights have failed negligently to be communicated, I advise her to speak freely, confident that nothing she discusses can be used against her in a court of law."

Woodbury nodded his head in agreement.

"Today, Chris opened; that means he was supposed to show up at ten to do setup. I was to work a double, so I came in just before eleven. When I came in, I smelled it. I went to the kitchen and found him laying there

Woodbury asked, "You have a key?"

"Yes, all the bartenders have a key. One of us has to open every morning. We have to be able to get in."

Woodbury continued, "Who else has a key?"

"I don't know. The manager has one, obviously. It's a hotel bar, so somebody at the hotel might have one."

"Okay, we can check on that. What did you do when you found the body?"

"I didn't know what to do." She looked at me. "So I called him and asked him to come down."

"Why did you call Freak?"

She hesitated slightly. "Actually, I didn't. I called Pegasus Investigations. I didn't realize until after I'd hung up that I was talking to him and not Mr. Jennings."

Woodbury nodded, "But you trust them both, so it didn't matter. I get that. It must be nice for a young lady like you to have two men she can trust. Most don't."

I wondered if he was thinking about his wife or his Mistress, but I knew better than to bring it up. Cooperating on an investigation didn't involve making rude comments about personal lifestyle decisions. April also didn't say anything. I wondered if the Great Detective had been teaching her the value of not saying anything.

I don't count the seconds of silence like my partner does, but we'd been sitting there for some time when one of the lab boys came over to the table holding an evidence bag.

He showed it to Woodbury and asked, "Have you figured out yet what 1 Corinthians 6:18 means?"

April shrieked and fainted. I nearly did the same.

"They say you always remember your first love. I'll definitely never forget mine. Honestly though, I'd give anything on earth to forget him. Unfortunately, he keeps haunting me. I remember his eyes: small, beady and cold like a bird's. I hate birds, you know."

April was sitting behind the desk in our office lobby talking about her past for the first time I could remember. When she'd fainted, I realized that she knew more about what was going on than I did. I figured Larry Joe would disown me if I let her answer any police questions about it. Woodbury hadn't liked it when I quit cooperating, but if he could have done anything about it, he opted against it. I escorted her back to the office without incident.

The Great Detective and I sat in the client chairs. The doors to both of our offices were open. Larry Joe was standing behind April with one hand on her shoulder trying to comfort her. I wondered briefly if I should be the one doing that, but decided it didn't matter. The important thing was that she knew we were all here for her.

"You hate birds like I hate spiders. How does that cause you to faint at the mere mention of Corinthians?" That's my partner. He loves to be silent, but when he speaks, he gets right to point.

April didn't seem to mind the question. "It's not just Corinthians. It's 1 Corinthians 6:18. That's the inscription he left on the bodies of my friends." She curled two fingers on each hand to indicate she was about to read a quotation. "Flee from sexual immorality. All other sins a man commits are outside his body, but he who sins sexually sins against his own body."

She put her hands back on the desk. "That's from the New International Version. That's the Bible he was carrying when they arrested him four years ago. He's supposed to die in jail. I don't understand why this is happening again."

"It should be easy enough to find out if he's still in jail," Larry Joe had no trace of his Texas accent. "What's his name and where was he sent to do his time?"

"He was sent to Casuarina Prison in Kwinana, Western Australia. His name is Jamie Salt."

Larry Joe reached for his cell phone. He stepped into my office and closed the door behind him.

I asked, "Western Australia?"

"That's where I grew up. I moved here after the…"

For the first time since she fainted at the bar, April appeared to be on the verge of losing it. I went behind the desk to comfort her. I picked up one of her hands from the desk and held it. "And it's a good thing you did. If you hadn't, Katherine's killer would still be free, and I'd be either dead or in jail. We caught a killer together once. We can do it again."

April pulled herself together quickly. "Yes, we did, but compared to Jamie Salt, that bitch is a pussy cat. I suppose I better tell you about Jamie."

"Yes, you should," I said.

"I met him a few months before I went off to University in Fremantle. I took a job as a waitress in a restaurant where he was the co-owner. He was charming, mature, handsome and even more religious than my parents. I'd just graduated from St Mary's Anglican Girls' School, so I'd had no experience with boys. To say he had me at hello would be an understatement."

With the hand I wasn't holding, she subtly caressed her face, much like the way a teenage boy does at a sad movie when he doesn't want his date to notice that he's wiping away tears. I didn't react at all and just let her continue.

"For two months, he was my world and I was his. We did everything together. I was sure I was the first princess to find her prince without having to kiss any frogs. Obviously, I was dead wrong. As time passed, he became more and more controlling. At first I thought it meant he loved me more. By the time I was ready to start university in Fremantle, I realized it didn't. I broke up with him, expecting to never see him again."

I asked, "But obviously, you did?"

"I did. He started stalking me. He sent me flowers with love notes or Bible verses on the cards. He'd call me several times a day. Even though I quit answering, he kept doing it. He'd leave long messages telling me that God wanted me to return to him. It was horrible."

She repeated the little wipe away tears move, and again, I chose not to comment. I couldn't think of any reason to let her know I'd even noticed, let alone interrupt her to do so.

"One night, I went out with two of my girlfriends. We got a little tipsy and started having a real good time, really trying to impress the boys. Since Jenny and Charlotte were both gorgeous, we were doing a good job of it. About midnight, we started dancing with each other."

The Great Detective interrupted, "I presume the dancing was of a provocative nature?"

April managed a slight smile, "Most guys find girls dancing together provocative no matter what the nature is, but yes. We made sure it was provocative. Jenny and Charlotte tongue kissed for several minutes; then they each kissed me. The boys were definitely impressed. Both the girls hooked up with guys. I still wasn't ready for another relationship with everything Jamie was putting me through, so I left them there and went back to my dormitory."

April's grip on my hand tightened, but she didn't pause. "I found Jenny dead the next morning when I left my dorm. She was in the hall with her throat slit. I banged on Charlotte's door, but she didn't answer. I don't know why, but I tried her door and it was unlocked. I went in and found her hanging from a rope tied around her ceiling fan. I found out later that each girl had a piece of paper with '1 Corinthians 6:18' typed on it in her pocket."

I asked, "Paper, not a metal dog tag"?

"It was paper with the girls; on his other three victims, it varied. He didn't care about the medium, just the message. My humanities professor was the next victim. Of course, nobody suspected it was Jamie even then. Professor Quigman was known for inviting every student who got an A in his class to a party at his house after each semester. Of course, he was also a pervert who gave twice as many A's to cute girls as anybody else."

This time she didn't try to hide the tears. She let go of my hand and used both hands to wipe away tears. Carl produced a box of tissues, and she used them until she was ready to continue. She reached for my hand again, and I held hers gently while she continued.

"I got an A in his class, which I'd like to think I earned scholastically and went to the party. It actually wasn't a bad party; good food, expensive wine and intelligent conversation for the most part. As each female guest would leave, Quigman would walk us to the car. Of course, he tried to get a goodnight kiss from us."

"Did he succeed?" My partner does get right to the point.

April blushed, "With me, yes, it didn't seem like a big deal. A couple of girls refused, one even slapped him, but I didn't think it was that big of a deal at the time. I still don't think it should have been."

"But it turned out to be," I ventured. "What happened to him?"

"His house burned down with him and his beautiful golden retriever in it. '1 Corinthians 6:18' was spray painted in red on the roof of his white sedan. The next two victims were guys I dated. If you don't mind, I'd rather not go into detail."

I didn't mind. I'd already learned more than I'd wanted to know about April's past. I'd certainly heard enough to know why she'd said she'd seen worse when she found Chris Austin's body. I looked at the Great Detective who looked at me and said nothing.

"Sure," I said. "I can't see any reason to get into that. I presume you finally convinced the police that everybody who kissed you was dying because your crazy ex-boyfriend killed them."

"No, they convinced me. Fremantle is a little college town and all the victims were associated with the college. We all believed we had a random serial killer on campus. It never occurred to me that I was even involved, let alone that Jamie was the killer. It's hard to imagine a Bible thumper as a serial killer even if he is stalking you. Of course, I didn't know about the 1 Corinthians 6:18 thing at first."

April tensed again and her hold on my hand tightened. "Look, I'm sure it's obvious to a couple of professional detectives. Hell, it might be obvious to me now, too. But I'd never been around anything like that before. I was just an overprotected nineteen year old girl whose first boyfriend turned out to be a psychotic serial killer. The girl I was then has nothing in common with the bartender at The Rodeo Bar who occasionally helps you guys out by pretending to be a detective."

Larry Joe came out of my office. "Jamie Salt is still serving life without the possibility of parole in a maximum security prison in Western Australia. My sources tell me that in Western Australia, a life sentence actually means for life."

"So we're dealing with a copycat serial killer?"

"We might be. However, Dallas doesn't have a monopoly on convicting innocent people."

"What are you suggesting?" April looked like she'd been slapped, "That Jamie didn't kill everybody that got close to me after we broke up?"

"Calm down there, little lady. I ain't suggesting a thing, just stating a simple fact. Now that you're over the shock, we need to go tell DPD what you know. It'll be plumb interesting to see if they get along any better with their compadres in Perth than they do with the ones in Mesquite."

After April and Larry Joe left to give her statements to the police, I looked at the Great Detective. "What do we do now?"

"That's the wrong question. What I do next is take my wife on our Tuesday night date. What you should do next is either solve the case, or figure out if the kiss that almost got you killed twice is also what caused you to finally be able to sleep in your own bed."

I didn't give him the satisfaction of asking how he knew about the kiss. Instead I asked him about the case. "If April's first boyfriend is in jail in Australia for killing everybody who kissed her, which boyfriend in Dallas is trying to do the same thing?"

As soon I said it, I realized that wasn't the right question, either. I also knew that the person who killed Rick Taylor and Chris Austin had never been April's boyfriend. There's a huge difference between being a boyfriend and thinking you're a boyfriend! With some people a pretty girl only needs to show a little love to blur the line.

50   Suicidal Plan

"Damn it, Freak, you can't expect me to arrest him just because you think he might be a killer. Give me some evidence."

"I understand, Detective Woodbury. You don't want to be the first cop in the history of Dallas to arrest somebody who is innocent. He's not. He's tried twice to kill me and he knows now that he's failed. I'm not going to feel safe leaving this office until he's behind bars. I thought you said you wanted to cooperate on this."

"I've cooperated. I showed his picture to Mr. Washington. He said it might be the guy, but he couldn't be sure. Even if he was sure, he wouldn't make much of a witness. Any defense attorney worth his salt could carve him to pieces."

I already knew the answer, but I asked anyway. "What did the Australian authorities say?"

"They say they got their man and he's in jail forever. The evidence was overwhelming and he virtually confessed. The case got a great deal of press and they think we've either got a copycat on our hands or...."

When it was obvious he wasn't going to finish the sentence, I asked, "Or what?"

"It's not important. The important thing is that I can't arrest a guy just because you think he's a killer."

"You can, but you won't. The fact that he has a concealed handgun permit even though he doesn't own a registered handgun doesn't interest you?"

"How do you know that?"

"It's the information age, Woodbury. In the two days since I figured out he tried to kill me I've learned more about him than I know about my parents. Nothing in his history that predates April's move to Dallas can be confirmed. Every school he's supposedly attended and every job he allegedly held prior to that date no longer exists and no records exist. "

"The same can be said about your friend April, or should I say Christie Spring since that's the name she was born with."

Technically, it was the name she was given immediately after she was born, but I saw no reason to mention that. "Sure, but we know why she started a new life when she did. You never answered my question about the concealed handgun permit."

"Sure, it's interesting, but not felonious. Maybe he planned to buy a gun when he got the permit, but never got around to it."

"Maybe, or maybe he already had the guns when he got the permit."

"Maybe," Woodbury admitted.

"If he kills me in broad daylight in front of witnesses, will you arrest him, then?"

"You're that sure?"

"Yes."

"Even though there's no evidence that he's ever even been to Australia, you're sure that he killed everybody Jamie Salt is in jail for killing and followed April to Dallas to continue killing."

"If I live long enough, remind me to show you how easy it is to become somebody else if you get tired of being who you are. If I'd wanted to, I could have left that hospital, blown up half of Harris County and disappeared into a new life. Nobody but God, if he exists, would have ever known it."

"I believe you, but you're a clever, devious son of a bitch with more tricks up your sleeve than most people can imagine."

"I hope I'm wrong about this, but I'm afraid that son of a bitch is even more devious. I do know that he's more dangerous than I am."

"How do you know he's more dangerous?"

"Because, I know he's completely insane. I'm only slightly crazy."

Woodbury stared at me for a long time. Twice he started to say something and stopped. The Great Detective was in his office with Sam The Man listening on the intercom. I suspected I was making him proud by remaining silent.

Eventually Woodbury spoke, "Okay, I'll do it. I can't promise how long we can keep him, but I'll have him arrested."

"Doesn't matter how long," I said. "All that matters is that I know when he'll be released. Oh, and it would be nice if he got released around ten-thirty on a weekday morning."

Woodbury stood up to leave. "I'll call you when the arrest is made and I'll stay on top of it. You'll know when he's going to be released before he does. I can't promise we'll release him at ten-thirty, but I'll try. I hope you have a good plan."

"I do. Was the 'or' from the Australian cops the absurd idea that April had snapped and started to repeat Jamie Salt's actions here?"

"How the Hell did you know that?"

I smiled. "I didn't until you asked the wrong question."

Woodbury shook his head. "A few months as an apprentice private dick and you think you're Sherlock Fucking Holmes. I hope you're as good as you think you are. If you're not, we're both screwed."

As soon as Woodbury left, Sam The Man and Carl came out of his office to join me. "You lied, you know?"

"Did I?"

"You don't have a good plan. You have a desperate plan that is probably going to end up with you dead and a serial killer laughing about what a sucker you are."

"If it's such a bad plan, why'd you agree to go along with it?"

Uncharacteristically, he answered immediately, "Because I don't have a better one."

I'd successfully convinced the Great Detective to go along with my plan to get the son of a bitch to shoot me again. I'd convinced Sam The Man to take some time off so he could try to make sure I survived again. I'd convinced Woodbury to arrest him, so we'd have time to put the plan in place without letting him shoot me when I wasn't ready for it.

I quietly reflected on what could go wrong. Since about a thousand things could go wrong, I continued reflecting for awhile.

Sam The Man broke my thought, "You know, it would be easier just to kill him."

"Sure it would, Osalumense. But we're not killers, we're detectives. The plan is to catch him in the act and have him arrested and convicted."

"You're a detective and your plan is to have him arrested. I'm just a simple man and I think you're making this harder than it needs to be."

"You ever kill anybody in cold blood?"

Sam The Man laughed. "I don't even know what cold blood is. I know how to kill for survival and to protect my country from its government, but that was always in hot blood. I haven't had to kill at all since I escaped to this land of the free. I hoped I'd never again have to do it. But, I think if you're sure the dude's killed a half dozen people, maybe just killing him would be the right thing to do."

"Well, maybe you should think less and let me make decisions. Are you going to help or not?"

"I'm in, you know that. I will always fight with you or for you, but if I happen to get the chance to kill that dude, I'll do it."

"That's fine, but don't forget, that's not your objective here. The Great Detective and I are going to take care of the rest."

They both nodded affirmatively, but neither one looked confident. I didn't care. Everything was in place except for one thing. I still needed to convince April to kiss me again.

51   Stage Props

"Not a chance, I won't do it. I absolutely won't do it!"

I knew she was going to say that. "Okay, then just pick the guy you want to be the next target and you can kiss him."

"You're not funny. You know that, don't you?"

We were in Larry Joe's conference room on Friday morning. I knew I hadn't been followed and the Great Detective assured me that he'd gotten April in without being noticed. I trusted him on that. He was more likely to bring her in dizzy and fainting from a million turns, u-turns and cutbacks than to let anybody follow them here.

"I'm not trying to be funny. We have to get this handled. You can't spend the rest of your life refusing to get close to anybody."

"Why can't I? It seems to be working for you."

I didn't honestly know if it was working for me or not, but I knew April didn't believe it was. I decided to go for the hard sell. "So, you're content for both of us to live the rest of our lives sleeplessly walking around at night contemplating the advantages and disadvantages of different methods of suicide?"

April looked at me intently. Her bright green eyes seemed to stare right through me as if she were trying to read my mind. Since nothing was on my mind except getting her to agree to the plan I didn't mind that.

"Fine, I'll kiss you, but if you live through this, you'll have to plan your next suicide attempt without me. I'm not helping you try again."

It wasn't exactly the buy-in I'd been hoping for, but it would work. I explained the plan to her and we walked out of the conference room. I asked my partner to help April get out unseen so she could go to work. When they were gone, I turned to Larry Joe. "Can you drive me up to Plano to The Queen of Hearts?"

"The Queen of Hearts?" he asked. I thought you'd given up show business."

"I've got to put on one more performance. If I don't knock 'em dead, it might be my last."

"I have to be in court in an hour. Adriana, can you take the boy wherever he needs to go?"

"Sure boss, what about your appointments?"

"Reschedule what you can and cancel the rest. Family is more important than business."

The Queen of Hearts is a costume and magic shop in old downtown Plano. It's been an institution since it opened in the early eighties and I've had friends on the staff since I started performing. Rachel saw me come in and rushed over to hug me. "It's the Absolutely Incredible Freak Show. It's so good to see you again. We heard you died, you know?"

Rachel's a petite brunette with long curly hair, bright blue eyes and an almost perfect body. We dated briefly years ago before we both realized that we were better suited as friends and co-stars than lovers. Dating a co-worker is a challenge even if your co-worker's job doesn't include whipping you with a riding crop and otherwise abusing your body for the amusement of a paying audience. After she hugged me, she stepped back and looked at Adriana. "Don't worry, we're just friends. I won't try to steal him from you."

"Adriana is Larry Joe's assistant. Apparently he's not making any money practicing law, so he hires her out as a chauffeur sometimes. Reports of my death were greatly exaggerated, as you can see. I missed you at my funeral, though."

"I don't do funerals, too depressing. What can we do you for?"

"I need a complete disguise, including clothes. The clothes need to be big enough to wear over SWAT team combat armor. I need my face to be completely unrecognizable, but still as handsome as possible."

Rachel clapped her hands together one time. "Bitchin', you've brought me a challenge. Adriana, you may want to go out on the square and shop. This could take a couple of hours."

Two and a half hours later I looked like a new man. Rachel had performed her magic perfectly. She'd also packed a case with everything I'd need to repeat the look as many times as I might need to repeat it. Thanks to padding and platform shoes I now stood four inches taller and looked sixty pounds heavier than normal.

I wore gray slacks that were long enough to cover up the platform shoes, a white dress shirt and a blue sport jacket. The shirt was white, but it was thick enough to hide the padding underneath it. If I could have added another five inches to my height, I'd look pretty much like the Great Detective heading out on a date with Emily.

I thought about texting Adriana to pick me up, but decided to try to find her. That was easy. As soon as I saw the Starbucks, I knew where she'd be. I walked over to her table and smiled at her when she looked up. "Does it hurt when an angel like you falls from heaven?" I asked.

"I don't know. I've never been an angel. Do you have the slightest idea how trite that pickup line is?"

"Actually I do. However, I knew that a woman of your sophistication and beauty wouldn't be impressed with any pickup line and I seldom use them, so I don't know any good ones."

I sat down as if I'd been invited. She didn't try to stop me. "I'm Adriana. Why don't you have a seat?"

I shook the hand she offered. "I'm Kirk, Kirk Johnson. You're too delightful to be from Plano. What brings you here from..." I hesitated slightly, "Southlake, maybe?"

"Colleyville, actually", She said. "Close guess; I'm here waiting for my friend."

I stood up and took a business card from my jacket pocket, "A cliché brush-off after a cliché pick up line. I suppose I deserve that." I handed her my Pegasus Investigations card.

"Wait, that wasn't a brush off." She glanced at the card; then looked back at me, "No way! Is that really you?"

"In the flesh, I take it you believed I was Kirk Johnson."

"Believed it? Damn it, I was already planning our wedding and trying to decide if Adriana Johnson would be a good name. You're just mean, you know?"

"Sorry," I said sincerely. "Any name you have will be a good name. Let's get out of here."

She agreed. I was now ready for the most difficult and critical performance of my short life. It was going to be a short life, indeed, if I couldn't pull it off.

52   Performance Anxiety

I had a suite at the Adam's Mark hotel on Olive Street. We were piling up expenses on a case with no client to bill, but it didn't matter. This case had become personal a long time ago. Besides, if I had to inherit a ton of cash and a disease that guaranteed I wouldn't live long enough to spend it all, the least I could do was spend some when the occasion warranted it.

This occasion definitely warranted it. Everything it would take to become Kirk Johnson was in the bedroom waiting for the time to use it. I was waiting to hear from Woodbury that he'd made the arrest, so we could put the plan in place. It was Tuesday night and I was playing three handed spades with the Emily and Carl. I'd spent four days in this suite practicing the performance I was about to give.

I could get into and out of the ballistics vest and other protective gear in about fifteen minutes. Putting the oversize clothes on over it took a few minutes longer. The time-consuming part was putting on the make up that completed the disguise. If I hurried, I could do it in less than an hour, but I hoped I didn't have to hurry. The more time I took, the better it worked.

As Emily dealt the cards, I said, "Some date night, huh? It reminds me of when I was in the hospital. I guess it's my lot in life to be a burden to y'all."

Emily looked at me sharply, "Shut up. If you're ever a burden, I'll tell you. An evening of cards in a five star hotel suite is better than most of the dates we go on. Mr. Cheapskate over there used to take me to the soup kitchen for date night, you know."

"It wasn't a soup kitchen; it was the food bank. We were both volunteers, and Tuesday night was the one time we always both worked. That's how you decided to make Tuesday date night."

Like they always do when it looks like they're arguing, they kissed each other almost in mid-sentence.

"Stop it, you two. I'm going to have to make you get your own room if you keep that up."

My cell phone rang before either of them could reply. I answered before the song got to the lyrics.

"We've arrested him. He'll be there all night. He should be released in the morning sometime. I'll try to make sure it's between ten and eleven." Woodbury sounded very pleased with himself, but not nearly as pleased as I was.

He hung up and I looked at the newlyweds who were again acting like newlyweds. I cleared my throat, "The game is afoot. Our quarry will spend the night at Lew Sterrett and be released sometime tomorrow morning."

I sent April a text message, 'its on – tom morn".

She replied right away, "on my way".

I sent back, "tom is tomorrow".

I got back, "duh – on my way now".

"April's on her way over." I told the newlyweds.

Emily smiled. "Great, now we can play something fun. I hate three handed card games."

The great detective had just opened a Miller Lite when Woodbury called. He'd thrown it away and had a glass of water in front of him now. "Isn't throwing away a full beer considered alcohol abuse?" I asked.

"Probably, but I'd like both of us to live long enough for me to stand trial for it."

In spite of her earlier comment, Emily insisted we keep playing three handed spades until there was a knock on the door about nine o'clock. I went to the door and called out. "Who is it?"

"It's your once and future girlfriend, Kirk. Open the door."

I did and April came in. She had a suitcase big enough for a five day trip with her. We played several hands of spades without mentioning what was going to happen tomorrow. April and I lost every one, partly because I'm a terrible spades players and partly because Emily was the only one actually concentrating and trying to win.

At a little after ten, Emily said, "We should go now, Darling. Let these two old lovebirds catch up on old times."

When they were gone, I finally asked April about the suitcase. "It's just an overnight bag, Kirk. The scene is that I spent the night here, so I'm going to spend the night here. I'll take the couch, you can have the bedroom."

"I smiled. No, you take the bed. At three bills a night, somebody should sleep in it once before I check out. I'll stay out here on the couch."

April shook her head sadly, but she didn't argue. She took her suitcase into the bedroom. She came out a few minutes later with the picture of Katherine Elizabeth I'd put in the bedroom. She carefully sat it on a table beside the one I put on the end table, so I could see it from the couch. "Do you ever not miss her?"

"No," I answered quickly. Then I decided to be more honest, "maybe for a few seconds now and then. If I do, I always feel guilty and miss her even more."

She turned and went back to the bedroom. At the doorway, she turned back and asked, "Do you think that's what she would want?"

She closed the door before I could answer, which wasn't hard since I didn't have an answer. I turned on the television and started channel surfing until I found a movie to watch.

Around one o'clock I was on the couch watching the opening credits of 'A Touch of Evil" with Charlton Heston and Janet Leigh. April came out and sat on the couch beside me. She took my hand and leaned against my shoulder. "If neither of us is going to sleep, we can at least watch the movie together."

We did just that, but neither of us was awake when it ended. As April lay sleeping beside me, I finally answered her question. "No, it isn't what she would want." That's the last thing I said or thought before I fell asleep. Fortunately, I'd set the alarm just in case I did sleep. The Great Detective always told me to plan for anything that might happen, not just what you expect to happen.

53   Old Lovers

"Why did he kill Chris? I never gave him the time of day, let alone kissed him."

"Two reasons. One, I think he's spiraling downhill fast, which is one reason I wanted Woodbury to arrest him. The second reason is because when you weren't working, Mr. Austin sometimes bragged about having had you to impress his customers."

I was dressed in my Kirk Johnson disguise and April was dressed for work. We were sitting in the hotel room waiting for the phone call that would put the plan in motion. Around ten, Woodbury called. "He's not going to get out until almost eleven, maybe even later. A lot of public intox cases last night have to be processed. I hope that doesn't spoil your plan."

I assured him it didn't and thanked him for calling. I told April the news and she pulled out her cell phone. "I better let the boss know I'm going to be late."

I only heard her end of the conversation. "I'm going to be late today. I'm helping out the Pegasus guys. No matter what you see me do or hear me say today, just act like everything is normal, okay?"

After a short pause, she said. "I'm holding you to that."

The conversation went on for a little bit longer before she hung up.

"Is he okay with it? I don't want to get you fired."

"He's fine, he knows to go along and he probably knows why. I trust him to handle this fine. I didn't tell him the plan because I want him to act surprised like he would if I really did this. He's mostly worried he might lose me to full-time detective work."

"He should be. He very well might."

April's eyes lit up like only hers can, "He should? He might?"

"Of course, don't tell me you don't love this stuff more than bartending."

"Sure I do, but last I heard bartending didn't qualify as relevant experience when applying for a job as a detective."

"It should. But, who cares? Circus freak and bike courier probably don't either."

"I didn't know you were a bike courier."

"Not me, I was talking about Carl. He got started by helping out part-time like you do now. The only difference is he was an ugly bike courier, not a gorgeous bartender."

"I didn't know that. I always assumed the bike was just a handy disguise. And he's not ugly, you know."

I had no desire to continue discussing my partner's looks or anything else not related to catching a murderer. I also didn't want to scare April by talking too much about what we were about to try, so I turned on the television and we watched something in silence. I don't know what it was.

Woodbury finally called at 11:15. "He's being released now. Good luck."

"Thanks."

I called the Great Detective to let him know. "He's out. Ten to one, he goes straight to Walt's"

"No bet, but if he doesn't, I'll let you know. I've got three guys working the tail with me. We won't lose him and he won't spot us. I don't care how paranoid he is after being arrested."

"Okay, April and I are ready for our curtain call."

I had the Bluetooth in my ear and we kept the connection as the Great Detective followed the killer from the jail to his date with his destiny. As expected, he went straight to Walt's. I ended the call and looked at April, "We're on. Are you ready?"

"Let me check my makeup." She strolled to the bathroom and came back less than five minutes later. Her face had a glow to it. She'd put on some kind of sparkly makeup.

"You don't think glitter is a bit much?"

"Here's a suggestion. I don't tell you how to play the tough guy with the suicide complex and you don't tell me how to play the temptress who'll never find true love."

I hit the call back button to reconnect with the Great Detective, and we timed our approach to the bar to make sure the killer saw us walking hand in hand down Commerce Street. When we were just outside the bar, April stopped and looked up at me. "You know it'll probably help when we do this if you make it look like kissing me is something you like doing."

"Don't worry," I said confidently. "We'll show him a kiss that makes Bogart and Bacall look like casual acquaintances by comparison."

216

She smiled, "It's even better when you help."

"Here's looking at you, kid."

"Wrong movie and wrong leading lady, let's do it."

Even casual acquaintances can't walk through a revolving door arm in arm without looking like lovers. Obviously, we didn't try. When we got into the bar, she spun around to face me and held both my hands between us at her chest level. "Darling, you have to let me go to work now. Give me a kiss."

I did just that. The kiss might not have been the best in the history of cinema, but it was definitely the best and the longest in the history of Walt Garrison's Rodeo Bar. When we finally separated, April looked radiant. That glitter makeup must really work. I made a mental note to apologize to her later for questioning her on her area of expertise.

"Find a table and I'll bring you something to eat. You simply can't go back home tomorrow without experiencing real Texas cuisine."

As planned, I found a table by the window looking out on Commerce Street. I tried to act like I'd never been here before as I sat down and looked over the menu. I also avoided making any eye contact with any of the customers.

"Who's your new boyfriend, April?" Seated around the bar were five regulars and a guy I didn't recognize. I wasn't sure which one had asked the question, but I figured it was one of the innocent regulars. The stranger wouldn't know April well enough to ask that, and the killer never said anything that loudly.

"Actually, he's my old boyfriend, Kirk Johnson. He's in town for a few days and he found my MySpace page to let me know he'd be here. Isn't that so romantic?"

Carl had hated that part of the script when we came up with it, but he's old. What did he expect us to use: the lonely hearts club? April was busy taking care of her customers, as I pretended to study the menu.

April's boss came over and set a glass of lemonade on my table. "April said you like lemonade. I hope she's not going to be an hour late every time you come to town."

I hate lemonade, of course. It was part of the performance. A performance that I knew had a rapt audience member at the bar. "Don't worry, Sir. It will never happen again. We just had to catch up on old times, you know." I tried to wink at him exactly the way Chris Austin would have winked. "Besides, if I play my cards right, I'm hoping she'll come up to see me before I come down here again. No offense, but it's damn hot down here."

"No offense taken." He turned back to the bar. "April, do you have everything under control? Can I go back to the office knowing our customers will receive the service this bar is famous for?"

"Yes sir! Sorry about being late, it won't happen again."

"I hope not." He said as he went to his office.

He wasn't the only one leaving. For the first time in the year I'd been coming here, I watched the man who most people never notice with the name most people never remember leave Walt Garrison's Rodeo Bar while April was still on duty and before he'd even insisted that only she could bring him his beer.

I put the Bluetooth in my ear and started dialing. If my theory was correct, Frank Arrington was no more his name than Freak Show was mine. Whatever his real name was, I knew he was going to try for the third time this month to kill me. I should have been scared; but I wasn't. I was pissed off and pumped up.

54   Professional Surveillance

"He's on the move," I told Carl when he answered.

"Yes, he is and we're on him. He's wandering aimlessly through a cash lot like a mall shopper who forgot where he parked."

I knew what that meant, "Or a car thief looking for his next ride. I hope Emily didn't park her SUV around here. Make sure you're well-hidden. We need him to get his ride if this is going to work."

"Freak, I'm the veteran, remember? I'm supposed to be giving you the unneeded reminders, okay?"

"Sorry about that, chief."

"Damn! This guy's good." He hung up before I could mention that we already knew that. I worried briefly that we might lose the guy, but then I remembered how well we'd planned this and relaxed. April brought over a plate of Buffalo wings with honey barbecue sauce.

"Finger food, in case you have to leave in a hurry," she said.

"Plus, it's something I've never ordered, in case he comes back."

She smiled and went back to the bar. The place was crowded as it usually is at lunch time. I'd turned the ringtone off on my cell phone, so it only vibrated when the Great Detective called me back.

"Yes," I answered.

"He took a blue Jeep Cherokee in less than six seconds. If I hadn't been watching him specifically, I wouldn't have noticed he stole it. He's headed north on Harry Hines right now. We're on him and we've got the license plate. If he stops anywhere, we'll put a tracking device on it. Otherwise, if we lose him we'll call in the cops. It's a new one; it's probably got a LoJack device."

When he hung up, I started on the wings. They were better than I expected. I wondered why I'd never had them before. The phone vibrated again.

"Yes."

"He went to a self storage facility at Royal Lane and Stemmons. Pat couldn't get close enough to see everything, but he saw him park by a unit near the back and change out the plates on the Jeep. He also loaded some stuff, but Pat couldn't see what it was.

He's headed back south. Pat's tailing him. Call him for the play by play."

"Okay. Did he get the number of his unit?"

"C-fifteen, why?"

"Aren't you the one who told me it's always better to know than to not know?"

"Sure I am. Call Pat, now."

I assured him that I would, but I didn't. First I called Sam The Man. I gave him the location of the self storage facility and the unit number and told him to get there as soon as he could.

"Why am I going there?"

"If he wins and we lose, he'll go back to unload his stuff. If he shows up there and you can't reach us, it'll be time for you to see if you can kill in cold blood."

"If it comes to that, I won't have to see. I already know. All that will be left to learn is if I become a bitch in prison or if I make everybody there my bitch."

"For the sake of every possible bitch in Huntsville, let's hope it doesn't come to that. Deep Ellum can barely handle you; no prison could possibly be ready."

With that done, I called Pat. He'd followed our suspect from Royal Lane back downtown. We both knew where he was headed and he didn't disappoint us. When Pat told me Frank Arrington turned onto Commerce, I hung up on Pat and called Jeff. He was standing in front of Walt's. His job was to warn me to duck if Frank showed any indication that he was trying to shoot me drive by style as he passed Walt's.

As the Cherokee approached, Jeff said, "Okay, stay on your toes. If I say dive, don't ask questions." He started whistling softly, so I'd know the connection was still open. I concentrated on not looking out the window or crawling under the table like a little baby. After what seemed like an eternity, he stopped whistling. "It's all good; he looked in as he passed, like we thought he would to make sure you're still there. Somebody will call you when we see where he sets up."

I hung up and waited for the next call. I didn't wait long.

"As you love to say, the game is afoot. He's parked in the left lane on Commerce a little bit east of the Starbucks. If he tries to shoot from the back of the SUV like he did before, you won't need me to warn you, you'll see him."

"And we both know that's not likely."

"Right, he'll probably try to shoot you in the back after you pass the Jeep. You should walk to the Jeep keeping an eye on the back door. If nothing happens, cross the street as you get to it. He won't be expecting that, so he'll have to adjust on the fly."

"Then he'll have to try to shoot me in the back across traffic, not an easy shot. Good thinking. Even if he hits, I'm wearing more protection than a dogtag this time"

"Don't get too cocky, body armor won't help you at all if he shoots you in the back of the head. You don't have to go through with this, you know. We probably have enough on him now to get the cops to at least check the self storage unit. They'd have to find something."

"We're not going to repeat this argument," I said firmly. "My job is to make him shoot me again in front of witnesses. Your job is to warn me when he's about to do it so I can duck. I appear to have succeeded at my job. When do we start on your job?"

"Let's give it an hour to cut down on the number of innocent bystanders in the area. It won't hurt if it makes him edgier either."

I've never agreed with the assumption that bystanders are always innocent, but I didn't mention it. Instead, I ate the rest of the wings, used the facilities and made sure my pistol was in a pocket I could pull it from quickly when I needed it. It hadn't been an hour, but I called anyway.

"Can we do this? I'm getting edgier than he is."

"Sure, Freak. If you're ready, we're ready. You can still back out, you know."

"No, I can't. It's personal. If it goes bad and I get killed, it will still have happened in front of witnesses. I'll die knowing he's going down for what he did because of me. If we call the cops now and there's no proof, or they fuck it up, he'll skate away having killed everybody April ever loved and laughing at me. I'd rather die than live with that."

"Not everybody, Freak, but, you're right. This is what we decided to do. We might as well do it. Tell April goodbye and start walking."

April was standing nervously nearby when I stood up. "Duty calls," I said.

"Yes, it does. Kiss me again. If you die today, I don't want our performance earlier to be my last kiss."

I kissed her again. "I'm not going to die today. Haven't you heard? I'm Superman."

As I walked out the door, I heard Carl's voice over the Bluetooth in my ear, "No, you aren't. You're the Absolutely Incredible Freak Show. Superman would never attempt a foolish stunt like this. I can't whistle worth a damn, so I'm just going to chatter softly until I see him start to fire. When I say 'dive', dive damn it."

"I will. I know who I am and who I'm not. I just wanted April to worry less. I haven't forgotten the plan. It's my plan, remember."

55   Texas Shootout

I walked out of Walt Garrison's Rodeo Bar for what I hoped wouldn't be the last time into a sunny, warm, but not too hot, Texas afternoon. Carl's voice came in softly over the Bluetooth. I couldn't really hear what he was saying, but it sounded like he was reading the box score from a baseball game. It didn't matter; he was only talking so I'd know the connection was still good.

I had a pistol in my pocket and I wondered briefly if Sam The Man didn't have a good point. I could shoot the son of a bitch before he got the chance to shoot me and end this thing. Of course, that wouldn't really end it, and it wouldn't do a thing to help Pegasus Investigations thrive.

Besides, he's better suited to survive a long prison stay than I am. If my plan was a suicidal plan, then so be it. Nobody lives forever, and most people die for less worthy reasons than this. If Katherine was right about the whole afterlife thing, she'd be happy to see me again.

The Great Detective raised his voice, "Freak! Are you focused? This isn't the time for daydreams or heartache."

I considered several comebacks, but I realized he was right before I decided on one. "I am now! Thanks. Is the Jeep I see in front of me his?"

"Yes, he's sitting in the front passenger seat. Just keep walking, I'll tell you if he reacts."

I walked slowly, partly because the platform shoes weren't built for speed and partly because with every step I was looking for the best place to dive when he started shooting. I trusted my partner to warn me about the first shot in time to duck it, but I expected the son of a bitch to keep shooting.

"He keeps adjusting the rearview mirror. I assume he's tracking you. He's still just sitting, though. He must be planning to let you walk past then shoot you from behind."

I passed the Starbucks and the Schlotzsky's. I asked, "Still nothing?"

"No, go ahead and cross the street. Don't look at the SUV. I want to see how he reacts."

I did exactly that. As I crossed Commerce, I got the feeling that I was being followed. Of course, I was being watched by one psychotic killer, my partner and at least two other private investigators that were being paid to make sure that if I died somebody went down for it. I quit thinking about that and went back to concentrating on crossing the street without staring at the Jeep Cherokee.

The Great Detective's voice rose again as I reached the sidewalk on the south side of Commerce, "Freak, somebody's following you."

"I thought so. Who is it?"

"I can't tell. I don't know if it matters, either. If Arrington doesn't try anything here, I'll get in behind you and find out."

I had passed the Joseph A. Banks Clothiers store and was about to pass the blue Jeep Cherokee. I was still trying not to look at it when Carl said, "Here we go. He's out of the Jeep. Keep walking and stay ready."

I kept walking as my partner muttered into his phone. I couldn't hear what he was saying, but it didn't matter. I just needed to hear him when the time came.

"Dive!" said my partner loudly.

I dove forward and heard a bullet hit the bricks to my right. I scrambled back toward the doorway I'd just passed. He fired several times. One hit my right hand before I could duck into the doorway. It only took seconds to learn that the doors were locked and I was stuck in the doorway.

"Freak, are you are okay?"

"For now, but this door doesn't open. What's he's doing?"

He's walking toward you carefully. I think he's sure he has you cornered. I'm going to try to beat him to you. If I don't, you better shoot first and ask questions later.

I leaned against the locked door and took my pistol from my pocket. My hand was bleeding, really bleeding. Even Rachel wasn't going to be able to convince her boss to return the deposit on this costume. More importantly, I didn't know if I'd be able to shoot straight with this hand.

Carl wasn't muttering anymore. I had my pistol in my hand hoping if I had to use it, that the first shot I ever fired at something other than a practice range target would hit its mark.

"Shit!" Carl seldom cusses, so this had to be bad.

"Officer this is important, that man is trying to commit murder."

I barely heard the other voice over the Bluetooth. "I don't think so. You're the one I see with the gun. Drop it and turn around."

"No," the Great Detective told the officer firmly. "Freak, he's crossed the street. Shoot him when he turns the corner. You might not get another chance."

I tried to steady the pistol, while I listened to Carl and the cop discuss who was violating the law. The discussion didn't seem to be going well, which didn't matter much to me. I was trapped in a doorway and a psychotic killer was closing in on me while a cop was preventing my partner from doing anything to save me.

I'd never tried to fire a pistol while my hand was bleeding from being shot, but it shouldn't be much harder than firing a pistol any other time since I wasn't feeling any pain. Of course, I'd never fired a pistol at anybody trying to kill me before.

"He's at the corner, Freak. Shoot the next thing you see."

I heard somebody yell, "Hold it!" Then I heard guns being fired outside the doorway followed by a thud.

I steadied the pistol across my left arm. I waited for the killer to turn the corner into the doorway. I was ready to fire at the next thing I saw. I steadied my arm. I still wasn't sure I'd be able to keep the gun steady, but I felt fairly sure I'd be able to pull the trigger. As I saw a shadow turn the corner, I heard a loud voice in my ear. "Freak, don't shoot."

By the time I realized the voice belonged to my partner, it was too late not to pull the trigger. I managed to drop my arm and the bullet hit the pavement and ricocheted across Commerce. Detective Woodbury stood there smiling. "Damn Freak, I save your life and you still want to shoot me. That's just wrong."

"You saved my life? What the Hell are you talking about?"

"I knew you'd do something stupid, so I followed you. When that guy took a shot at you, I decided it was police business. When he followed you to this doorway with a pistol in his hand, I shot him. I presume we'll find evidence to connect him to several homicides now that his civil rights aren't an issue."

"How'd you know who I was? This is a good disguise."

"Easy, the man we had staking out the Rodeo Bar saw April kiss you. In spite of the description he gave me of the man April kissed, I knew it had to be you. Don't forget, I've seen your stage show, I know how capable you are of donning different disguises. By the way, he was quite impressed with your kiss."

Carl joined us in the doorway, accompanied by a beat cop. "Sir, this guy threatened to sue if I didn't let him talk to you before I took him in."

"What are you taking him in for?"

"Brandishing a weapon and resisting arrest."

"I told you to detain him, not arrest him. Get the Hell out of here."

The Great Detective looked at Woodbury. "You told him to detain me?"

"It seemed like a good idea at the time. When a private citizen shoots another citizen, the burden of proof is on him to explain his reasons for shooting. When a police detective shoots a suspect, the burden of proof shifts. That son of a bitch needed shot, but I didn't want you to have to answer for it."

"Or get the credit for it," I suggested.

"That either," Woodbury answered smiling broadly. "I told you, y'all are going to get me promoted again."

I smiled, "Maybe it would have been better if we hadn't taken the stolen guitar case."

56   Another Kiss

Carl shook his head sadly. "Just once I'd like us to solve a big case without spending any time in a hospital."

On a Friday or Saturday night or any holiday, Parkland's emergency room has longer waiting lines than Six Flags in June. Mid-afternoon Wednesday on the last day of May, Parkland looked more like any other hospital. Woodbury brought me here to have my hand examined. The doctor looked at it and insisted that I stay here at least four hours to recover and be observed again before leaving.

I didn't argue, pain isn't an issue, but severe blood loss can be serious even for me. Actually, it can be more serious for me with no pain to warn me if something is going wrong. The Great Detective came with us from the scene of the shooting. After making sure I got a private room, Woodbury went back to the crime scene to make sure he got credit for it. April and Larry Joe had joined us pretty soon after. April sat beside the bed holding my good hand.

I smiled, "Well, at least we have a client to bill this time. As soon as the police close the case, we can give Charlie Ray his guitar case and collect our fee and expenses."

I looked at Larry Joe, "How much do we bill him for your time? I've always been your pro bono client, so I don't even know what your rate is."

Larry Joe laughed "If Charlie Ray could afford my services; I don't reckon he'd have been in that dang mess in the first place. Just bill Charlie Ray for everything you did until that guitar stealin' varmint got hisself shot and Ah'll pay for the rest."

Carl didn't like that idea. "Lawrence, we don't need your charity. Even if we did, it wouldn't be tax deductible."

If being called Lawrence bothered my Godfather he didn't let it show. "Settle down, Pardner. I know y'all ain't a charity case."

Carl looked at me and I returned his look without comment. I wasn't being silent to impress him; I simply had nothing to add.

The silence didn't last long, and when Larry Joe ended it, he sounded like a lawyer, not a cowpoke. "I have a client who is paying my firm its usual rate to look into the Jamie Salt conviction. She can easily afford my rates, and I will bill your work and expenses at your standard rates."

April's grip on my hand tightened, "Who is your client?"

Larry Joe tone was soothing as he answered her, "Jamie's mother. When I called to check on his status, somebody let her know about it. She called me to find out why I was asking about him. I didn't tell her much, but she asked me if she could hire me, and I agreed."

He looked at April, "I know this is hard for you, and I'll drop it if you want. But if Jamie didn't kill your friends, he deserves decent representation. If he did kill them, then he'll serve his time. No matter what you may have heard about me, I don't make my living by helping serial killers escape justice."

April's grip on my hand did not loosen, "I don't understand. I thought Frank Arrington was a copycat killer. Didn't Jamie confess?"

"No, he put up very little defense, but he didn't confess. According to his mother, he felt guilty about stalking you, but he realized he was never going to have you. He also didn't think he'd ever be able to stop wanting you. She says he decided he might as well die in prison if he was going to have to live without you."

"God, that's almost more pathetic. Don't drop the case on my account. Did she say anything about me?"

"Surprisingly, she had nothing but good things to say about you. Usually, a mother will side with her darling little boy and blame the girl for everything when something like this happens. She doesn't."

"She's a good woman, and she can definitely afford your fees. Are you sure Jamie's innocent?"

McCoy saw Woodbury enter the room and immediately turned on his drawl. "Not at all, Missy. But Ah'm sure aimin' to make sure he gets another shot at a fair trial."

"Who're you trying to get out of jail this time, McCoy? Not one of my arrests, I hope."

"Not yours, Pardner. Lessin' you was marshallin' in the Outback before you moseyed onto DPD. Jamie Salt's ma hired me to see if he got railroaded."

April squeezed my hand tighter, but said nothing. I could tell she wanted to either scream or cry, but she did neither. She just tightened her grip on my hand.

Woodbury stood there grinning like the Cheshire Cat. "You may have an easy case, McCoy. We found some very interesting things in the van. The arsenal included a .32 Ruger which matches the caliber that killed Rick Taylor and a .338 AWS Magnum, which matches the caliber which shot Superman earlier. The boys who know tell me the AWS is the assault rifle of choice in Australia."

As he discussed the contents of the van, I remembered that Sam The Man was still guarding the mini-warehouse. I sent him a text message to let him know it was over and we had won.

Larry Joe didn't share Woodbury's confidence. "Ah reckon that's plumb helpful, but I ain't sure that'll free the boy."

"It might not. Why don't we step outside and discuss it. They found more than an arsenal. None of it is a matter of public record, but it won't hurt to share it with you privately."

Carl watched them leave and asked incredulously, "He'll share with McCoy, but not us. What the Hell is he thinking? He knows we can be trusted to keep a secret, doesn't he."

"He does." I answered, "He also knows we can all feel pain even if it's in different ways. If something in that Jeep clears Jamie Salt, then it may be something April shouldn't hear about. For that matter, you and I may not want to hear about it either. He just didn't want to insult us by suggesting that we wouldn't."

"Woodbury's discovered tact? You think anybody in Deep Ellum would believe that?"

"No, but for his sake, I'm not going to tell anybody down there."

He smiled, "I won't either, but I need to talk to Emily anyway, and I have to tell somebody." The great detective hummed happily to himself as he pulled out his cell phone and walked out of my hospital room.

I'm not sure how long April and I sat silently. It was a comfortable silence, but somehow it seemed stilted. I tried to decide what Humphrey Bogart would say at this moment, but I couldn't decide. Even if I was Bogart, I didn't know if April was Ingrid Bergman or Lauren Bacall.

Eventually April said softly, "Well, we did it, again. You caught the bad guy and proved you're tougher than bullets again. Have you started planning your next suicide attempt?"

"It wasn't a suicide attempt. I wanted to live and I did. I also wanted to catch that son of a bitch, and I did that, too. He died and I lived. I don't need a pep talk or a lecture from you, right now."

"Yes, you do! At some point, you really do need to start living again. This grieving widower act hurts your image as a tough guy. Hell, you told me yourself that Woodbury thinks you're soft, and he's too weak to even divorce his bitch of a wife."

"I've been living. If I'm not living, how can I be grieving? For that matter, how could I have caught a serial killer?"

"No, I mean really living, not just going through the motions like you're the only one who's ever lost a loved one. You need to start doing things. Dare I say it, maybe even date?"

"You might be right. You have anybody in mind?"

She smiled the million watt smile that caused Frank Arrington to kill people on two continents, and to try three times to add me to the list.

"I do," she said and then she kissed me.

ACKNOWLEDGEMENTS

First, I'd like to thank Lezlie K. King, the co-author of The Freak Show Case. Without her, the first novel in the Pegasus Investigations series might never have been completed, so there would never have been a sequel, much less a series.

Therefore, I must also thank everybody who bought the first book, or recommended it to a friend or family member. The starving artist mythos is a powerful image, but it's an awful reality. Trust me on that one.

As always, I must thank the waiters and waitresses who almost never complained about the writer with the laptop camping at a four top. Lastly, and perhaps, most importantly, I thank Christie Paterson for her contribution to this story.